Lost American Fiction

There are no firm guidelines for selection of the Lost American Fiction volumes. The only rule is that to be considered for republication a book must have been originally published at least twenty-five years ago. One quality we look for might be called "life": does the work live?—does it have a voice of its own?—does it present convincing characters? Another test for including a work in this series is its historical value: does it illuminate the literary or social history of its time?

The editor and the press feel that the Lost American Fiction series has largely achieved what it set out to do. Twenty-seven books have been given another chance. Some have found new audiences. Some will vanish again. We do not claim that all of the volumes are lost masterpieces; and there has been considerable disagreement from readers about individual titles. We never anticipated uniformity of response. That readers would find the Lost American Fiction volumes worth reading and would be prompted to make their own appraisals is all we expected.

M. J. B.

Lost American Fiction
EDITED BY MATTHEW J. BRUCCOLI

THE PLASTIC AGE
A Novel

by Percy Marks

With an Afterword by R. V. Cassill

SOUTHERN ILLINOIS UNIVERSITY PRESS
Carbondale and Edwardsville

Feffer & Simons, Inc.
London and Amsterdam

Library of Congress Cataloging in Publication Data

Marks, Percy, 1891–
  The plastic age.

  (Lost American fiction)
  Reprint of the ed. published by Century Co., New
York.
  I. Title.
PZ3.M3423Pl   1980   [PS3525.A6657] 823'.912   80-17959
ISBN 0-8093-0984-X

Copyright 1924 by The Century Co.
Afterword by R. V. Cassill Copyright © 1980 by
  Southern Illinois University Press
All rights reserved
Printed by offset lithography in the United States of
  America

TO
MY MOTHER

THE PLASTIC AGE

THE PLASTIC AGE

CHAPTER I

WHEN an American sets out to found a college, he hunts first for a hill. John Harvard was an Englishman and indifferent to high places. The result is that Harvard has become a university of vast proportions and no color. Yale flounders about among the New Haven shops, trying to rise above them. The Harkness Memorial tower is successful; otherwise the university smells of trade. If Yale had been built on a hill, it would probably be far less important and much more interesting.

Hezekiah Sanford was wise; he found first his hill and then founded his college, believing probably that any one ambitious enough to climb the hill was a man fit to wrestle with learning and, if need be, with Satan himself. Satan was ever before Hezekiah, and he fought him valiantly, exorcising him every morning in chapel and every evening at prayers. The first students of Sanford College learned Latin and Greek and to fear the devil.

3

There are some who declare that their successors learn less.

Hezekiah built Sanford Hall, a fine Georgian building, performed the duties of trustees, president, dean, and faculty for thirty years, and then passed to his reward, leaving three thousand acres, his library of five hundred books, mostly sermons, Sanford Hall, and a charter that opened the gates of Sanford to all men so that they might "find the true light of God and the glory of Jesus in the halls of this most liberal college."

More than a century had passed since Hezekiah was laid to rest in Haydensville's cemetery. The college had grown miraculously and changed even more miraculously. Only the hill and its beautiful surroundings remained the same. Indian Lake, on the south of the campus, still sparkled in the sunlight; on the east the woods were as virgin as they had been a hundred and fifty years before. Haydensville, still only a village, surrounded the college on the west and north.

Hezekiah's successors had done strange things to his campus. There were dozens of buildings now surrounding Sanford Hall, and they revealed all the types of architecture popular since Hezekiah had thundered his last defiance at Satan. There were fine old colonial buildings, their windows outlined by English ivy; ponderous Romanesque buildings made of stone, grotesque and hideous; a pseudo-Gothic chapel with a tower of surpassing loveliness; and four laboratories of the purest factory design. But despite the conglomerate and sometimes absurd architecture—a Doric temple neighbored a Byzantine mosque—the campus was beautiful. Lawns, often terraced, stretched everywhere, and the great elms lent a dignity to Sanford College that no architect, however stupid, could quite efface.

This first day of the new college year was glorious in the golden haze of Indian summer. The lake was silver blue, the long reflections of the trees twisting and bending as a soft breeze ruffled the surface into tiny waves. The hills already brilliant with color—scarlet, burnt orange, mauve, and purple—flamed up to meet the clear blue sky; the elms softly rustled their drying leaves; the white houses of the village retreated coyly behind maples and firs and elms: everywhere there was peace, the peace that comes with strength that has been stronger than time.

As Hugh Carver hastened up the hill from the station, his two suit-cases banged his legs and tripped him. He could hardly wait to reach the campus. The journey had been intolerably long —Haydensville was more than three hundred miles from Merrytown, his home—and he was wild to find his room in Surrey Hall. He wondered how he would like his room-mate, Peters. . . . What's

his name? Oh, yes, Carl. . . . The registrar had
written that Peters had gone to Kane School. . . .
Must be pretty fine. Ought to be first-class to
room with. . . . Hugh hoped that Peters would n't
think that he was too country. . . .

Hugh was a slender lad who looked considerably
less than his eighteen years. A gray cap concealed
his sandy brown hair, which he parted on the side
and which curled despite all his brushing. His crys-
talline blue eyes, his small, neatly carved nose, his
sensitive mouth that hid a shy and appealing smile,
were all very boyish. He seemed young, almost
pathetically young.

People invariably called him a nice boy, and he
did n't like it; in fact, he wanted to know how they
got that way. They gave him the pip, that's
what they did. He guessed that a fellow who
could run the hundred in 10:2 and out-box anybody in high school was n't such a baby. Why, he
had overheard one of the old maid teachers call
him sweet. Sweet! Cripes, that old hen made
him sick. She was always pawing him and sticking
her skinny hands in his hair. He was darn glad
to get to college where there were only men
teachers.

Women always wanted to get their hands into his
hair, and boys liked him on sight. Many of those
who were streaming up the hill before and behind

him, who passed him or whom he passed, glanced at his eager face and thought that there was a guy they'd like to know.

An experienced observer would have divided those boys into three groups: preparatory school boys, carelessly at ease, well dressed, or, as the college argot has it, "smooth"; boys from city schools, not so well dressed perhaps, certainly not so sure of themselves; and country boys, many of them miserably confused and some of them clad in Kollege Kut Klothes that they would shamefacedly discard within a week.

Hugh finally reached the top of the hill, and the campus was before him. He had visited the college once with his father and knew his way about. Eager as he was to reach Surrey Hall, he paused to admire the pseudo-Gothic chapel. He felt a little thrill of pride as he stared in awe at the magnificent building. It had been willed to the college by an alumnus who had made millions selling rotten pork.

Hugh skirted two of the factory laboratories, hurried between the Doric temple and Byzantine mosque, paused five times to direct confused classmates, passed a dull red colonial building, and finally stood before Surrey Hall, a large brick dormitory half covered by ivy.

He hurried up-stairs and down a corridor until

he found a door with 19 on it. He knocked.

"What th' hell! Come in." The voice was impatiently cheerful.

Hugh pushed open the door and entered the room to meet wild confusion—and his room-mate. The room was a clutter of suit-cases, trunks, clothes, banners, unpacked furniture, pillows, pictures, golf-sticks, tennis-rackets, and photographs— dozens of photographs, all of them of girls apparently. In the middle of the room a boy was on his knees before an open trunk. He had sleek black hair, parted meticulously in the center, a slender face with rather sharp features and large black eyes that almost glittered. His lips were full and very red, almost too red, and his cheeks seemed to be colored with a hard blush.

"Hullo," he said in a clear voice as Hugh came in. "Who are you?"

Hugh flushed slightly. "I 'm Carver," he answered, "Hugh Carver."

The other lad jumped to his feet, revealing, to Hugh's surprise, golf knickers. He was tall, slender, and very neatly built.

"Hell!" he exclaimed. "I ought to have guessed that." He held out his hand. "I 'm Carl Peters, the guy you 've got to room with—and God help you."

Hugh dropped his suit-cases and shook hands. "Guess I can stand it," he said with a quick laugh to hide his embarrassment. "Maybe you 'll need a little of God's help yourself." Diffident and unsure, he smiled—and Peters liked him on the spot.

"Chase yourself," Peters said easily. "I know a good guy when I see one. Sit down somewhere —er, here." He brushed a pile of clothes off a trunk to the floor with one sweep of his arm. "Rest yourself after climbing that goddamn hill. Christ! It 's a bastard, that hill is. Say, your trunk 's down-stairs. I saw it. I 'll help you bring it up soon 's you 've got your wind."

Hugh was rather dazzled by the rapid, staccato talk, and, to tell the truth, he was a little shocked by the profanity. Not that he was n't used to profanity; he had heard plenty of that in Merrytown, but he did n't expect somehow that a college man— that is, a prep-school man—would use it. He felt that he ought to make some reply to Peters's talk, but he did n't know just what would do. Peters saved him the trouble.

"I 'll tell you, Carver—oh, hell, I 'm going to call you Hugh—we 're going to have a swell joint here. Quite the darb. Three rooms, you know; a bedroom for each of us and this big study. I 've brought most of the junk that I had at Kane, and I s'pose you 've got some of your own."

"Not much," Hugh replied, rather ashamed of what he thought might be considered stinginess.

He hastened to explain that he did n't know what Carl would have; so he thought that he had better wait and get his stuff at college.

"That 's the bean," exclaimed Carl. He had perched himself on the window-seat. He threw one well shaped leg over the other and gazed at Hugh admiringly. "You certainly used the old bean. Say, I 've got a hell of a lot of truck here, and if you 'd 'a' brought much, we 'd 'a' been swamped. . . . Say, I 'll tell you how we 'll fix this dump." He jumped up, led Hugh on a tour of the rooms, discussed the disposal of the various pieces of furniture with enormous gusto, and finally pointed to the photographs.

"Hope you don't mind my harem," he said, making a poor attempt to hide his pride.

"It 's some harem," replied Hugh in honest awe. Again he felt ashamed. He had pictures of his father and mother, and that was all. He 'd write to Helen for one right away. "Where 'd you get all of 'em? You 've certainly got a collection."

"Sure have. The album of hearts I 've broken. When I 've kissed a girl twice I make her give me her picture. I 've forgotten the names of some of these janes. I collected ten at Bar Harbor this summer and three at Christmas Cove. Say, this kid—" he fished through a pile of pictures—"was the hottest little devil I ever met." He passed to Hugh a cabinet photograph of a standard flapper.

"Pet? My God!" He cast his eyes ceilingward ecstatically.

Hugh's mind was a battle-field of disapproval and envy. Carl dazzled and confused him. He had often listened to the recitals of their exploits by the Merrytown Don Juans, but this good-looking, sophisticated lad evidently had a technique and breadth of experience quite unknown to Merrytown. He wanted badly to hear more, but time was flying and he had n't even begun to unpack.

"Will you help me bring up my trunk?" he asked half shyly.

"Oh, hell, yes. I 'd forgotten all about that. Come on."

They spent the rest of the afternoon unpacking, arranging and rearranging the furniture and pictures. They found a restaurant and had dinner. Then they returned to 19 Surrey and rearranged the furniture once more, pausing occasionally to chat while Carl smoked. He offered Hugh a cigarette. Hugh explained that he did not smoke, that he was a sprinter and that the coaches said that cigarettes were bad for a runner.

"Right-o," said Carl, respecting the reason thoroughly. "I can't run worth a damn myself, but I 'm not bad at tennis—not very good, either. Say, if you 're a runner you ought to make a fraternity easy. Got your eye on one?"

"Well," said Hugh, "my father 's a Nu Delt."

"The Nu Delts. Phew! High-hat as hell."
He looked at Hugh enviously. "Say, you certainly
are set. Well, my old man never went to college,
but I want to tell you that he left us a whale of a
lot of jack when he passed out a couple of years
ago."

"What!" Hugh exclaimed, staring at him in
blank astonishment.

In an instant Carl was on his feet, his flashing
eyes dimmed by tears. "My old man was the best
scout that ever lived—the best damned old scout
that ever lived." His sophistication was all gone;
he was just a small boy, heartily ashamed of himself and ready to cry. "I want you to know that,"
he ended defiantly.

At once Hugh was all sympathy. "Sure, I
know," he said softly. Then he smiled and added,
"So 's mine."

Carl's face lost its lugubriousness in a broad grin.
"I 'm a fish," he announced. "Let 's hit the hay."

"You said it!"

CHAPTER II

HUGH wrote two letters before he went to bed, one to his mother and father and the other to Helen Simpson. His letter to Helen was very brief, merely a request for her photograph.

Then, his mind in a whirl of excitement, he went to bed and lay awake dreaming, thinking of Carl, the college, and, most of all, of Helen and his walk with her the day before.

He had called on her to say good-by. They had been "going together" for a year, and she was generally considered his girl. She was a pretty child with really beautiful brown hair, which she had foolishly bobbed, lively blue eyes, and an absurdly tiny snub nose. She was little, with quick, eager hands—a shallow creature who was proud to be seen with Hugh because he had been captain of the high-school track team. But she did wish that he was n't so slow. Why, he had kissed her only once, and that had been a silly peck on the cheek. Perhaps he was just shy, but sometimes she was almost sure that he was "plain dumb."

They had walked silently along the country road
to the woods that skirted the town.   An early frost
had already touched the foliage with scarlet and
orange.   They sat down on a fallen log, and Hugh
gazed at a radiant maple-tree.

Helen let her hand drop lightly on his.   "Thinking of me?" she asked softly.

Hugh squeezed her hand.   "Yes," he whispered,
and looked at the ground while he scuffed some
fallen leaves with the toe of his shoe.

"I am going to miss you, Hughie—oh, awfully.
Are you going to miss me?"

He held her hand tightly and said nothing.   He
was aware only of her hand.   His throat seemed
to be stopped, choked with something.

A bird that should have been on its way south
chirped from a tree near by.   The sound made
Hugh look up.   He noticed that the shadows were
lengthening.   He and Helen would have to start
back pretty soon or he would be late for dinner.
There was still packing to do; his mother had said
that his father wanted to have a talk with him—
and through all his thoughts there ran like a fiery
red line the desire to kiss the girl whose hand was
clasped in his.

He turned slightly toward her.   "Hughie," she
whispered and moved close to him.   His heart
stopped as he loosened her hand from his and put

his arm around her. With a contented sigh she rested her head on one shoulder and her hand on the other. "Hughie dear," she breathed softly.

He hesitated no longer. His heart was beating so that he could not speak, but he bent and kissed her. And there they sat for half an hour more, close in each other's embrace, speaking no words, but losing themselves in kisses that seemed to have no end.

Finally Hugh realized that darkness had fallen. He drew the yielding girl to her feet and started home, his arm around her. When they reached her gate, he embraced her once more and kissed her as if he could never let her go. A light flashed in a window. Frightened, he tried to leave, but she clung to him.

"I must go," he whispered desperately.

"I 'm going to miss you awfully." He thought that she was weeping—and kissed her again. Then as another window shot light into the yard, he forced her arms from around his neck.

"Good-by, Helen. Write to me." His voice was rough and husky.

"Oh, I will. Good-by—darling."

He walked home tingling with emotion. He wanted to shout; he felt suddenly grown up. Golly, but Helen was a little peach. He felt her arms around his neck again, her lips pressed maddeningly to his. For an instant he was dizzy. . . .

As he lay in bed in 19 Surrey thinking of Helen, he tried to summon that glorious intoxication again. But he failed. Carl, the college, registration—a thousand thoughts intruded themselves. Already Helen seemed far away, a little nebulous. He wondered why. . . .

CHAPTER III

FOR the next few days Carl and Hugh did little but wait in line. They lined up to register; they lined up to pay tuition; they lined up to shake hands with President Culver; they lined up to talk for two quite useless minutes with the freshman dean; they lined up to be assigned seats in the commons. Carl suggested that he and Hugh line up in the study before going to bed so that they would keep in practice. Then they had to attend lectures given by various members of the faculty about college customs, college manners, college honor, college everything. After the sixth of them, Hugh, thoroughly weary and utterly confused, asked Carl if he now had any idea of what college was.

"Yes," replied Carl; "it's a young ladies' school for very nice boys."

"Well," Hugh said desperately, "if I have to listen to about two more awfully noble lectures, I'm going to get drunk. I have a hunch that college isn't anything like what these old birds say it is. I hope not, anyway."

"Course it isn't. Say, why wait for two more

of the damn things to kill you off?" He pulled a flask out of his desk drawer and held it out invitingly.

Hugh laughed. "You told me yourself that that stuff was catgut and that you would n't drink it on a bet. Besides, you know that I don't drink. If I 'm going to make my letter, I 've got to keep in trim."

"Right you are. Wish I knew what to do with this poison. If I leave it around here, the biddy 'll get hold of it, and then God help us. I 'll tell you what: after it gets dark to-night we 'll take it down and poison the waters of dear old Indian Lake."

"All right. Say, I 've got to pike along; I 've got a date with my faculty adviser. Hope I don't have to stand in line."

He did n't have to stand in line—he was permitted to sit—but he did have to wait an hour and a half. Finally a student came out of the inner office, and a gruff voice from within called, "Next!"

"Just like a barber shop," flashed across Hugh's mind as he entered the tiny office.

An old-young man was sitting behind a desk shuffling papers. He glanced up as Hugh came in and motioned him to a chair beside him. Hugh sat down and stared at his feet.

"Um, let 's see. Your name 's—what?"

"Carver, sir. Hugh Carver."

The adviser, Professor Kane, glanced at some

notes. "Oh, yes, from Merrytown High School,
fully accredited.   Are you taking an A.B. or a
B.S.?"

"I—I don't know."

"You have to have one year of college Latin for
a B.S. and at least two years of Greek besides for
an A.B."

"Oh!" Hugh was frightened and confused.
He knew that his father was an A.B., but he had
heard the high-school principal say that Greek was
useless nowadays.   Suddenly he remembered: the
principal had advised him to take a B.S.; he had
said that it was more practical.

"I guess I 'd better take a B.S.," he said softly.

"Very well." Professor Kane, who had n't yet
looked at Hugh, picked up a schedule card. "Any
middle name?" he asked abruptly.

"Yes, sir—Meredith."

Kane scribbled H. M. Carver at the top of the
card and then proceeded to fill it in rapidly.   He
hastily explained the symbols that he was using,
but he did not say anything about the courses.
When he had completed the schedule, he copied it
on another card, handed one to Hugh, and stuck
the other into a filing-box.

"Anything else?" he asked, turning his blond,
blank face toward Hugh for the first time.

Hugh stood up.   There were a dozen questions
that he wanted to ask.   "No, sir," he replied.

"Very well, then. I am your regular adviser. You will come to me when you need assistance. Good day."

"Good day, sir," and as Hugh passed out of the door, the gruff voice bawled, "Next!" The boy nearest the door rose and entered the sanctum.

Hugh sought the open air and gazed at the hieroglyphics on the card. "Guess they mean something," he mused, "but how am I going to find out?" A sudden fear made him blanch. "I bet I get into the wrong places. Oh, golly!"

Then came the upper-classmen, nearly seven hundred of them. The quiet campus became a bedlam of excitement and greetings. "Hi, Jack. Didya have a good summer?" . . . "Well, Tom, ol' kid, I sure am glad to see you back." . . . "Put her there, ol' scout; it 's sure good to see you." Everywhere the same greetings: "Didya have a good summer? Glad to see you back." Every one called every one else by his first name; every one shook hands with astonishing vigor, usually clutching the other fellow by the forearm at the same time. How cockily these lads went around the campus! No confusion or fear for them; they knew what to do.

For the first time Hugh felt a pang of homesickness; for the first time he realized that he was n't yet part of the college. He clung close to Carl and

one or two other lads in Surrey with whom he
picked up an acquaintance, and Carl clung close to
Hugh, careful to hide the fact that he felt very
small and meek. For the first time *he* realized
that he was just a freshman—and he did n't like it.
Then suddenly the tension, which had been gath-
ering for a day or so, broke. Orders went out
from the upper-classmen that all freshmen put on
their baby bonnets, silly little blue caps with a
bright orange button. From that moment every
freshman was doomed. Work was their lot, and
plenty of it. "Hi, freshman, carry up my trunk.
Yeah, you, freshman—you with the skinny legs.
You and your fat friend carry my trunk up to the
fourth floor—and if you drop it, I 'll break your
fool necks." . . . "Freshman! go down to the station and get my suit-cases. Here are the checks.
Hurry back if you know what 's good for you."
. . . "Freshman! go up to Hill Twenty-eight and
put the beds together." . . . "Freshman! come up
to my room. I want you to hang pictures."
    Fortunately the labor did not last long, but while
it lasted Hugh was hustled around as he never had
been before. And he loved it. He loved his blue
cap and its orange button; he loved the upper-
classmen who called him freshman and ordered him
around; he loved the very trunks that he lugged
so painfully up-stairs. He was being recognized,
merely as a janitor, it is true, but recognized; at

last he was a part of Sanford College. Further,
one of the men who had ordered him around the
most fiercely wore a Nu Delta pin, the emblem of
his father's fraternity. He ran that man's errands
with such speed and willingness that the hero decided that the freshman was "very, very dumb."

That night Hugh and Carl sat in 19 Surrey and
rested their aching bones, one on a couch, the other
in a leather Morris chair.

"Hot stuff, was n't it?" said Hugh, stretching
out comfortably.

"Hot stuff, hell! How do they get that way?"

"Never mind; we 'll do the ordering next year."

"Right you are," said Carl decisively, lighting a
cigarette, "and won't I make the little frosh walk."
He gazed around the room, his face beaming with
satisfaction. "Say, we 're pretty snappy here,
are n't we?"

Hugh, too, looked around admiringly. The
walls were almost hidden by banners, a huge Sanford blanket—Hugh's greatest contribution—Carl's
Kane blanket, the photographs of the "harem,"
posters of college athletes and movie bathing-girls,
pipe-racks, and three Maxfield Parrish prints.

"It certainly is fine," said Hugh proudly. "All
we need is a barber pole and a street sign."

"We 'll have 'em before the week is out." This
with great decision.

CHAPTER IV

CARL'S adviser had been less efficient than Hugh's; therefore he knew what his courses were, where the classes met and the hours, the names of his instructors, and the requirements other than Latin for a B.S. degree. Carl said that he was taking a B.S. because he had had a year of Greek at Kane and was therefore perfectly competent to make full use of the language; he could read the letters on the front doors of the fraternity houses.

The boys found that their courses were the same but that they were in different sections. Hugh was in a dilemma; he could make nothing out of his card.

"Here," said Carl, "give the thing to me. My adviser was a good scout and wised me up. This P.C. is n't paper cutting as you might suppose; it 's gym. You 'll get out of that by signing up for track. P.C. means physical culture. Think of that! You can sign up for track any time tomorrow down at the gym. And E 1, 7 means that you 're in English 1, Section 7; and M is math. You 're in Section 3. Lat means Latin, of course —Section 6. My adviser—he tried pretty hard to be funny—said that G.S. was n't glorious salvation but general science. That meets in the big lecture hall in Cranston. We all go to that. And H 1, 4 means that you are in Section 4 of History 1. See? That 's all there is to it. Now this thing"—he held up a printed schedule—"tells you where the classes meet."

With a great deal of labor, discussion, and profanity they finally got a schedule made out that meant something to Hugh. He heaved a Brobdingnagian sigh of relief when they finished.

"Well," he exclaimed, "that 's that! At last I know where I 'm going. You certainly saved my life. I know where all the buildings are; so it ought to be easy."

"Sure," said Carl encouragingly; "it 's easy. Now there 's nothing to do till to-morrow until eight forty-five when we attend chapel to the glory of the Lord. I think I 'll pray to-morrow; I may need it. Christ! I hate to study."

"Me, too," Hugh lied. He really loved books, but somehow he could n't admit the fact, which had suddenly become shameful, to Carl. "Let 's go to the movies," he suggested, changing the subject for safety.

"Right-o!" Carl put on his freshman cap and flung Hugh's to him. "Gloria Nielsen is there, and she 's a pash baby. Ought to be a good fillum."

The Blue and Orange—it was the only movie theater in town—was almost full when the boys arrived. Only a few seats near the front were still vacant. A freshman started down the aisle, his "baby bonnet" stuck jauntily on the back of his head.

"Freshman!" . . . "Kill him!" . . . "Murder the frosh!" Shouts came from all parts of the house, and an instant later hundreds of peanuts shot swiftly at the startled freshman. "Cap! Cap! Cap off!" There was a panic of excitement. Upper-classmen were standing on their chairs to get free throwing room. The freshman snatched off his cap, drew his head like a scared turtle down into his coat collar, and ran for a seat. Hugh and Carl tucked their caps into their coat pockets and attempted to stroll nonchalantly down the aisle. They had n't taken three steps before the bombardment began. Like their classmate, they ran for safety.

Then some one in the front of the theatre threw a peanut at some one in the rear. The fight was on! Yelling like madmen, the students stood on their chairs and hurled peanuts, the front and rear of the house automatically dividing into enemy camps. When the fight was at its hottest, three girls entered.

"Wimmen! Wimmen!" As the girls walked down the aisle, infinitely pleased with their reception, five hundred men stamped in time with their steps.

No sooner were the girls seated than there was a scramble in one corner, an excited scuffling of feet. "I 've got it!" a boy screamed. He stood on his chair and held up a live mouse by its tail. There was a shout of applause and then—"Play catch!"

The boy dropped the writhing mouse into a peanut bag, screwed the open end tight-closed, and then threw the bag far across the room. Another boy caught it and threw it, this time over the girls' heads. They screamed and jumped upon their chairs, holding their skirts, and dancing up and down in assumed terror. Back over their heads, back and over, again and again the bagged mouse was thrown while the girls screamed and the boys roared with delight. Suddenly one of the girls threw up her arm, caught the bag deftly, held it for a second, and then tossed it into the rear of the theater.

Cheers of terrifying violence broke loose: "Ray! Ray! Atta girl! Hot dog! Ray, ray!" And then the lights went out.

"Moosick! Moosick! Moo-sick!" The audience stamped and roared, whistled and howled. "Moosick! We want moosick!"

The pianist, an undergraduate, calmly strolled down the aisle.

"Get a move on!" . . . "Earn your salary!"
. . . "Give us moosick!"

The pianist paused to thumb his nose casually at
the entire audience, and then amid shouts and hisses
sat down at the piano and began to play "Love
Nest."

Immediately the boys began to whistle, and as
the comedy was utterly stupid, they relieved their
boredom by whistling the various tunes that the
pianist played until the miserable film flickered out.

Then the "feature" and the fun began. During
the stretches of pure narrative, the boys whistled,
but when there was any real action they talked.
The picture was a melodrama of "love and hate,"
as the advertisement said.

The boys told the actors what to do; they revealed to them the secrets of the plot. "She's
hiding behind the door, Harold. No, no! Not
that way. Hey, dumbbell—behind the door."
. . . "Catch him, Gloria; he's only shy!" . . .
"No, that's not him!"

The climactic fight brought shouts of encourag-
ment—to the villain. "Kill him!" . . . "Shoot
one to his kidneys!" . . . "Ahhhhh," as the villain hit the hero in the stomach. . . . "Muss his
hair. Atta boy!" . . . "Kill the skunk!" And finally groans of despair when the hero won his inevitable victory.

But it was the love scenes that aroused the great-

est ardor and joy. The hero was given careful
instructions. "Some neckin', Harold!" . . . "Kiss
her! Kiss her! Ahhh!" . . . "Harold, Harold,
you're getting rough! . . . "She's vamping you,
Harold!" . . . "Stop it; Gloria; he's a good boy."
And so on until the picture ended in the usual close-
up of the hero and heroine silhouetted in a tender
embrace against the setting sun. The boys breathed
"Ahhhh" and "Ooooh" ecstatically—and laughed.
The meretricious melodrama did not fool them, but
they delighted in its absurdities.

The lights flashed on and the crowd filed out,
"wise-cracking" about the picture and commenting
favorably on the heroine's figure. There were
shouts to this fellow or that fellow to come on over
and play bridge, and suggestions here and there
to go to a drug store and get a drink.

Hugh and Carl strolled home over the dark
campus, both of them radiant with excitement, Hugh
frankly so.

"Golly, I did enjoy that," he exclaimed. "I
never had a better time. It was sure hot stuff. I
don't want to go to the room; let's walk for a
while."

"Yeah, it was pretty good," Carl admitted.
"Nope, I can't go walking; gotta write a letter."

"Who to? The harem?"

Carl hunched his shoulders until his ears touched

his coat collar. "Gettin' cold. Fall's here.
Nope, not the harem. My old lady."

Hugh looked at him bewildered. He was finding Carl more and more a conundrum. He consistently called his mother his old lady, insisted that
she was a damned nuisance—and wrote to her
every night. Hugh was writing to his mother only
twice a week. It was very confusing. . . .

CHAPTER V

CAPWELL CHAPEL—it bore the pork merchant's name as an eternal memorial to him—was as impressive inside as out. The stained-glass windows had been made by a famous New York firm; the altar had been designed by an even more famous sculptor. The walls, quite improperly, were adorned with paintings of former presidents, but the largest painting of all—it was fairly Gargantuan—was of the pork merchant, a large, ruddy gentleman, whom the artist, a keen observer, had painted truly—complacently porcine, benevolently smug.

The seniors and juniors sat in the nave, the sophomores on the right side of the transept, the freshmen on the left. Hugh gazed upward in awe at the dim recesses of the vaulted ceiling, at the ornately carved choir where gowned students were quietly seating themselves, at the colored light streaming through the beautiful windows, at the picture of the pork merchant. The chapel bells ceased tolling; rich, solemn tones swelled from the organ.

President Culver in cap and gown, his purple

hood falling over his shoulders, entered followed by his faculty, also gowned and hooded. The students rose and remained standing until the president and faculty were seated. The organ sounded a final chord, and then the college chaplain rose and prayed—very badly. He implored the Lord to look kindly "on these young men who have come from near and far to drink from this great fount of learning, this well of wisdom."

The prayer over, the president addressed the students. He was a large, erect man with iron-gray hair and a rugged intelligent face. Although he was sixty years old, his body was vigorous and free from extra weight. He spoke slowly and impressively, choosing his words with care and enunciating them with great distinctness. His address was for the freshmen: he welcomed them to Sanford College, to its splendid traditions, its high ideals, its noble history. He spoke of the famous men it numbered among its sons, of the work they had done for America and the world, of the work he hoped future Sanford men, they, the freshmen, would some day do for America and the world. He mentioned briefly the boys from Sanford who had died in the World War "to make the world safe for democracy," and he prayed that their sacrifice had not been in vain. Finally, he spoke of the chapel service, which the students were required to attend. He hoped that they would find inspiration in it, knowledge and strength. He assured them that the service would always be non-sectarian, that there would never be anything in it to offend any one of any race, creed, or religion. With a last exhortation to the freshmen to make the most of their great opportunities, he ended with the announcement that they would rise and sing the sixty-seventh hymn.

Hugh was deeply impressed by the speech but disturbed by the students. From where he sat he got an excellent view of the juniors and seniors. The seniors, who sat in the front of the nave, seemed to be paying fairly good attention; but the juniors—many of them, at least—paid no attention at all. Some of them were munching apples, some doughnuts, and many of them were reading "The Sanford News," the college's daily paper. Some of the juniors talked during the president's address, and once he noticed four of them doubled up as if overcome by laughter. To him the service was a beautiful and impressive occasion. He could not understand the conduct of the upper-classmen. It seemed, to put it mildly, irreverent.

Every one, however, sang the doxology with great vigor, some of the boys lifting up a "whisky" tenor that made the chapel ring, and to which Hugh happily added his own clear tenor. The benediction was pronounced by the chaplain, the seniors marched out slowly in twos, while the other students and the faculty stood in their places; then the president, followed by the faculty, passed out of the great doors. When the back of the last faculty gown had disappeared, the under-classmen broke for the door, pushing each other aside, swearing when a toe was stepped on, yelling to each other, some of them joyously chanting the doxology. Hugh was caught in the rush and carried along with the mob, feeling ashamed and distressed; this was no way to leave a church.

Once outside, however, he had no time to think of the chapel service; he had five minutes in which to get to his first class, and the building was across the campus, a good two minutes' walk. He patted his cap to be sure that it was firmly on the back of his head, clutched his note-book, and ran as hard as he could go, the strolling upper-classmen, whom he passed at top speed, grinning after him in tolerant amusement.

Hugh was the first one in the class-room and wondered in a moment of panic if he was in the right place. He sat down dubiously and looked at his watch. Four minutes left. He would wait two, and then if nobody came he would—he gasped; he could n't imagine what he *would* do. How could he find the right class-room? Maybe his class did n't come at this hour at all. Suppose he and Carl had made a mistake. If they had, his whole schedule was probably wrong. "Oh, golly," he thought, feeling pitifully weak, "won't that be hell? What can I do?"

At that moment a countrified-looking youth entered, looking as scared as Hugh felt. His face was pale, and his voice trembled as he asked timidly, "Do you know if this is Section Three of Math One?"

Hugh was immediately strengthened. "I think so," he replied. "Anyhow, let's wait and find out."

The freshman sighed in huge relief, took out a not too clean handkerchief, and mopped his face. "Criminy!" he exclaimed as he wriggled down the aisle to a seat by Hugh, "I was sure worried. I thought I was in the wrong building, though I was sure that my adviser had told me positively that Math was in Matthew Six."

"I guess we're all right," Hugh comforted him as two other freshmen, also looking dubious, entered. They were followed by four more, and then by a stampeding group, all of them pop-eyed, all of them in a rush. In the next minute five freshmen dashed in and then dashed out again, utterly bewildered, obviously terrified, and not knowing where to go or what to do. "Is this Math One, Section Three?" every man demanded of the room as he entered; and every one yelled, "Yes," or, "I think so."

Just as the bell rang at ten minutes after the

hour, the instructor entered. It was Professor Kane.

"This is Mathematics One, Section Three," Kane announced in a dry voice. "If there is any one here who does not belong here, he will please leave." Nobody moved; so he shuffled some cards in his hand and asked the men to answer to the roll-call.

"Adams, J. H."

"Present, sir."

Kane looked up and frowned. "Say 'here,'" he said severely. "This is not a grammar-school."

"Yes, sir," stuttered Adams, his face first white then purple. "Here, sir."

" 'Here' will do; there is no need of the 'sir.' Allsop, K. E."

"Here"—in a very faint voice.

"Speak up!"

"Here." This time a little louder.

And so it went, hardly a man escaping without some admonishment. Hugh's throat went dry; his tongue literally stuck to the roof of his mouth: he was sure that he would n't be able to say "Here" when it came his turn, and he could feel his heart pounding in dreadful anticipation.

"Carver, H. M."

"Here!"

There! it was out! Or had he really said it? He looked at the professor in terror, but Kane was already calling, "Dana, R. T." Hugh sank back in his chair; he was trembling.

Kane announced the text-book, and when Hugh caught the word "trigonometry" he actually thrilled with joy. He had had trig in high school. Whoops! Would he hit Math I in the eye? He'd knock it for a goal. . . . Then conscience spoke. Ought n't he to tell Kane that he had already had trig? He guessed quite rightly that Kane had not understood his high-school credentials, which had given him credit for "advanced mathematics." Kane had taken it for granted that that was advanced algebra. Hugh felt that he ought to explain the mistake, but fear of the arid, impersonal man restrained him. Kane had told him to take Math I; and Kane was law.

Unlike most of Hugh's instructors, Kane kept the class the full hour the first day, seating them in alphabetical order—he had to repeat the performance three times during the week as new men entered the class—lecturing them on the need of doing their problems carefully and accurately, and discoursing on the value of mathematics, trigonometry in particular, in the study of science and engineering. Hugh was not interested in science, engineering, or mathematics, but he listened carefully, trying hard to follow Kane's cold discourse. At the end of the hour he told his neighbor as they left the room that he guessed that Professor Kane knew an awful lot, and his neighbor agreed with him.

Hugh's other instructors proved less impressive than Kane; in fact, Mr. Alling, the instructor in Latin, was altogether disconcerting.

"Plautus," he told the class, "wrote comedies, farces—not exercises in translation. He was also, my innocents, occasionally naughty—oh, really naughty. What's worse, he used slang, common every-day slang—the kind of stuff that you and I talk. Now, I have an excellent vocabulary of slang, obscenity, and profanity; and you are going to hear most of it. Think of the opportunity. Don't think that I mean just 'damn' and 'hell.' They are good for a laugh in a theater any day, but Plautus was not restrained by our modern conventions. *You* will confine yourselves, please, to English undefiled, but I shall speak the modern equivalent to a Roman gutter-pup's language whenever necessary. You will find this course very illuminating—in some ways. And, who knows? you may learn something not only about Latin but about Rome."

Hugh thought Mr. Alling was rather flippant and lacking in dignity. Professor Kane was more like a college teacher. Before the term was out he hated Kane with an intensity that astonished him, and he looked forward to his Latin classes with an eagerness of which he was almost ashamed.

Plautus in the Alling free and colloquial transla-
tions was enormously funny.

Professor Hartley, who gave the history lectures,
talked in a bass monotone and never seemed to
pause for breath. His words came in a slow
steady stream that never rose nor fell nor paused—
until the bell rang. The men in the back of the
room slept. Hugh was seated near the front; so
he drew pictures in his note-book. The English
instructor talked about punctuation as if it were
very unpleasant but almost religiously important;
and what the various lecturers in general science
talked about—ten men gave the course—Hugh
never knew. In after years all that he could remember about the course was that one man spoke
broken English and that a professor of physics had
made huge bulbs glow with marvelous colors.

Hugh had one terrifying experience before he
finally got settled to his work. It occurred the second day of classes. He was comfortably seated
in what he thought was his English class—he had
come in just as the bell rang—when the instructor
announced that it was a class in French. What
was he to do? What would the instructor do if he
got up and left the room? What would happen if
he didn't report at his English class? What
would happen to him for coming into his English
class late? These questions staggered his mind.
He was afraid to stay in the French class. Cau-

tiously he got up and began to tiptoe to the door.

"Wrong room?" the instructor asked pleasantly.

Hugh flushed. "Yes, sir." He stopped dead still, not knowing what to do next.

He was a typical rattled freshman, and the class, which was composed of sophomores, laughed. Hugh, angry and humiliated, started for the door, but the instructor held up a hand that silenced the class; then he motioned for Hugh to come to his desk.

"What class are you looking for?"

"English One, sir, Section Seven." He held out his schedule card, reassured by the instructor's kindly manner.

The instructor looked at the card and then consulted a printed schedule.

"Oh," he said, "your adviser made a mistake. He got you into the wrong group list. You belong in Sanders Six."

"Thank you, sir." Hugh spoke so softly that the waiting class did not hear him, but the instructor smiled at the intensity of his thanks. As he left the room, he knew that every one was looking at him; his legs felt as if they were made of wood. It wasn't until he had closed the door that his knee-joints worked naturally. But the worst was still ahead of him. He had to go to his English class in Sanders 6. He ran across the campus, his heart beating wildly, his hands desperately clenched.

When he reached Sanders 6, he found three other freshmen grouped before the door.

"Is this English One, Section Seven?" one asked tremulously.

"I think so," whispered the second. "Do you know?" he asked, turning to Hugh.

"Yes; I am almost sure."

They stood there looking at each other, no one quite daring to enter Sanders 6, no one quite daring to leave. Suddenly the front door of the building slammed. A bareheaded youth rushed up the stairs. He was a repeater; that is, a man who had failed the course the preceding year and was taking it over again. He brushed by the scared freshmen, opened the door, and strode into Sanders 6, closing the door behind him.

The freshmen looked at each other, and then the one nearest the door opened it. The four of them filed in silently.

The class looked up. "Sit in the back of the room," said the instructor.

And that was all there was to that. In his senior year Hugh remembered the incident and wondered at his terror. He tried to remember why he had been so badly frightened. He could n't; there did n't seem to be any reason at all.

CHAPTER VI

ABOUT a week after the opening of college, Hugh returned to Surrey Hall one night feeling unusually virtuous and happy. He had worked religiously at the library until it had closed at ten, and he had been in the mood to study. His lessons for the next day were all prepared, and prepared well. He had strolled across the moon-lit campus, buoyant and happy. Some one was playing the organ in the dark chapel; he paused to listen. Two students passed him, humming softly,

> "Sanford, Sanford, mother of men,
> Love us, guard us, hold us true . . ."

The dormitories were dim masses broken by rectangles of soft yellow light. Somewhere a banjo twanged. Another student passed.

"Hello, Carver," he said pleasantly. "Nice night."

"Oh, hello, Jones. It sure is."

The simple greeting completed his happiness. He felt that he belonged, that Sanford, the "mother of men," had taken him to her heart. The music in the chapel swelled, lyric, passionate—up! up! almost a cry. The moonlight was golden between the heavy shadows of the elms. Tears came into the boy's eyes; he was melancholy with joy.

He climbed the stairs of Surrey slowly, reluctant to reach his room and Carl's flippancy. He passed an open door and glanced at the men inside the room.

"Hi, Hugh. Come in and bull a while."

"Not to-night, thanks." He moved on down the hall, feeling a vague resentment; his mood had been broken, shattered.

The door opposite his own room was slightly open. A freshman lived there, Herbert Morse, a queer chap with whom Carl and Hugh had succeeded in scraping up only the slightest acquaintance. He was a big fellow, fully six feet, husky and quick. The football coach said that he had the makings of a great half-back, but he had already been fired off the squad because of his irregularity in reporting for practice. Except for what the boys called his stand-offishness—some of them said that he was too damned high-hat—he was extremely attractive. He had red, almost copper-colored, hair, and an exquisite skin, as delicate as a child's. His features were well carved, his nose slightly aquiline—a magnificent looking fellow, almost imperious; or as Hugh once said to Carl, "Morse looks kinda noble."

As Hugh placed his hand on the door-knob of
No 19, he heard something that sounded suspiciously like a sob from across the hall. He paused
and listened. He was sure that he could hear
some one crying.

"Wonder what's wrong," he thought, instantly
disturbed and sympathetic.

He crossed the hall and tapped lightly on
Morse's door. There was no answer; nor was
there any when he tapped a second time. For a
moment he was abashed, and then he pushed open
the door and entered Morse's room.

In the far corner Morse was sitting at his desk,
his head buried in his arms, his shoulders shaking.
He was crying fiercely, terribly; at times his whole
body jerked in the violence of his sobbing.

Hugh stood by the door embarrassed and rather
frightened. Morse's grief brought a lump to his
throat. He had never seen any one cry like that
before. Something had to be done. But what
could he do? He had no right to intrude on
Morse, but he couldn't let the poor fellow go on
suffering like that. As he stood there hesitant,
shaken, Morse buried his head deeper in his arms,
moaned convulsively, twisting and trembling after
a series of sobs that seemed to tear themselves
from him. That was too much for Hugh. He
couldn't stand it. Some force outside of him sent
him across the room to Morse. He put his

hand on a quivering shoulder and said gently: "What is it, Morse? What's the matter?"

Morse ran his hand despairingly through his red hair, shook his head, and made no answer.

"Come on, old man; buck up." Hugh's voice trembled; it was husky with sympathy. "Tell me about it. Maybe I can help."

Then Morse looked up, his face stained with tears, his eyes inflamed, almost desperate. He stared at Hugh wonderingly. For an instant he was angry at the intrusion, but his anger passed at once. He could not miss the tenderness and sympathy in Hugh's face; and the boy's hand was still pressing with friendly insistence on his shoulder. There was something so boyishly frank, so clean and honest about Hugh that his irritation melted into confidence; and he craved a confidant passionately.

"Shut the door," he said dully, and reached into his trousers pocket for his handkerchief. He mopped his face and eyes vigorously while Hugh was closing the door, and then blew his nose as if he hated it. But the tears continued to come, and all during his talk with Hugh he had to pause occasionally to dry his eyes.

Hugh stood awkwardly in the middle of the rug, not knowing whether to sit down or not. Morse was clutching his handkerchief in his hand and staring at the floor. Finally he spoke up.

"Sit down," he said in a dead voice, "there."

Hugh sank into the chair Morse indicated and then gripped his hands together. He felt weak and frightened, and absolutely unable to say anything. But Morse saved him the trouble.

"I suppose you think I am an awful baby," he began, his voice thick with tears, "but I just can't help it. I—I just can't help it. I don't want to cry, but I do." And then he added defiantly, "Go ahead and think I 'm a baby if you want to."

"I don't think you 're a baby," Hugh said softly; "I 'm just sorry; that 's all. . . . I hope I can help." He smiled shyly, hopefully.

His smile conquered Morse. "You 're a good kid, Carver," he cried impulsively. "A darn good kid. I like you, and I 'm going to tell you all about it. And I—I—I won't care if you laugh."

"I won't laugh," Hugh promised, relieved to think that there was a possibility of laughing. The trouble could n't be so awfully bad.

Morse blew his nose, stuck his handkerchief into his pocket, pulled it out again and dabbed his eyes, returned it to his pocket, and suddenly stood up.

"I 'm homesick!" he blurted out. "I 'm—I 'm homesick, damned homesick. I 've been homesick ever since I arrived. I—I just can't stand it."

For an instant Hugh did have a wild desire to laugh. Part of the desire was caused by nervous relief, but part of it was caused by what seemed to

him the absurdity of the situation: a big fellow like
Morse blubbering, bawling for home and mother!

"You can't know," Morse went on, "how awful
it is—awful! I want to cry all the time. I can't
listen in classes. A prof asked me a question to-
day, and I did n't know what he had been talking
about. He asked me what he had said. I had to
say I did n't know. The whole class laughed, and
the prof asked me why I had come to college.
God! I nearly died."

Hugh's sympathy was all captured again. He
knew that he *would* die if he ever made a fool
of himself in the class-room.

"Gosh!" he exclaimed. "What did you say?"

"Nothing. I could n't think of anything. For
a minute I thought that my head was going to bust.
He quit razzing me and I tried to pay attention,
but I could n't; all I could do was think of home.
Lord! I wish I was there!" He mopped at his
eyes and paced up and down the room nervously.

"Oh, you 'll get over that," Hugh said comfort-
ingly. "Pretty soon you 'll get to know lots of
fellows, and then you won't mind about home."

"That 's what I keep telling myself, but it don't
work. I can't eat or sleep. I can't study. I
can't do anything. I tell you I 've got to go
home. I 've *got* to!" This last with desperate
emphasis.

Hugh smiled. "You 're all wrong," he asserted

positively. "You're just lonely; that's all. I
bet that you'll be crazy about college in a month—
same as the rest of us. When you feel blue, come
in and see Peters and me. We'll make you grin;
Peters will, anyway. You can't be blue around
him."

Morse sat down. "You don't understand.
I'm not lonely. It isn't that. I could talk to
fellows all day long if I wanted to. I don't want
to talk to 'em. I can't. There's just one person
that I want to talk to, and that's my mother."
He shot the word "mother" out defiantly and
glared at Hugh, silently daring him to laugh, which
Hugh had sense enough not to do, although he
wanted to strongly. The great big baby, wanting
his mother! Why, he wanted his mother, too, but
he didn't cry about it.

"That's all right," he said reassuringly; "you'll
see her Christmas vacation, and that isn't very long
off."

"I want to see her now!" Morse jumped to his
feet and raised his clenched hands above his head.
"Now!" he roared. "Now! I've got to. I'm
going home on the midnight." He whirled about
to his desk and began to pull open the drawers, pil-
ing their contents on the top.

"Here!" Hugh rushed to him and clutched his
arms. "Don't do that." Morse struggled, angry
at the restraining hands, ready to strike them off.

Hugh had a flash of inspiration. "Think how disappointed your mother will be," he cried, hanging on to Morse's arms; "think of her."

Morse ceased struggling. "She will be disappointed," he admitted miserably. "What can I do?" There was a world of despair in his question.

Hugh pushed him into the desk-chair and seated himself on the edge of the desk. "I'll tell you," he said. He talked for half an hour, cheering Morse, assuring him that his homesickness would pass away, offering to study with him. At first Morse paid little attention, but finally he quit sniffing and looked up, real interest in his face. When Hugh got a weak smile out of him, he felt that his work had been done. He jumped off the desk, leaned over to slap Morse on the back, and told him that he was a good egg but a damn fool.

Morse grinned. "You're a good egg yourself," he said gratefully. "You've saved my life."

Hugh was pleased and blushed. "You're full of bull. . . . Remember, we do Latin at ten tomorrow." He opened the door. "Good night."

"Good night." And Hugh heard as he closed the door, "Thanks a lot."

When he opened his own door, he found Carl sitting before a blazing log fire. There was no other light in the room. Carl had written his nightly letter to the "old lady," and he was a little homesick himself—softened into a tender and pensive mood. He did not move as Hugh sat down in a big chair on the other side of the hearth and said softly, "Thinking?"

"Un-huh. Where you been?"

"Across the hall in Morse's room." Then as Carl looked up in surprise, he told him of his experience with their red-headed neighbor. "He'll get over it," he concluded confidently. "He's just been lonely."

Carl puffed contemplatively at his pipe for a few minutes before replying. Hugh waited, watching the slender boy stretched out in a big chair before the fire, his ankles crossed, his face gentle and boyish in the ruddy, flickering light. The shadows, heavy and wavering, played magic with the room; it was vast, mysterious.

"No," said Carl, pausing again to puff his pipe; "no, he won't get over it. He'll go home."

"Aw, shucks. A big guy like that isn't going to stay a baby all his life." Hugh was frankly derisive. "Soon as he gets to know a lot of fellows, he'll forget home and mother."

Carl smiled vaguely, his eyes dreamy as he gazed into the hypnotizing flames. The mask of sophistication had slipped off his face; he was pleasantly in the control of a gentle mood, a mood that erased the last vestige of protective coloring.

He shook his head slowly. "You don't understand, Hugh. Morse is sick, *sick*—not lonesome. He's got something worse than flu. Nobody can, stand what he's got."

Hugh looked at him in bewilderment. This was a new Carl, some one he had n't met before. Gone was the slang flippancy, the hard roughness. Even his voice was softened.

Carl knocked his pipe empty on the knob of an andiron, sank deeper into his chair, and began to speak slowly.

"I think I'm going to tell you a thing or two about myself. We've got to room together, and I—well, I like you. You're a good egg, but you don't get me at all. I guess you've never run up against anybody like me before." He paused. Hugh said nothing, afraid to break into Carl's mood. He was intensely curious. He leaned forward and watched Carl, who was staring dreamily into the fire.

"I told you once, I think," he continued, "that my old man had left us a lot of jack. That's true. We're rich, awfully rich. I have my own account and can spend as much as I like. The sky's the limit. What I did n't tell you is that we're *nouveau riche*—no class at all. My old man made all his money the first year of the war. He was a commission-merchant, a middleman. Money just rolled in, I guess. He bought stocks with it, and they boomed; and he had sense enough to sell them

when they were at the top. Six years ago we
did n't have hardly anything. Now we 're rich.

"My old man was a good scout, but he did n't
have much education; neither has the old lady.
Both of 'em went through grammar-school; that 's
all.

"Well, they knew they were n't real folks, not
regular people, and they wanted me to be. See?
That 's why they sent me to Kane. Well, Kane
is n't strong for *nouveau riche* kids, not by a damn
sight. At first old Simmonds—he 's the head master—would n't take me, said that he did n't have
room; but my old man begged and begged, so finally
Simmonds said all right."

Again he paused, and Hugh waited. Carl was
speaking so softly that he had trouble in hearing
him, but somehow he did n't dare to ask him to
speak louder.

"I sha'n't forget the day," Carl went on, "that
the old man left me at Kane. I was scared, and
I did n't want to stay. But he made me; he said
that Kane would make a gentleman out of me. I
was homesick, homesick as hell. I know how
Morse feels. I tried to run away three times, but
they caught me and brought me back. Cry? I
bawled all the time when I was alone. I could n't
sleep for weeks; I just laid in bed and bawled.
God! it was awful. The worst of it was the meals.
I did n't know how to eat right, you see, and the

master who sat at the table with our form would correct me. I used to want to die, and sometimes I would say that I was sick and did n't want any food so that I would n't have to go to meals. The fellows razzed the life out of me; some of 'em called me Paddy. The reason I came here to Sanford was that no Kane fellows come here. They go mostly to Williams, but some of 'em go to Yale or Princeton.

"Well, I had four years of that, and I was homesick the whole four years. Oh, I don't mean that they kept after me all the time—that was just the first few months—but they never really accepted me. I never felt at home. Even when I was with a bunch of them, I felt lonesome. . . . And they never made a gentleman out of me, though my old lady thinks they did."

"You 're crazy," Hugh interrupted indignantly. "You 're as much a gentleman as anybody in college."

Carl smiled and shook his head. "No, you don't understand. You 're a gentleman, but I 'm not. Oh, I know all the tricks, the parlor stunts. Four years at Kane taught me those, but they 're just tricks to me. I don't know just how to explain it— but I know that you 're a gentleman and I 'm not."

"You 're just plain bug-house. You make me feel like a fish. Why, I 'm just from a country high school. I 'm not in your class." Hugh sat up and leaned eagerly toward Carl, gesticulating excitedly.

"As if that made any difference," Carl replied, his voice sharp with scorn. "You see, I'm a bad egg. I drink and gamble and pet. I have n't gone the limit yet on—on account of my old lady—but I will."

Hugh was relieved. He had wondered more than once during the past week "just how far Carl had gone." Several times Carl had suggested by sly innuendos that there was n't anything that he had n't done, and Hugh had felt a slight disapproval—and considerable envy. His own standards were very high, very strict, but he was ashamed to reveal them.

"I 've never gone the limit either," he confessed shyly.

Carl threw back his head and laughed. "You poor fish; don't you suppose I know that?" he exclaimed.

"How did you know?" Hugh demanded indignantly. "I might 've. Why, I was out with a girl just before I left home and—"

"You kissed her," Carl concluded for him. "I don't know how I knew, but I did. You 're just kinda pure; that 's all. I 'm not pure at all; I 'm just a little afraid—and I keep thinkin' of my old lady. I 've started to several times, but I 've always thought of her and quit."

He sat silent for a minute or two and then continued more gently. "My old lady never came to Kane. She never will come here, either. She wants to give me a real chance. See? She knows she is n't a lady—but—but, oh, God, Hugh, she 's white, white as hell. I guess I think more of her than all the rest of the world put together. That 's why I write to her every night. She writes to me every day, too. The letters have mistakes in them, but—but they keep me straight. That is, they have so far. I know, though, that some night I 'll be out with a bag and get too much liquor in me— and then good-by, virginity."

"You 're crazy, Carl. You know you won't."

Carl rose from the chair and stretched hugely.

"You 're a good egg, Hugh," he said in the midst of a yawn, "but you 're a damn fool."

Hugh started. That was just what he had said to Morse.

He never caught Carl in a confidential mood again. The next morning he was his old flippant self, swearing because he had to study his Latin, which was n't "of any damned use to anybody."

In the following weeks Hugh religiously clung to Morse, helped him with his work, went to the movies with him, inveigled him into going on several long walks. Morse was more cheerful and almost pathetically grateful. One day, however,

Hugh found an unstamped letter on the floor. He opened it wonderingly.

Dear Hugh [he read]. You've been awfully good to me but I can't stand it. I'm going home to-day. Give my regards to Peters. Thanks for all you've done for me.

BERT MORSE.

CHAPTER VII

FOR a moment after reading Morse's letter Hugh was genuinely sorry, but almost immediately he felt irritated and hurt.

He handed the letter to Carl, who entered just as he finished reading it, and exploded: "The simp! And after I wasted so much time on him."

Carl read the letter. "I told you so." He smiled impishly. "You were the wise boy; you *knew* that he would get over it."

Hugh should really have felt grateful to Morse. It was only a feeling of responsibility for him that had made Hugh prepare his own lessons. Day after day he had studied with Morse in order to cheer him up; and that was all the studying he had done. Latin and history had little opportunity to claim his interest in competition with the excitement around him.

Crossing the campus for the first few weeks of college was an adventure for every freshman. He did not know when he would be seized by a howling group of sophomores and forced to make an ass of himself for their amusement. Sometimes he was required to do "esthetic dancing," sometimes to

sing, or, what was more common, to make a speech.
And no matter how hard he tried, the sophomores
were never pleased.   If he danced, they laughed at
him, guyed him unmercifully, called attention to his
legs, his awkwardness, urged him to go faster, insisted that he get some "pash" into it.   If he sang,
and the frightened freshman usually sang off key,
they interrupted him after a few notes, told him
to sing something else, interrupted that, and told
him "for God's sake" to dance.   The speech-
making, however, provided the most fun, especially
if the freshman was cleverer than his captors.
Then there was a battle of wits, and if the freshman too successfully defeated his opponents, he was
dropped into a watering-trough that had stood on
the campus for more than a century.   Of justice
there was none, but of sport there was a great
plenty.   The worst scared of the freshmen really
enjoyed the experience.   By a strange sort of in-
verted logic, he felt that he was something of a
hero; at least, for a brief time he had occupied the
public eye.   He had been initiated; he was a Sanford man.

One freshman, however, found those two weeks
harrowing.   That was Merton Billings, the fat
man of the class.   Day after day he was captured
by the sophomores and commanded to dance.   He
was an earnest youth and entirely without a sense of
humor.   Dancing to him was not only hard work

but downright wicked. He was a member of the Epworth League, and he took his membership seriously. Even David, he remembered, had "got in wrong" because he danced; and he had no desire to emulate David. Within two days the sophomores discovered his religious ardor, his horror of drinking, smoking, and dancing. So they made him dance while they howled with glee at his bobbing stomach; his short, staggering legs; his red jowls, jigging and jouncing; his pale blue eyes, protruding excitedly from their sockets; his lips pressed tight together, periodically popping open for breath. He was very funny, very angry, and very much ashamed. Every night he prayed that he might be forgiven his sin. A month later when the intensity of his hatred had subsided somewhat, he remembered to his horror that he had not prayed that his tormentors be forgiven their even greater sin. He rectified the error without delay, not neglecting to ask that the error be forgiven, too.

Hugh was forced to sing, to dance, and to make a speech, but he escaped the watering-trough. He thought the fellows were darned nice to let him off, and they thought that he was too darned nice to be ducked. Although Hugh did n't suspect it, he was winning immediate popularity. His shy, friendly smile, his natural modesty, and his boyish enthusiasm were making a host of friends for him.

He liked the "initiations" on the campus, but he

did not like some of them in the dormitories.   He
did n't mind being pulled out of bed and shoved under a cold shower.   He took a cold shower every
morning, and if the sophomores wanted to give
him another one at night—all right, he was willing.
He had to confess that "Eliza Crossing the Ice"
had been enormous fun.   The freshmen were commanded to appear in the common room in their
oldest clothes.   Then all of them, the smallest lad
excepted, got down on their hands and knees, form-
ing a circle.   The smallest lad, "Eliza," was given
a big bucket full of water.   He jumped upon the
back of the man nearest to him and ran wildly
around the circle, leaping from back to back, the
bucket swinging crazily, the water splashing in every
direction and over everybody.

Hugh liked such "stunts," and he liked putting
on a show with three other freshmen for the amusement of their peers, but he did object to the vulgarity and cruelty of much that was done.

The first order the sophomores often gave was,
"Strip, freshman."   Just why the freshmen had to
be naked before they performed, Hugh did not
know, but there was something phallic about the
proceedings that disgusted him.   Like every athlete, he thought nothing of nudity, but he soon discovered that some of the freshmen were intensely
conscious of it.   True, a few months in the gymnasium cured them of that consciousness, but at first

many of them were eternally wrapping towels about themselves in the gymnasium, and they took a shower as if it were an act of public shame. The sophomores recognized the timidity that some of the freshmen had in revealing their bodies, and they made full capital of it. The shyer the freshman, the more pointed their remarks, the more ingeniously nasty their tricks.

"I don't mind the razzing myself," Hugh told Carl after one particularly strenuous evening, "but I don't like the things they said to poor little Wilkins. And when they stripped 'em and made Wilkins read that dirty story to Culver, I wanted to fight."

"It was kinda rotten," Carl agreed, "but it was funny."

"It was n't funny at all," Hugh said angrily.

Carl looked at him in surprise. It was the first time that he had seen him aroused.

"It was n't funny at all," Hugh repeated; "it was just filthy. I 'd 'a' just about died if I 'd 'a' been in Wilkins's place. The poor kid! They 're too damn dirty, these sophomores. I did n't think that college men could be so dirty. Why, not even the bums at home would think of such things. And I 'm telling you right now that there are three of those guys that I 'm layin' for. Just wait till the class rush. I 'm going to get Adams, and then I 'm going to get Cooper—yes, I 'm going to get him

even if he is bigger 'n me—and I 'm going to get
Dodge. I did n't say anything when they made me
wash my face in the toilet bowl, but, by God! I 'm
going to get 'em for it."

Three weeks later he made good this threat. He
was a clever boxer, and he succeeded in separating
each of the malefactors from the fighting mob.
He would have been completely nonplussed if he
could have heard Adams and Dodge talking in their
room after the rush.

"Who gave you the black eye?" Adams asked
Dodge.

"That freshman Carver," he replied, touching
the eye gingerly. "Who gave you that welt on
the chin?"

"Carver! And, say, he beat Hi Cooper to a
pulp. He 's a mess."

They looked at each other and burst out laughing.

"Lord," said Dodge, "I 'm going to pick my
freshmen next time. Who 'd take a kid with a
smile like his to be a scrapper? He 's got the nicest smile in college. Why, he looks meek as a
lamb."

"You never can tell," remarked Adams, rubbing
his chin ruefully.

Dodge was examining his eye in the mirror.
"No, you never can tell. . . . Damn it, I 'm going
to have to get a beefsteak or something for this
lamp of mine."

"Say, he ought to be a good man for the frater-nity," Adams said suddenly.

"Who?" Dodge's eye was absorbing his entire attention.

"Carver, of course. He ought to make a damn good man."

"Yeah—you bet. We 've got to rush him sure."

CHAPTER VIII

THE dormitory initiations had more than angered Hugh; they had completely upset his mental equilibrium: his every ideal of college swayed and wabbled. He was n't a prig, but he had come to Sanford with very definite ideas about the place, and those ideas were already groggy from the unmerciful pounding they were receiving.

His father was responsible for his illusions, if one may call them illusions. Mr. Carver was a shy, sensitive man well along in his fifties, with a wife twelve years his junior. He pretended to cultivate his small farm in Merrytown, but as a matter of fact he lived off of a comfortable income left him by his very capable father. He spent most of his time reading the eighteenth-century essayists, John Donne's poetry, the "Atlantic Monthly," the "Boston Transcript," and playing Mozart on his violin. He did not understand his wife and was thoroughly afraid of his son; Hugh had an animal vigor that at times almost terrified him.

At his wife's insistence he had a talk with Hugh the night before the boy left for college. Hugh

had wanted to run when he met his father in the
library after dinner for that talk. He loved the
gentle, gray-haired man with the fine, delicate features and soft voice. He had often wished that he
knew his father. Mr. Carver was equally eager
to know Hugh, but he had no idea of how to go
about getting acquainted with his son.

They sat on opposite sides of the fireplace, and
Mr. Carver gazed thoughtfully at the boy. Why
had n't Betty had this talk with Hugh? She knew
him so much better than he did; they were more
like brother and sister than mother and son. Why,
Hugh called her Betty half the time, and she seemed
to understand him perfectly.

Hugh waited silently. Mr. Carver ran a thin
hand through his hair and then sharply desisted;
he must n't let the boy know that he was nervous.
Then he settled his horn-rimmed pince-nez more
firmly on his nose and felt in his waistcoat for a
cigar. Why did n't Hugh say something? He
snipped the end of the cigar with a silver knife.
Slowly he lighted the cigar, inhaled once or twice,
coughed mildly, and finally found his voice.

"Well, Hugh," he said in his gentle way.

"Well, Dad." Hugh grinned sheepishly. Then
they both started; Hugh had never called his father
Dad before. He thought of him that way always,
but he could never bring himself to dare anything

but the more formal Father. In his embarrassment he had forgotten himself.

"I—I—I'm sorry, sir," he stuttered, flushing painfully.

Mr. Carver laughed to hide his own embarrassment. "That's all right, Hugh." His smile was very kindly. "Let it be Dad. I think I like it better."

"That's fine!" Hugh exclaimed.

The tension was broken, and Mr. Carver began to give the dreaded talk.

"I hardly know what to say to you, Hugh," he began, "on the eve of your going away to college. There is so much that you ought to know, and I have no idea of how much you know already."

Hugh thought of all the smutty stories he had heard—and told. Instinctively he knew that his father referred to what a local doctor called "the facts of life."

He hung his head and said gruffly, "I guess I know a good deal—Dad."

"That's splendid!" Mr. Carver felt the full weight of a father's responsibilities lifted from his shoulders. "I believe Dr. Hanson gave you a talk at school about—er, sex, did n't he?"

"Yes, sir." Hugh was picking out the design in the rug with the toe of his shoe and at the same time unconsciously pinching his leg. He pinched so hard that he afterward found a black and blue spot, but he never knew how it got there.

"Excellent thing, excellent thing, these talks by medical men." He was beginning to feel at ease. "Excellent thing. I am glad that you are so well informed; you are old enough."

Hugh was n't well informed; he was pathetically ignorant. Most of what he knew had come from the smutty stories, and he often did not understand the stories that he laughed at most heartily. He was consumed with curiosity.

"If there is anything you want to know, don't hesitate to ask," his father continued. He had a moment of panic lest Hugh would ask something, but the boy merely shook his head—and pinched his leg.

Mr. Carver puffed his cigar in great relief. "Well," he continued, "I don't want to give you much advice, but your mother feels that I ought to tell you a little more about college before you leave. As I have told you before, Sanford is a splendid place, a—er, a splendid place. Fine old traditions and all that sort of thing. Splendid place. You will find a wonderful faculty, wonderful. Most of the professors I had are gone, but I am sure that the new ones are quite as good. Your opportunities will be enormous, and I am sure that you will take advantage of them. We have been very proud of your high school record, your mother and I, and we know that you will do quite as well in college. By the way, I hope you'll take a course in the eighteenth-century essayists; you will find them very stimulating—Addison especially.

"I—er, your mother feels that I ought to say something about the dissipations of college. I—I'm sure that I don't know what to say. I suppose that there are young men in college who dissipate—I remember that I knew one or two—but certainly most of them are gentlemen. Crude men—vulgarians do not commonly go to college. Vulgarity has no place in college. You may, I presume, meet some men not altogether admirable, but it will not be necessary for you to know them. Now, as to the fraternity . . ."

Hugh forgot to pinch his leg and looked up with avid interest in his face. The Nu Deltas!

Mr. Carver leaned forward to stir the fire with a brass poker before he continued. Then he settled back in his chair and smoked comfortably. He was completely at ease now. The worst was over.

"I have written to the Nu Deltas about you and told them that I hoped that they would find you acceptable, as I am sure they will. As a legacy, you will be among the first considered." For an hour more he talked about the fraternity, Hugh, his embarrassment swallowed by his interest, eagerly asking questions. His father's admiration for the fraternity was second only to his admiration for the college, and before the evening was over he had filled Hugh with an idolatry for both.

He left his father that night feeling closer to him than he ever had before. He was going to be a college man like his father—perhaps a Nu Delta, too. He wished that they had got chummy before. When he went to bed, he lay awake dreaming, thinking sometimes of Helen Simpson and of how he had kissed her that afternoon, but more often of Sanford and Nu Delta. He was so deeply grateful to his father for talking to him frankly and telling him everything about college. He was darned lucky to have a father who was a college grad and could put him wise. It was pretty tough on the fellows whose fathers had never been to college. Poor fellows, they did n't know the ropes the way he did. . . .

He finally fell off to sleep, picturing himself in the doorway of the Nu Delta house welcoming his father to a reunion.

That talk was returning to Hugh repeatedly. He wondered if Sanford had changed since his father's day or if his father had just forgotten what college was like. Everything seemed so different from what he had been told to expect. Perhaps he was just soft and some of the fellows were n't as crude as he thought they were.

CHAPTER IX

HUGH was by no means continuously depressed; as a matter of fact, most of the time he was agog with delight, especially over the rallies that were occurring with increasing frequency as the football season progressed. Sometimes the rallies were carefully prepared ceremonies held in the gymnasium; sometimes they were entirely spontaneous.

A group of men would rush out of a dormitory or fraternity house yelling, "Peerade, peerade!" Instantly every one within hearing would drop his books—or his cards—and rush to the yelling group, which would line up in fours and begin circling the campus, the line ever getting longer as more men came running out of the dormitories and fraternity houses. On, on they would go, arm in arm, dancing, singing Sanford songs, past every dormitory on the campus, past every fraternity house—pausing occasionally to give a cheer, always, however, keeping one goal in mind, the fraternity house where the team lived during the football season. Then when the cheer-leaders and the team were heading the procession, the mob would make for the football field, with the cry of "Wood, freshmen, wood!" ringing down the line.

Hugh was always one of the first freshmen to break from the line in his eagerness to get wood. In an incredibly short time he and his classmates had found a large quantity of old lumber, empty boxes, rotten planks, and not very rotten gates. When a light was applied to the clumsy pile of wood, the flames leaped up quickly—some one always seemed to have a supply of kerosene ready— and revealed the excited upper-classmen sitting on the bleachers.

"Dance, freshmen, dance!"

Then the freshmen danced around the fire, holding hands and spreading into an ever widening circle as the fire crackled and the flames leaped upward. Slowly, almost impressively, the upper-classmen chanted:

"Round the fire, the freshmen go,
Freshmen go,
Freshmen go;
Round the fire the freshmen go
To cheer Sanford."

The song had a dozen stanzas, only the last line of each being different. The freshmen danced until the last verse was sung, which ended with the Sanford cheer:

"Closer now the freshmen go,
Freshmen go,
Freshmen go;
Closer now the freshmen go
To cheer—

SANFORD!
Sanford! Rah, rah!
Sanford! Sanford!
San—San—San—
San—ford, San—ford—San—FORD!"

While the upper-classmen were singing the last stanza the freshmen slowly closed in on the dying fire. At the first word of the cheer, they stopped, turned toward the grand stand, and joined the cheering. That over, they broke and ran for the bleachers, scrambling up the wooden stands, shoving each other out of the way, laughing and shouting.

The football captain usually made a short and very awkward speech, which was madly applauded; perhaps the coach said a few words; two or three cheers were given; and finally every one rose, took off his hat if he wore one—nearly every one but the freshmen went bareheaded—and sang the college hymn, simply and religiously. Then the crowd broke, straggling in groups across the campus, chatting, singing, shouting to each other. Suddenly lights began to flash in the dormitory windows. In

less than an hour after the first cry of "Peerade!"
the men were back in their rooms, once more studying, talking, or playing cards.

It was the smoker rallies, though, that Hugh
found the most thrilling, especially the last one before the final game of the season, the "big game"
with Raleigh College.   There were 1123 students
in Sanford, and more than 1000 were at the rally.
A rough platform had been built at one end of the
gymnasium.   On one side of it sat the band, on the
other side the Glee Club—and before it the mass of
students, smoking cigarettes, corn-cob pipes, and,
occasionally, a cigar.   The "smokes" had been fur-
nished free by a local tobacconist; so everybody
smoked violently and too much.   In half an hour it
was almost impossible to see the ceiling through the
dull blue haze, and the men in the rear of the gymnasium saw the speakers on the platform dimly
through a wavering mist.

The band played various Sanford songs, and
everybody sang.   Occasionally Wayne Gifford, the
cheer-leader, leaped upon the platform, raised a
megaphone to his mouth, and shouted, "A regular
cheer for Sanford—a regular cheer for Sanford."
Then he lifted his arms above his head, flinging the
megaphone aside with the same motion, and waited
tense and rigid until the students were on their feet.
Suddenly he turned into a mad dervish, twisting,
bending, gesticulating, leaping, running back and

forth across the platform, shouting, and finally throwing his hands above his head and springing high into the air at the concluding "San—FORD!"

The Glee Club sang to mad applause; a tenor twanged a ukulele and moaned various blues; a popular professor told stories, some of them funny, most of them slightly off color; a former cheer-leader told of the triumphs of former Sanford teams—and the atmosphere grew denser and denser, bluer and bluer, as the smoke wreathed upward. The thousand boys leaned intently forward, occasionally jumping to their feet to shout and cheer, and then sinking back into their chairs, tense and excited. As each speaker mounted the platform they shouted: "Off with your coat! Off with your coat!" And the speakers, even the professor, had to shed their coats before they were permitted to say a word.

When the team entered, bedlam broke loose. Every student stood on his chair, waved his arms, slapped his neighbor on the back or hugged him wildly, threw his hat in the air, if he had one—and, so great was his training, keeping an eye on the cheer-leader, who was on the platform going through a series of indescribable contortions. Suddenly he straightened up, held his hands above his head again, and shouted through his megaphone: "A regular cheer for the team—a regular cheer for the team. Make it big—BIG! Ready—!"

Away whirled the megaphone, and he went through exactly the same performance that he had used before in conducting the regular cheer. Gifford looked like an inspired madman, but he knew exactly what he was doing. The students cheered lustily, so lustily that some of them were hoarse the next day. They continued to yell after the cheer was completed, ceasing only when Gifford signaled for silence.

Then there were speeches by each member of the team, all enthusiastically applauded, and finally the speech of the evening, that of the coach, Jack Price. He was a big, compactly built man with regular features, heavy blond hair, and pale, cold blue eyes. He threw off his coat with a belligerent gesture, stuck his hands into his trousers pockets, and waited rigidly until the cheering had subsided. Then he began:

"Go ahead and yell. It's easy as hell to cheer here in the gym; but what are you going to do Saturday afternoon?"

His voice was sharp with sarcasm, and to the shouts of "Yell! Fight!" that came from all over the gymnasium, he answered, "Yeah, maybe—maybe."

He shifted his position, stepping toward the front of the platform, thrusting his hands deeper into his pockets.

"I 've seen a lot of football games, and I 've seen lots of rooters, but this is the goddamndest gang of yellow-bellied quitters that I 've ever seen. What happened last Saturday when we were behind? I 'm asking you; what happened? You quit! Quit like a bunch of whipped curs. God! you 're yellow, yellow as hell. But the team went on fighting—and it won, won in spite of you, won for a bunch of yellow pups. And why? Because the team 's got guts. And when it was all over, you cheered and howled and serpentined and felt big as hell. Lord Almighty! you acted as if you 'd done something."

His right hand came out of his pocket with a jerk, and he extended a fighting, clenched fist toward his breathless audience. "I 'll tell you something," he said slowly, viciously; "the team can't win alone day after to-morrow. *It can't win alone!* You 've got to fight. Damn it! *You 've got to fight!* Raleigh 's good, damn good; it has n't lost a game this season—and we 've got to win, *win!* Do you hear? We 've got to win! And there 's only one way that we can win, and that 's with every man back of the team. Every goddamned mother's son of you. The team 's good, but it can't win unless you fight—*fight!*"

Suddenly his voice grew softer, almost gentle. He held out both hands to the boys, who had become so tense that they had forgotten to smoke. "We 've got to win, fellows, for old Sanford. Are you back of us?"

"*Yes!*" The tension shattered into a thousand yells. The boys leaped on the chairs and shouted until they could shout no more. When Gifford called for "a regular cheer for Jack Price" and then one for the team—"Make it the biggest you ever gave"—they could respond with only a hoarse croak.

Finally the hymn was sung—at least, the boys tried loyally to sing it—and they stood silent and almost reverent as the team filed out of the gymnasium.

Hugh walked back to Surrey Hall with several men. No one said a word except a quiet good night as they parted. Carl was in the room when he arrived. He sank into a chair and was silent for a few minutes.

Finally he said in a happy whisper, "Was n't it wonderful, Carl?"

"Un-huh. Damn good."

"Gosh, I hope we win. We 've *got* to!"

Carl looked up, his cheeks redder than usual, his eyes glittering. "God, yes!" he breathed piously.

CHAPTER X

THE football season lasted from the first of October to the latter part of November, and during those weeks little was talked about, or even thought about, on the campus but football. There were undergraduates who knew the personnel of virtually every football team in the country, the teams that had played against each other, their relative merits, the various scores, the outstanding players of each position. Half the students at Sanford regularly made out "All American" teams, and each man was more than willing to debate the quality of *his* team against that of any other. Night after night the students gathered in groups in dormitory rooms and fraternity houses, discussing football, football, football; even religion and sex, the favorite topics for "bull sessions," could not compete with football, especially when some one mentioned Raleigh College. Raleigh was Sanford's ancient rival; to defeat her was of cosmic importance.

There was a game every Saturday. About half the time the team played at home; the other games were played on the rivals' fields. No matter how far away the team traveled, the college traveled with it. The men who had the necessary money went by train; a few owned automobiles: but most of the undergraduates had neither an automobile nor money for train fare. They "bummed" their way. Some of them emulated professional tramps and "rode the beams," but most of them started out walking, trusting that kind-hearted motorists would pick them up and carry them at least part way to their destination. Although the distances were sometimes great, and although many motorists are not kind, there is no record of any man who ever started for a game not arriving in time for the referee's first whistle. Somehow, by hook or by crook—and it was often by crook—the boys got there, and, what is more astonishing, they got back. On Monday morning at 8:45 they were in chapel, usually worn and tired, it is true, ready to bluff their way through the day's assignments, and damning any instructor who was heartless enough to give them a quiz. Some of them were worn out from really harsh traveling experiences; some of them had more exciting adventures to relate behind closed doors to selected groups of confidants.

Football! Nothing else mattered. And as the weeks passed, the excitement grew, especially as the day drew near for the Raleigh game, which this year was to be played on the Sanford field. What were Sanford's chances? Would Harry Slade, Sanford's great half-back, make All American?

"Damn it to hell, he ought to. It 'll be a stinkin' shame if he don't." Would Raleigh's line be able to stop Slade's end runs? Slade! Slade! He was the team, the hope and adoration of the whole college.

Three days before the "big game" the alumni began to pour into town, most of them fairly recent graduates, but many of them gray-haired men who boasted that they had n't missed a Sanford-Raleigh game in thirty years. Hundreds of alumni arrived, filling the two hotels to capacity and overrunning the fraternity houses, the students doubling up or seeking hospitality from a friend in a dormitory.

In the little room in the rear of the Sanford Pool and Billiard Parlors there was almost continual excitement. Jim McCarty, the proprietor, a big, jovial, red-faced man whom all the students called Mac, was the official stake-holder for the college. Bets for any amount could be placed with him. Money from Raleigh flowed into his pudgy hands, and he placed it at the odds offered with eager Sanford takers. By the day of the game his safe held thousands of dollars, most of it wagered at five to three, Raleigh offering odds. There was hardly an alumnus who did not prove his loyalty to Sanford by visiting Mac's back room and putting down a few greenbacks, at least. Some were more loyal than others; the most loyal placed a thousand dollars—at five to two.

There was rain for two days before the game, but on Friday night the clouds broke. A full moon seemed to shine them away, and the whole campus rejoiced with great enthusiasm. Most of the alumni got drunk to show their deep appreciation to the moon, and many of the undergraduates followed the example set by their elders.

All Friday afternoon girls had been arriving, dozens of them, to attend the fraternity dances. One dormitory had been set aside for them, the normal residents seeking shelter in other dormitories. No man ever objected to resigning his room to a girl. He never could tell what he would find when he returned to it Monday morning. Some of the girls left strange mementos. . . .

No one except a few notorious grinds studied that night. Some of the students were, of course, at the fraternity dances; some of them sat in dormitory rooms and discussed the coming game from every possible angle; and groups of them wandered around the campus, peering into the fraternity houses, commenting on the girls, wandering on humming a song that an orchestra had been playing, occasionally pausing to give a "regular cheer" for the moon.

Hugh was too much excited to stay in a room; so with several other freshmen he traveled the campus. He passionately envied the dancers in the fraternity houses but consoled himself with the thought, "Maybe I 'll be dancing at the Nu Delt house next year." Then he had a spasm of fright. Perhaps the Nu Delts—perhaps no fraternity would bid him. The moon lost its brilliance; for a moment even the Sanford-Raleigh game was forgotten.

The boys were standing before a fraternity house, and as the music ceased, Jack Collings suggested: "Let 's serenade them. You lead, Hugh."

Hugh had a sweet, light tenor voice. It was not at all remarkable, just clear and true; but he had easily made the Glee Club and had an excellent chance to be chosen freshman song-leader.

Collings had brought a guitar with him. He handed it to Hugh, who, like most musical undergraduates, could play both a guitar and a banjo. "Sing that 'I arise from dreams of thee' thing that you were singing the other night. We 'll hum."

Hugh slipped the cord around his neck, tuned the guitar, and then thrummed a few opening chords. His heart was beating at double time; he was very happy: he was serenading girls at a fraternity dance. Couples were strolling out upon the veranda, the girls throwing warm wraps over their shoulders, the men lighting cigarettes and tossing the burnt matches on the lawn. Their white shirt-fronts gleamed eerily in the pale light cast by the Japanese lanterns with which the veranda was hung.

Hugh began to sing Shelley's passionate lyric, set

so well to music by Tod B. Galloway.   His mother
had taught him the song, and he loved it.

> "I arise from dreams of thee
> In the first sweet sleep of night,
> When the winds are breathing low
> And the stars are shining bright.
> I arise from dreams of thee,
> And a spirit in my feet
> Hath led me—who knows how?
> To thy chamber-window, Sweet!"

Two of the boys, who had heard Hugh sing the
song before, hummed a soft accompaniment.   When
he began the second verse several more began to
hum; they had caught the melody.   The couples on
the veranda moved quietly to the porch railing,
their chatter silent, their attention focused on a
group of dim figures standing in the shadow of an
elm.   Hugh was singing well, better than he ever
had before.   Neither he nor his audience knew that
the lyric was immortal, but its tender, passionate
beauty caught and held them.

> "The wandering airs they faint
> On the dark, the silent stream—
> The champak odors fail
> Like sweet thoughts in a dream;
> The nightingale's complaint
> It dies upon her heart,
> As I must die on thine
> O beloved as thou art!"

"Oh lift me from the grass!
I die, I faint, I fail!
Let thy love in kisses rain
On my cheeks and eyelids pale.
My cheek is cold and white, alas!
My heart beats loud and fast;
Oh! press it close to thine again
Where it will break at last."

There was silence for a moment after Hugh finished. The shadows, the moonlight, the boy's soft young voice had moved them all. Suddenly a girl on the veranda cried, "Bring him up!" Instantly half a dozen others turned to their escorts, insisting shrilly: "Bring him up. We want to see him."

Hugh jerked the guitar cord from around his neck, handed the instrument to Collings, and tried to run. A burst of laughter went up from the freshmen. They caught him and held him fast until the Tuxedo-clad upper-classmen rushed down from the veranda and had him by the arms. They pulled him, protesting and struggling, upon the veranda and into the living-room.

The girls gathered around him, praising, demanding more. He flushed scarlet when one enthusiastic maiden forced her way through the ring, looked hard at him, and then announced positively, "I think he's sweet." He was intensely embarrassed, in an agony of confusion—but very happy. The girls liked his clean blondness, his blushes, his startled smile. How long they would have held him there in the center of the ring while they admired and teased him, there is no telling; but suddenly the orchestra brought relief by striking up a foxtrot.

"He's mine!" cried a pretty black-eyed girl with a cloud of bobbed hair and flaming cheeks. Her slender shoulders were bare; her round white arms waved in excited, graceful gestures; her corn-colored frock was a gauzy mist. She clutched Hugh's arm. "He's mine," she repeated shrilly. "He's going to dance with me."

Hugh's cheeks burned a deeper scarlet. "My clothes," he muttered, hesitating.

"Your clothes! My dear, you look sweet. Take off your cap and dance with me."

Hugh snatched off his cap, his mind reeling with shame, but he had no time to think. The girl pulled him through the crowd to a clear floor. Almost mechanically, Hugh put his arm around her and began to dance. He *could* dance, and the girl had sense enough not to talk. She floated in his arm, her slender body close to his. When the music ceased, she clapped her little hands excitedly and told Hugh that he danced "won-der-ful-ly." After the third encore she led him to a dark corner in the hall.

"You're sweet, honey," she said softly. She

turned her small, glowing face up to his. "Kiss me," she commanded.

Dazed, Hugh gathered her into his arms and kissed her little red mouth. She clung to him for a minute and then pushed him gently away.

"Good night, honey," she whispered.

"Good night." Hugh's voice broke huskily. He turned and walked rapidly down the hall, upon the veranda, and down the steps. His classmates were waiting for him. They rushed up to him, demanding that he tell them what had happened.

He told them most of it, especially about the dance; but he neglected to mention the kiss. Shyness overcame any desire that he had to strut. Besides, there was something about that kiss that made it impossible for him to tell any one, even Carl. When he went to bed that night, he did not think once about the coming football game. Before his eyes floated the girl in the corn-colored frock. He wished he knew her name. . . . Closer and closer she came to him. He could feel her cool arms around his neck. "What a wonderful, wonderful girl! Sweeter than Helen—lots sweeter. . . . She's like the night—and moonlight. . . . Like moonlight and—" The music of the "Indian Serenade" began to thrill through his mind:

> "I arise from dreams of thee
> In the first sweet sleep of night. . . .

Oh, she's sweet, sweet—like music and moonlight. . . ." He fell asleep, repeating "music and moonlight" over and over again—"music and moonlight. . . ."

The morning of the "big game" proved ideal, crisp and cold, crystal clear. Indian summer was near its close, but there was still something of its dreamy wonder in the air, and the hills still flamed with glorious autumn foliage. The purples, the mauves, the scarlets, the burnt oranges were a little dimmed, a little less brilliant—the leaves were rustling dryly now—but there was beauty in dying autumn, its splendor slowly fading, as there was in its first startling burst of color.

Classes that Saturday morning were a farce, but they were held; the administration, which the boys damned heartily, insisted upon it. Some of the instructors merely took the roll and dismissed their classes, feeling that honor had been satisfied; but others held their classes through the hour, lecturing the disgusted students on their lack of interest, warning them that examinations were n't as far off as the millennium.

Hugh felt that he was lucky; he had only one class—it was with Alling in Latin—and it had been promptly dismissed. "When the day comes," said Alling, "that Latin can compete with football, I'll —well, I'll probably get a living wage. You had better go before I get to talking about a living wage. It is one of my favorite topics." He waved his hand toward the door; the boys roared with delight and rushed out of the room, shoving each other and laughing. They ran out of the building; all of them were too excited to walk.

By half-past one the stands were filled. Most of the girls wore fur coats, as did many of the alumni, but the students sported no such luxuries; nine tenths of them wore "baa-baa coats," gray jackets lined with sheep's wool. Except for an occasional banner, usually carried by a girl, and the bright hats of the women, there was little color to the scene. The air was sharp, and the spectators huddled down into their warm coats.

The rival cheering sections, seated on opposite sides of the field, alternated in cheering and singing, each applauding the other's efforts. The cheering was n't very good, and the singing was worse; but there was a great deal of noise, and that was about all that mattered to either side.

A few minutes before two, the Raleigh team ran upon the field. The Raleigh cheering section promptly went mad. When the Sanford team appeared a minute later, the Sanford cheering section tried its best to go madder, the boys whistling and yelling like possessed demons. Wayne Gifford brought them to attention by holding his hands above his head. He called for the usual regular cheer for the team and then for a short cheer for each member of it, starting with the captain, Sherman Walford, and ending with the great half-back, Harry Slade.

Suddenly there was silence. The toss-up had been completed; the teams were in position on the field. Slade had finished building a slender pyramid of mud, on which he had balanced the ball. The referee held up his hand. "Are you ready, Sanford?" Walford signaled his readiness. "Are you ready, Raleigh?"

The shrill blast of the referee's whistle—and the game was on. The first half was a see-saw up and down the field. Near the end of the half Raleigh was within twenty yards of the Sanford line. Shouts of "Score! Score! Score!" went up from the Raleigh rooters, rhythmic, insistent. "Hold 'em! Hold 'em! Fight! Fight! Fight!" the Sanford cheering section pleaded, almost sobbing the words. A forward pass skilfully completed netted Raleigh sixteen yards. "Fight! Fight! Fight!"

The timekeeper tooted his little horn; the half was over. For a moment the Sanford boys leaned back exhausted; then they leaped to their feet and yelled madly, while the Raleigh boys leaned back or against each other and swore fervently. Within two minutes the tension had departed. The rival cheering sections alternated in singing songs, applauded each other vigorously, whistled at a frightened dog that tried to cross the field and nearly lost its mind entirely when called by a thousand masters, waited breathlessly when the cheer-leaders announced the results from other football games that had been telegraphed to the field, applauded if Harvard was losing, groaned if it was n't, sang some more, relaxed and felt consummately happy.

Sanford immediately took the offensive in the second half. Slade was consistently carrying the ball. Twice he brought it within Raleigh's twenty-five-yard line. The first time Raleigh held firm, but the second time Slade stepped back for a drop-kick. The spectators sat silent, breathless. The angle was difficult. Could he make it? Would the line hold?

Quite calmly Slade waited. The center passed the ball neatly. Slade turned it in his hands, paid not the slightest attention to the mad struggle going on a few feet in front of him, dropped the ball —and kicked. The ball rose in a graceful arc and passed safely between the goal-posts.

Every one, men and women alike, the Raleigh adherents excepted, promptly turned into extraordinarily active lunatics. The women waved their banners and shrieked, or if they had no banners, they waved their arms and shrieked; the men danced up and down, yelled, pounded each other on the back, sometimes wildly embraced—many a woman was kissed by a man she had never seen before and never would again, nor did she object—Wayne Gifford was turning handsprings, and many of the students were feebly fluttering their hands, voiceless, spent with cheering, weak from excitement.

Early in the fourth quarter, however, Raleigh got its revenge, carrying the ball to a touch-down after a series of line rushes. Sanford tried desperately to score again, but its best efforts were useless against the Raleigh defense.

The final whistle blew; and Sanford had lost. Cheering wildly, tossing their hats into the air, the Raleigh students piled down from the grand stand upon the field.   With the cheer-leaders at the head, waving their megaphones, the boys rapidly formed into a long line in uneven groups, holding arms, dancing, shouting, winding in and out around the field, between the goal-posts, tossing their hats over the bars, waving their hands at the Sanford men standing despondently in their places—in and out, in and out, in the triumphant serpentine.   Finally they paused, took off their hats, cheered first their own team, then the Sanford team, and then sang their hymn while the Sanford men respectfully uncovered, silent and despairing.

When the hymn was over, the Sanford men quietly left the grand stand, quietly formed into a long line in groups of fours, quietly marched to the college flagpole in the center of the campus. A Sanford banner was flying from the pole, a blue banner with an orange S. Wayne Gifford loosened the ropes. Down fluttered the banner, and the boys reverently took off their hats. Gifford caught the banner before it touched the ground and gathered it into his arms. The song-leader stepped beside him. He lifted his hand, sang a note, and then the boys sang with him, huskily, sadly, some of them with tears streaming down their cheeks:

> "Sanford, Sanford, mother of men,
> Love us, guard us, hold us true.
> Let thy arms enfold us;
> Let thy truth uphold us.
> Queen of colleges, mother of men—
> Alma mater, Sanford—hail!
> Alma mater—Hail!—Hail!"

Slowly the circle broke into small groups that straggled wearily across the campus. Hugh, with two or three others, was walking behind two young professors—one of them, Alling, the other, Jones of the economics department. Hugh was almost literally broken-hearted; the defeat lay on him like an awful sorrow that never could be lifted. Every inch of him ached, but his despair was greater than his physical pain. The sharp, clear voice of Jones broke into his half-deadened consciousness.

"I can't understand all this emotional excitement," said Jones crisply. "A football game is a football game, not a national calamity. I enjoy the game myself, but why weep over it? I don't think I ever saw anything more absurd than those boys singing with tears running into their mouths."

Shocked, the boys looked at each other. They started to make angry remarks but paused as Alling spoke.

"Of course, what you say, Jones, is quite right," he remarked calmly, "quite right. But, do you know, I pity you."

"Alling's a good guy," Hugh told Carl later; "he's human."

CHAPTER XI

AFTER the Sanford-Raleigh game, the college seemed to be slowly dying. The boys held countless post-mortems over the game, explaining to each other just how it had been lost or how it could have been won. They watched the newspapers eagerly as the sport writers announced their choice for the so-called All American team. If Slade was on the team, the writer was conceded to "know his dope"; if Slade was n't, the writer was a "dumbbell." But all this pseudo-excitement was merely picking at the covers; there was no real heart in it. Gradually the football talk died down; freshmen ceased to write themes about Sanford's great fighting spirit; sex and religion once more became predominant at the "bull sessions."

Studies, too, began to find a place in the sun. Hour examinations were coming, and most of the boys knew that they were miserably prepared. Lights were burning in fraternity houses and dormitories until late at night, and mighty little of their glow was shed on poker parties and crap games. The college had begun to study.

When Hugh finally calmed down and took stock, he was horrified and frightened to discover how far he was behind in all his work. He had done his lessons sketchily from day to day, but he really knew nothing about them, and he knew that he did n't. Since Morse's departure, he had loafed, trusting to luck and the knowledge he had gained in high school. So far he had escaped a summons from the dean, but he daily expected one, and the mere thought of hour examinations made him shiver. He studied hard for a week, succeeding only in getting gloriously confused and more frightened. The examinations proved to be easier than he had expected; he did n't fail in any of them, but he did not get a grade above a C.

The examination flurry passed, and the college was left cold. Nothing seemed to happen. The boys went to the movies every night, had a peanut fight, talked to the shadowy actors; they played cards, pool, and billiards, or shot craps; Saturday nights many of them went to a dance at Hastings, a small town five miles away; they held bull sessions and discussed everything under the sun and some things beyond it; they attended a performance of Shaw's "Candida" given by the Dramatic Society and voted it a "wet" show; and, incidentally, some of them studied. But, all in all, life was rather tepid, and most of the boys were merely marking time and waiting for Christmas vacation.

For Hugh the vacation came and went with a rush. It was glorious to get home again, glorious to see his father and mother, and, at first, glorious to see Helen Simpson. But Helen had begun to pall; her kisses hardly compensated for her conversation. She gave him a little feeling of guilt, too, which he tried to argue away. "Kissing is n't really wrong. Everybody pets; at least, Carl says they do. Helen likes it but . . ." Always that "but" intruded itself. "But it does n't seem quite right when—I don't really love her." When he kissed her for the last time before returning to college, he had a distinct feeling of relief: well, that would be off his mind for a while, anyway.

It was a sober, quiet crowd of students—for the first time they were students—that returned to their desks after the vacation. The final examinations were ahead of them, less than a month away; and those examinations hung over their heads like the relentless, glittering blade of a guillotine. The boys studied. "College life" ceased; there was a brief period of education.

Of course, they did not desert the movies, and the snow and ice claimed them. Part of Indian Lake was scraped free of snow, and every clear afternoon hundreds of boys skated happily, explaining afterward that they had to have some exercise if they were going to be able to study. On those afternoons the lake was a pretty sight, zestful, alive with color. Many of the men wore blue sweaters, some of them brightly colored Mackinaws, all of them knitted toques. As soon as the cold weather arrived, the freshmen had been permitted to substitute blue toques with orange tassels for their "baby bonnets." The blue and orange stood out vividly against the white snow-covered hills, and the skates rang sharply as they cut the glare ice.

There was snow-shoeing, skiing, and sliding "to keep a fellow fit so that he could do good work in his exams," but much as the boys enjoyed the winter sports, a black pall hung over the college as the examination period drew nearer and nearer. The library, which had been virtually deserted all term, suddenly became crowded. Every afternoon and evening its big tables were filled with serious-faced lads earnestly bending over books, making notes, running their fingers through their hair, occasionally looking up with dazed eyes, or twisting about miserably.

The tension grew greater and greater. The upper-classmen were quiet and businesslike, but most of the freshmen were frankly terrified. A few of them packed their trunks and slunk away, and a few more openly scorned the examinations and their frightened classmates; but they were the exceptions. All the buoyancy seemed gone out of the college; nothing was left but an intense strain. The dormitories were strangely quiet at night. There was

no playing of golf in the hallways, no rolling of bats
down the stairs, no shouting, no laughter; a man
who made any noise was in danger of a serious beating. Even the greetings as the men passed each
other on the campus were quiet and abstracted.
They ceased to cut classes. Everybody attended,
and everybody paid close attention even to the most
tiresome instructors.

Studious seniors began to reap a harvest out of
tutoring sections. The meetings were a dollar "a
throw," and for another dollar a student could get
a mimeographed outline of a course. But the tutoring sections were only for the "plutes" or the
athletes, many of whom were subsidized by fraternities or alumni. Most of the students had to
learn their own lessons; so they often banded together in small groups to make the task less ardu-
ous, finding some relief in sociability.

The study groups, quite properly called seminars,
would have shocked many a worthy professor had
he been able to attend one; but they were truly
educative, and to many students inspiring. The
professor had planted the seed of wisdom with
them; it was at the seminars that they tried honestly, if somewhat hysterically and irreverently, to
make it grow.

Hugh did most of his studying alone, fearing that
the seminars would degenerate into bull sessions,
as many of them did; but Carl insisted that he join

one group that was going "to wipe up that goddamned English course to-night."

There were only five men at the seminar, which
met in Surrey 19, because Pudge Jamieson, who was
"rating" an A in the course and was therefore an
authority, said that he would n't come if there were
any more. Pudge, as his nickname suggests, was
plump. He was a round-faced, jovial youngster
who learned everything with consummate ease,
wrote with great fluency and sometimes real beauty,
peered through his horn-rimmed spectacles amusedly
at the world, and read every "smut" book that he
could lay his hands on. His library of erotica was
already famous throughout the college, his volumes
of Balzac's "Droll Stories," Rabelais complete,
"Mlle. de Maupin," Burton's "Arabian Nights,"
and the "Decameron" being in constant demand.
He could tell literally hundreds of dirty stories,
always having a new one on tap, always looking
when he told it like a complacent cherub.

There were two other men in the seminar.
Freddy Dickson, an earnest, anemic youth, seemed
to be always striving for greater acceleration and
never gaining it; or as Pudge put it, "The trouble
with Freddy is that he's always shifting gears."
Larry Stillwell, the last man, was a dark, handsome youth with exceedingly regular features,
pomaded hair parted in the center and shining

sleekly, fine teeth, and rich coloring: a "smooth" boy who prided himself on his conquests and the fact that he never got a grade above a C in his courses. There was no man in the freshman class with a finer mind, but he declined to study, declaring firmly that he could not waste his time acquiring impractical tastes for useless arts.

"Now everybody shut up," said Pudge, seating himself in a big chair and laboriously crossing one leg over the other. "Put some more wood on the fire, Hugh, will you?"

Hugh stirred up the fire, piled on a log or so, and then returned to his chair, hoping against belief that something really would be accomplished in the seminar. All the boys, he excepted, were smoking, and all of them were lolling back in dangerously comfortable attitudes.

"We've got to get going," Pudge continued, "and we aren't going to get anything done if we just sit around and bull. I'm the prof, and I'm going to ask questions. Now, don't bull. If you don't know, just say, 'No soap,' and if you do know, shoot your dope." He grinned. "How's that for a rime?"

"Atta boy!" Carl exclaimed enthusiastically.

"Shut up! Now, the stuff we want to get at to-night is the poetry. No use spending any time on the composition. My prof said that we would have to write themes in the exam, but we can't do anything about that here. You're all getting by on your themes, anyway, are n't you?"

"Yeah," the listening quartet answered in unison, Larry Stillwell adding dubiously, "Well, I'm getting C's."

"Larry," said Carl in cold contempt, "you're a goddamn liar. I saw a B on one of your themes the other day and an A on another. What are you always pulling that low-brow stuff for?"

Larry had the grace to blush. "Aw," he explained in some confusion, "my prof's full of hooey. He does n't know a C theme from an A one. He makes me sick. He—"

"Aw, shut up!" Freddy Dickson shouted. "Let's get going; let's get going. We gotta learn this poetry. Damn! I don't know anything about it. I did n't crack the book till two days ago."

Pudge took charge again. "Close your gabs, everybody," he commanded sternly. "There's no sense in going over the prose lit. You can do that better by yourselves. God knows I'm not going to waste my time telling you bone-heads what Carlyle means by a hero. If you don't know Odin from Mohammed by this time, you can roast in Dante's hell for all of me. Now listen; the prof said that they were going to make us place lines, and, of course, they'll expect us to know what the

poems are about.   Hell! how some of the boys are
going to fox 'em."   He paused to laugh.   "Jim
Hicks told me this afternoon that 'Philomela' was
by Shakspere."   The other boys did not understand the joke, but they all laughed heartily.

"Now," he went on, "I'll give you the name of
a poem, and then you tell me what it's about and
who wrote it."

He leafed rapidly through an anthology.   "Carl,
who wrote 'Kubla Khan'?"

Carl puffed his pipe meditatively.   "I'm going
to fox you, Pudge," he said, frankly triumphant;
"I know.   Coleridge wrote it.   It seems to be
about a Jew who built a swell joint for a wild woman
or something like that.   I can't make much out of
the damn thing."

"That's enough.   Smack for Carl," said Pudge
approvingly.   "Smack" meant that the answer was
satisfactory.   "Freddy, who wrote 'La Belle Dame
sans Merci'?"

Freddy twisted in his chair, thumped his head
with his knuckles, and finally announced with a
groan of despair, "No soap."

"Hugh?"

"No soap."

"Larry?"

"Well," drawled Larry, "I think Jawn Keats
wrote it.   It's one of those bedtime stories with
a kick.   A knight gets picked up by a jane.   He

puts her on his prancing steed and beats it for the tall timber. Keats is n't very plain about what happened there, but I suspect the worst. Anyhow, the knight woke up the next morning with an awful rotten taste in his mouth."

"Smack for Larry. Your turn, Carl. Who wrote 'The West Wind'?"

"You can't get me on that boy Masefield, Pudge. I know all his stuff. There is n't any story; it's just about the west wind, but it's a goddamn good poem. It's the cat's pajamas."

"You said it, Carl," Hugh chimed in, "but I like 'Sea Fever' better.

> "I must go down to the seas again,
> To the lonely sea and the sky. . . .

Gosh! that's hot stuff. 'August, 1914''s a peach, too."

"Yeah," agreed Larry languidly; "I got a great kick when the prof read that in class. Masefield's all right. I wish we had more of his stuff and less of Milton. Lord Almighty, how I hate Milton! What th' hell do they have to give us that tripe for?"

"Oh, let's get going," Freddy pleaded, running a nervous hand through his mouse-colored hair. "Shoot a question, Pudge."

"All right, Freddy." Pudge tried to smile wickedly but succeeded only in looking like a beam-

ing cherub. "Tell us who wrote the 'Ode on Intimations of Immortality from Recollections of Early
Childhood.' Cripes! what a title!"

Freddy groaned. "I know that Wadsworth
wrote it, but that is all that I do know about it."

"Wordsworth, Freddy," Carl corrected him.
"Wordsworth. Henry W. Wordsworth."

"Gee, Carl, thanks. I thought it was William."

There was a burst of laughter, and then Pudge
explained. "It is William, Freddy. Don't let
Peters razz you. Just for that, Carl, *you* tell what
it 's about."

"No soap," said Carl decisively.

"I know," Hugh announced, excited and pleased.

"Shoot!"

"Well, it 's this reincarnation business. Wordsworth thought you lived before you came on to this
earth, and everything was fine when you were a
baby but it got worse when you got older. That 's
about all. It 's kinda bugs, but I like some of it."

"It is n't bugs," Pudge contradicted flatly; "it 's
got sense. You do lose something as you grow
older, but you gain something, too. Wordsworth
admits that. It 's a wonderful poem, and you 're
dumbbells if you can't see it." He was very serious as he turned the pages of the book and laid his
pipe on the table at his elbow. "Now listen. This
stanza has the dope for the whole poem." He
read the famous stanza simply and effectively:

"Our birth is but a sleep and a forgetting;
The soul that rises with us, our life's Star,
Hath had elsewhere its setting
And cometh from afar;
Not in entire forgetfulness,
And not in utter nakedness,
But trailing clouds of glory do we come
From God who is our home:
Heaven lies about us in our infancy!
Shades of the prison house begin to close
Upon the growing Boy,
But he beholds the light, and whence it flows,
He sees it in his joy;
The Youth who daily farther from the east
Must travel, still is Nature's priest,
And by the vision splendid
Is on his way attended;
At length the Man perceives it die away,
And fade into the light of common day."

There was a moment's silence when he finished, and then Hugh said reverently: "That *is* beautiful. Read the last stanza, will you, Pudge?"

So Pudge read the last stanza, and then the boys got into an argument over the possible truth of the thesis of the poem. Freddy finally brought them back to the task in hand with his plaintive plea, "We 've gotta get going." It was two o'clock in the morning when the seminar broke up, Hugh admitting to Carl after their visitors departed that he had not only learned a lot but that he had enjoyed the evening heartily.

The college grew quieter and quieter as the day for the examinations approached. There were seminars on everything, even on the best way to prepare cribs. Certain students with low grades and less honor would somehow gravitate together and discuss plans for "foxing the profs." Opinions differed. One man usually insisted that notes in the palm of the left hand were safe from detection, only to be met by the objection that they had to be written in ink, and if one's hand perspired, "and it was sure as hell to," nothing was left but an inky smear. Another held that a fellow could fasten a rubber band on his forearm and attach the notes to those, pulling them down when needed and then letting them snap back out of sight into safety. "But," one of the conspirators was sure to object, "what th' hell are you going to do if the band breaks?" Some of them insisted that notes placed in the inside of one's goloshes—all the students wore them but took them off in the examination-room—could be easily read. "Yeah, but the proctors are wise to that stunt." And so *ad infinitum*. Eventually all the "stunts" were used and many more. Not that all the students cheated. Everything considered, the percentage of cheaters was not great, but those who did cheat usually spent

enough time evolving ingenious methods of preparing cribs and in preparing them to have learned
their lessons honestly and well.

The night before the first examinations the campus was utterly quiet. Suddenly bedlam broke
loose. Somehow every dormitory that contained
freshmen became a madhouse at the same time.
Hugh and Carl were in Surrey 19 earnestly studying. Freddy Dickson flung the door open and
shouted hysterically, "The general science exam's
out!"

Hugh and Carl whirled around in their desk-
chairs.

"What?" They shouted together.

"Yeah! One of the fellows saw it. A girl that
works at the press copied down the exam and gave
it to him."

"What fellow? Where's the exam?"

"I don't know who the guy is, but Hubert Manning saw the exam."

Hugh and Carl were out of their chairs in an
instant, and the three boys rushed out of Surrey in
search of Manning. They found him in his room
telling a mob of excited classmates that he hadn't
seen the exam but that Harry Smithson had.
Away went the crowd in search of Smithson, Carl
and Hugh and Freddy in the midst of the excited,
chattering lads. Smithson hadn't seen the exam,

but he had heard that Puddy McCumber had a copy. . . . Freshmen were running up and down stairs in the dormitories, shouting, "Have you seen the exam?" No, nobody had *seen* the exam, but some of the boys had been told definitely what the questions were going to be. No two seemed to agree on the questions, but everybody copied them down and then rushed on to search for a *bona fide* copy. They hurried from dormitory to dormitory, constantly shouting the same question, "Have you seen the exam?" There were men in every dormitory with a new list of questions, which were hastily scratched into note-books by the eager seekers. Until midnight the excitement raged; then the campus quieted down as the freshmen began to study the long lists of questions.

"God!" said Carl as he scanned his list hopelessly, "these damn questions cover everything in the course and some things that I know damn well were n't in it. What a lot of nuts we were. Let 's go to bed."

"Carl," Hugh wailed despondently, "I 'm going to flunk that exam. I can't answer a tenth of these questions. I can't go to bed; I 've got to study. Oh, Lord!"

"Don't be a triple-plated jackass. Come on to bed. You 'll just get woozy if you stay up any longer."

"All right," Hugh agreed wearily. He went to bed, but many of the boys stayed up and studied, some of them all night.

The examinations were held in the gymnasium. Hundreds of class-room chairs were set in even rows. Nothing else was there, not even the gymnasium apparatus. A few years earlier a wily student had sneaked into the gymnasium the night before an examination and written his notes on a dumbbell hanging on the wall. The next day he calmly chose the seat in front of the dumbbell—and proceeded to write a perfect examination. The annotated dumbbell was found later, and after that the walls were stripped clean of apparatus before the examinations began.

At a few minutes before nine the entire freshman class was grouped before the doors of the gymnasium, nervously talking, some of them glancing through their notes, others smoking—some of them so rapidly that the cigarettes seemed to melt, others walking up and down, muttering and mumbling; all of them so excited, so tense that they hardly knew what they were doing. Hugh was trying to think of a dozen answers to questions that popped into his head, and he could n't think of anything.

Suddenly the doors were thrown open. Yelling, shoving each other about, fairly dancing in their eagerness and excitement, the freshmen rushed into the gymnasium. Hugh broke from the mob as quickly as possible, hurried to a chair, and snatched up a copy of the examination that was lying on its broad arm. At the first glance he thought that he could answer all the questions; a second glance revealed four that meant nothing to him. For a moment he was dizzy with hope and despair, and then, all at once, he felt quite calm. He pulled off his goloshes and prepared to go to work.

Within three minutes the noise had subsided. There was a rustling as the boys took off their baa-baa coats and goloshes, but after that there was no sound save the slow steps of the proctors pacing up and down the aisle. Once Hugh looked up, thinking desperately, almost seizing an idea that floated nebulous and necessary before him. A proctor that he knew caught his eye and smiled fatuously. Hugh did not smile back. He could have cried in his fury. The idea was gone forever.

Some of the students began to write immediately; some of them leaned back and stared at the ceiling; some of them chewed their pencils nervously; some of them leaned forward mercilessly pounding a knee; some of them kept running one or both hands through their hair; some of them wrote a little and then paused to gaze blankly before them or to tap their teeth with a pen or pencil: all of them were concentrating with an intensity that made the silence electric.

That proctor's idiotic smile had thrown Hugh's thoughts into what seemed hopeless confusion, but a small incident almost immediately brought order and relief. The gymnasium cat was wandering around the rear of the gymnasium. It attracted the attention of several of the students—and of a proctor. Being very careful not to make any noise, he picked up the cat and started for the door. Almost instantly every student looked up; and then the stamping began. Four hundred freshmen stamped in rhythm to the proctor's steps. He blushed violently, tried vainly to look unconcerned, and finally disappeared through the door with the cat. Hugh had stamped lustily and laughed in great glee at the proctor's confusion; then he returned to his work, completely at ease, his nervousness gone.

One hour passed, two hours. Still the freshmen wrote; still the proctors paced up and down. Suddenly a proctor paused, stared intently at a youth who was leaning forward in his chair, walked quickly to him, and picked up one of his goloshes. The next instant he had a piece of paper in his hand and was walking down the gymnasium after beckoning to the boy to follow him. The boy shoved his feet into his goloshes, pulled on his baa-baa coat, and, his face white and strained, marched down the aisle. The proctor spoke a few words to him at the door. He nodded, opened the door, left the gymnasium—and five hours later the college.

Thus the college for ten days: the better students moderately calm, the others cramming information into aching heads, drinking unbelievable quantities of coffee, sitting up, many of them, all night, attending seminars or tutoring sessions, working for long hours in the library, finally taking the examination, only to start a new nerve-racking grind in preparation for the next one.

If a student failed in a course, he received a "flunk notice" from the registrar's office within four days after the examination, so that four days after the last examination every student knew whether he had passed his courses or not. All those who failed to pass three courses were, as the students put it, "flunked out," or as the registrar put it, "their connection with the college was severed." Some of the flunkees took the news very casually, packed their trunks, sold their furniture, and departed; others frankly wept or hastened to their instructors to plead vainly that their grades be raised: all of them were required to leave Haydensville at once.

Hugh passed all of his courses but without distinction. His B in trigonometry did not give him great satisfaction inasmuch as he had received an A in exactly the same course in high school; nor was he particularly proud of his B in English, since he knew that with a little effort he could have "pulled" an A. The remainder of his grades were C's and D's, mostly D's. He felt almost as much ashamed as Freddy Dickson, who somehow had n't "got going" and had been flunked out. Carl received nothing less than a C, and his record made Hugh more ashamed of his own. Carl never seemed to study, but he had n't disgraced himself.

Hugh spent many bitter hours thinking about his record. What would his folks think? Worse, what would they *say?* Finally he wrote to them:

Dear Mother and Dad:

I have just found out my grades. I think that they will be sent to you later. Well, I did n't flunk out but my record is n't so hot. Only two of my grades are any good. I got a B in English and Math but the others are all C's and D's. I know that you will be ashamed of me and I 'm awfully sorry. I 've thought of lots of excuses to write to you, but I guess I won't write them. I know that I did n't study hard enough. I had too much fun.

I promise you that I 'll do better next time. I know that I can. Please don't scold me.

Lots of love,

HUGH.

All that his mother wrote in reply was, "Of course, you will do better next time." The kindness hurt dreadfully. Hugh wished that she had scolded him.

CHAPTER XII

THE college granted a vacation of three days between terms, but Hugh did not go home, nor did many of the other undergraduates. There was excitement in the air; the college was beginning to stew and boil again. Fraternity rushing was scheduled for the second week of the new term.

The administration strictly prohibited the rushing of freshmen the first term; and, in general, the fraternities respected the rule. True, the fraternity men were constantly visiting eligible freshmen, chatting with them, discussing everything with them except fraternities. That subject was barred.

Hugh and Carl received a great many calls from upper-classmen the first term, and Hugh had been astonished at Carl's reticence and silence. Carl, the flippant, the voluble, the "wise-cracker," lost his tongue the minute a man wearing a fraternity pin entered the room. Hugh was forced to entertain the all-important guest. Carl never explained how much he wanted to make a good fraternity, not any fraternity, only a *good* one; nor did he explain that his secret studying the first term had been inspired by his eagerness to be completely eligible. A good fraternity would put the seal of aristocracy on him; it would mean everything to the "old lady."

For the first three nights of the rushing season the fraternities held open house for all freshmen, but during the last three nights no freshman was supposed to enter a fraternity house unless invited.

The first three nights found the freshmen traveling in scared groups from fraternity house to fraternity house, sticking close together unless rather vigorously pried apart by their hosts. Everybody was introduced to everybody else; everybody tried rather hopelessly to make conversation, and nearly everybody smoked too much, partly because they were nervous and partly because the "smokes" were free.

It was the last three nights that counted. Both Hugh and Carl received invitations from most of the fraternities, and they stuck together, religiously visiting them all. Hugh hoped that they would "make" the same fraternity and that that fraternity would be Nu Delta. They were together so consistently during the rushing period that the story went around the campus that Carver and Peters were "going the same way," and that Carver had said that he would n't accept a bid from any fraternity unless it asked Peters, too.

Hugh heard the story and could n't understand

it. Everybody seemed to take it for granted that he would be bid. Why did n't they take it equally for granted that Carl would be bid as well? He thought perhaps it was because he was an athlete and Carl was n't; but the truth was, of course, that the upper-classmen perceived the *nouveau riche* quality in Carl quite as clearly as he did himself. He knew that his money and the fact that he had gone to a fashionable prep school would bring him bids, but would they be from the right fraternities? That was the all-important question.

Those last three days of rushing were nerve-racking. At night the invited freshmen—and that meant about two thirds of the class—were at the fraternity houses until eleven; between classes and during every free hour they were accosted by earnest fraternity men, each presenting the superior merits of his fraternity. The fraternity men were wearier than the freshmen. They sat up until the small hours every morning discussing the freshmen they had entertained the night before.

Hugh was in a daze. Over and over he heard the same words with only slight variations. A fraternity man would slap a fat book with an excited hand and exclaim: "This is 'Baird's Manual,' the final authority on fraternities, and it 's got absolutely all the dope. You can see where we stand. Sixty chapters! You don't join just this one, y' understand; you join all of 'em. You 're welcome wherever you go." Or, if the number of chapters happened to be small, "Baird's Manual" was referred to again. "Only fifteen chapters, you see. We don't take in new chapters every time they ask. We're darned careful to know what we're signing up before we take anybody in." The word "aristocratic" was carefully avoided, but it was just as carefully suggested.

It seemed to Hugh that he was shown a photograph of every fraternity house in the country. "Look," he would be told by his host, "look at that picture to the right of the fireplace. That's our house at Cornell. Isn't it the darb? And look at that one. It's our house at California. Some palace. They've got sunken gardens. I was out there last year to our convention. The boys certainly gave us a swell time."

All this through a haze of tobacco smoke and over the noise of a jazz orchestra and the chatter of a dozen similar conversations. Hugh was excited but not really interested. The Nu Deltas invited him to their house every evening, but they were not making a great fuss over him. Perhaps they weren't going to give him a bid. . . . Well, he'd go some other fraternity. No, he wouldn't, either. Maybe the Nu Deltas would bid him later after he'd done something on the track.

Although actual pledging was not supposed to be done until Saturday night, Hugh was receiving what amounted to bids all that day and the night before. Several times groups of fraternity men got into a room, closed the door, and then talked to him until he was almost literally dizzy. He was wise enough not to make any promises. His invariable answer was: "I don't know yet. I won't know until Saturday night."

Carl was having similar experiences, but neither of them had been talked to by Nu Deltas. The president of the chapter, Merle Douglas, had said to Hugh in passing, "We 've got our eye on you, Carver," and that was all that had been said. Carl did not have even that much consolation. But he was n't so much interested in Nu Delta as Hugh was; Kappa Zeta or Alpha Sigma would do as well. Both of these fraternities were making violent efforts to get Hugh, but they were paying only polite attention to Carl.

On Friday night Hugh was given some advice that he had good reason to remember in later years. At the moment it did not interest him a great deal.

He had gone to the Delta Sigma Delta house, not because he had the slightest interest in that fraternity but because the Nu Deltas had not urged him to remain with them. The Delta Sigma Deltas welcomed him enthusiastically and turned him over to their president, Malcolm Graham, a tall, serious senior with sandy hair and quiet brown eyes.

"Will you come up-stairs with me, Carver? I want to have a talk with you," he said simply.

Hugh hesitated. He did n't mind being talked *to*, but he was heartily sick of being talked *at*.

Graham noticed his hesitation and smiled. "Don't worry; I 'm not going to shanghai you, and I 'm not going to jaw you to death, either."

Hugh smiled in response. "I 'm glad of that," he said wearily. "I 've been jawed until I don't know anything."

"I don't doubt it. Come on; let 's get away from this racket." He took Hugh by the arm and led him up-stairs to his own room, which was pleasantly quiet and restful after the noise they had left.

When they were both seated in comfortable chairs, Graham began to talk. "I know that you are being tremendously rushed, Carver, and I know that you are going to get a lot of bids, too. I 've been watching you all through this week, and you seem dazed and confused to me, more confused even than the average freshman. I think I know the reason."

"What is it?" Hugh demanded eagerly.

"I understand that your father is a Nu Delt."

Hugh nodded.

"And you 're afraid that they are n't going to bid you."

Hugh was startled. "How did you know?" He never thought of denying the statement.

"I guessed it. You were obviously worried; you visited other fraternities; and you did n't seem to enjoy the attention that you were getting. I 'll tell you right now that you are worrying about nothing; the Nu Delts will bid you. They are just taking you for granted; that 's all. You are a legacy, and you have accepted all their invitations to come around. If you had stayed away one night, there would have been a whole delegation rushing around the campus to hunt you up."

Hugh relaxed. For the time being he believed Graham implicitly.

"Now," Graham went on, "it 's the Nu Delts that I want to talk about. Oh, I 'm not going to knock them," he hastened to add as Hugh eyed him suspiciously. "I know that you have heard plenty of fraternities knocking each other, but I am sure that you have n't heard any knocking in this house."

"No I have n't," Hugh admitted.

"Well, you are n't going to, either. The Nu Delts are much more important than we are. They are stronger locally, and they 've got a very powerful national organization. But I don't think that you have a very clear notion about the Nu Delts or us or any other fraternity. I heard you talking about fraternities the other night, and, if you will forgive me for being awfully frank, you were talking a lot of nonsense."

Hugh leaned forward eagerly. He was n't offended, and for the first time that week he did n't feel that he was being rushed.

"Well, you have a lot of sentimental notions about fraternities that are all bull; that's all. You think that the brothers are really brothers, that they stick by each other and all that sort of thing. You seem to think, too, that the fraternities are democratic. They are n't, or there would n't be any fraternities. You don't seem to realize that fraternities are among other things political organizations, fighting each other on the campus for dear life. You've heard fraternities this week knocking each other. Well, about nine tenths of what's been said is either lies or true of every fraternity on the campus. These fraternities are n't working together for the good of Sanford; they're working like hell to ruin each other. You think that you are going to like every man in the fraternity you join. You won't. You'll hate some of them."

Hugh was aroused and indignant. "If you feel that way about it, why do you stay in a fraternity?"

Graham smiled gravely. "Don't get angry, please. I stay because the fraternity has its virtues as well as its faults. I hated the fraternity the first two years, and I'm afraid that you're going to, too. You see, I had the same sort of notions you have—and it hurt like the devil when

they were knocked into a cocked hat.   The fraternity is a pleasant club: it gets you into campus activities; and it gives you a social life in college that
you can't get without it.   It isn't very important
to most men after they graduate.   Just try to raise
some money from the alumni some time, and you 'll
find out.   Some of them remain undergraduates
all their lives, and they think that the fraternity is
important, but most of them hardly think of it except when they come back to reunions.   They 're
more interested in their clubs or the Masons or
something of that sort."

"My father has n't remained an undergraduate
all his life, but he 's interested in the Nu Delts,"
Hugh countered vigorously.

"I suppose he is," Graham tactfully admitted,
"but you 'll find that most men are n't.   But that
does n't matter.   You are n't an alumnus yet;
you 're a freshman, and a fraternity is a darn nice
thing to have around while you are in college.

"What I am going to say now," he continued,
hesitating, "is pretty touchy, and I hope that you
won't be offended.   I have been trying to impress
on you that the fraternity is most important while
you are in college, and, believe me, it 's damned
important.   A fellow has a hell of a time if he gets
into the wrong fraternity. . . . I am sure that you
are going to get a lot of bids.   Don't choose hastily.   Spend to-morrow thinking the various bunches

over—and choose the one that has the fellows that you like best, no matter what its standing on the campus is. Be sure that you like the fellows; that is all-important. We want you to come to us. I think that you would fit in here, but I am not going to urge you. Think us over. If you like us, accept our bid; if you don't, go some fraternity where you do like the fellows. And that's my warning about the Nu Delts. Be sure that you like the fellows, or most of them, anyway, before you accept their bid. Have you thought them over?"

"No," Hugh admitted, "I have n't."

He did n't like Graham's talk; he thought that it was merely very clever rushing. He did Graham an injustice. Graham had been strongly attracted to Hugh and felt sure that he would be making a serious mistake if he joined Nu Delta. Hugh's reaction, however, was natural. He had been rushed in dozens of ingenious ways for a week; he had little reason, therefore, to trust Graham or anybody else.

Graham stood up. "I have a feeling, Carver," he said slowly, "that I have flubbed this talk. I am sure that you'll know some day that I was really disinterested and wanted to do my best for you."

Hugh was softened and smiled shyly as he lifted himself out of his chair. "I know you did," he said with more gratitude in his voice than he quite felt, "and I 'm very grateful, but I 'm so woozy now that I don't know what to think."

"I don't wonder. To tell you the truth, I am, too. I have n't got to bed earlier than three o'clock any night this week, and right now I hardly care if we pledge anybody to-morrow night." He continued talking as they walked slowly down the stairs. "One more bit of advice. Don't go anywhere else to-night. Go home to bed, and to-morrow think over what I 've told you. And," he added, holding out his hand, "even if you don't come our way, I hope I see a lot of you before the end of the term."

Hugh clasped his hand. "You sure will. Thanks a lot. Good night."

"Good night."

Hugh did go straight to his room and tried to think, but the effort met with little success. He wanted desperately to receive a bid from Nu Delta, and if he did n't—well, nothing else much mattered. Graham's assertion that Nu Delta would bid him no longer brought him any comfort. Why should Graham know what Nu Delta was going to do?

Shortly after eleven Carl came in and threw himself wearily into a chair. For a few minutes neither boy said anything; they stared into the fire and frowned. Finally Carl spoke.

"I can go Alpha Sig if I want," he said softly.

Hugh looked up. "Good!" he exclaimed, honestly pleased. "But I hope we can both go Nu Delt. Did they come right out and bid you?"

"Er—no. Not exactly. It's kinda funny." Carl obviously wanted to tell something and did n't know how to go about it.

"What do you mean 'funny'? What happened?"

Carl shifted around in his chair nervously, filled his pipe, lighted it, and then forgot to smoke.

"Well," he began slowly, "Morton—you know that Alpha Sig, Clem Morton, the senior—well, he got me off into a corner to-night and talked to me quite a while, shot me a heavy line of dope. At first I did n't get him at all. He was talking about how they needed new living-room furniture and that sort of thing. Finally I got him. It's like this—well, it's this way: they need money. Oh, hell! Hugh, don't you see? They want money— and they know I've got it. All I've got to do is to let them know that I'll make the chapter a present of a thousand or two after initiation—and I can be an Alpha Sig."

Hugh was sitting tensely erect and staring at Carl dazedly.

"You mean," he asked slowly, "that they want you to buy your way in?"

Carl gave a short, hard laugh. "Well, nobody said anything vulgar like that, Hugh, but you've got the big idea."

"The dirty pups! The goddamn stinkers! I hope you told Morton to go straight to hell." Hugh jumped up and stood over Carl excitedly.

"Keep your shirt on, Hugh. No, I did n't tell him to go to hell. I did n't say anything, but I know that all I 've got to do to get an Alpha Sig bid to-morrow night is to let Morton know that I 'd like to make the chapter a present. And I 'm not sure—but I think maybe I 'll do it."

"What!" Hugh cried. "You would n't, Carl! You know damn well you would n't." He was almost pleading.

"Hey, quit yelling and sit down." He got up, shoved Hugh back into his chair, and then sat down again. "I want to make one of the Big Three; I 've *got* to. I don't believe that either Nu Delt or Kappa Zete is going to bid me. See? This is my only chance—and I think that I 'm going to take it." He spoke deliberately, staring pensively into the fire.

"I don't see how you can even think of such a thing," Hugh said in painful wonderment. "Why, I 'd rather never join a fraternity than buy myself into one."

"You are n't me."

"No, I 'm not you. Listen, Carl." Hugh turned in his chair and faced Carl, who kept his eyes on the dying fire. "I 'm going to say something awfully mean, but I hope you won't get mad.

. . . You remember you told me once that you were n't a gentleman. I did n't believe you, but if you buy yourself into that—that bunch of—of gutter-pups, I 'll—I 'll—oh, hell, Carl, I 'll have to believe it." He was painfully embarrassed, very much in earnest, and dreadfully unhappy.

"I told you that I was n't a gentleman," Carl said sullenly. "Now you know it."

"I don't know anything of the sort. I 'll never believe that you could do such a thing." He stood up again and leaned over Carl, putting his hand on his shoulder. "Listen, Carl," he said soberly, earnestly, "I promise that I won't go Nu Delt or any other fraternity unless they take you, too, if you 'll promise me not to go Alpha Sig."

Carl looked up wonderingly. "What!" he exclaimed. "You 'll turn down Nu Delt if they don't bid me, too?"

"Yes, Nu Delt or Kappa Zete or any other bunch. Promise me," he urged; "promise me."

Carl understood the magnitude of the sacrifice offered, and his eyes became dangerously soft. "God! you 're white, Hugh," he whispered huskily, "white as hell. You go Nu Delt if they ask you— but I promise you that I won't go Alpha Sig even if they bid me without pay." He held out his hand, and Hugh gripped it hard. "I promise," he repeated, "on my word of honor."

At seven o'clock Saturday evening every freshman who had any reason at all to think that he
would get a bid—and some that had no reason—
collected in nervous groups in the living-room of
the Union.   At the stroke of seven they were permitted to move up to a long row of tables which
were covered with large envelopes, one for every
freshman.   They were arranged in alphabetical order, and in an incredibly short time each man found
the one addressed to him.   Some of the envelopes
were stuffed with cards, each containing the freshman's name and the name of the fraternity bidding
him; some of them contained only one or two cards
—and some of them were empty.   The boys who
drew empty envelopes instantly left the Union without a word to anybody; the others tried to find a
free space where they could scan their cards unob-
served.   They were all wildly excited and nervous.
One glance at the cards, and their faces either
lighted with joy or went white with disappointment.

Hugh found ten cards in his envelope—and one
of them had Nu Delta written on it.   His heart
leaped; for a moment he thought that he was going
to cry.   Then he rushed around the Union looking
for Carl.   He found him staring at a fan of cards,
which he was holding like a hand of bridge.

"What luck?" Hugh cried.

Carl handed him the cards.   "Lamp those," he

said, "and then explain. They've got me stopped."

He had thirteen bids, one from every fraternity in good standing, including the so-called Big Three.

When Hugh saw the Nu Delta card he yelled with delight.

"I got a Nu Delt, too." His voice was trembling with excitement. "You'll go with me, won't you?"

"Of course, Hugh. But I don't understand."

"Oh, what's the dif? Let's go."

He tucked his arm in Carl's, and the two of them passed out of the Union on their way to the Nu Delta house. Later both of them understood. Carl's good looks, his excellent clothes, his money, and the fact that he had been to an expensive preparatory school were enough to insure him plenty of bids even if he had been considerably less of a gentleman than he was.

Already the campus was ringing with shouts as freshmen entered fraternity houses, each freshman being required to report at once to the fraternity whose bid he was accepting.

When Carl and Hugh walked up the Nu Delta steps, they were seized by waiting upper-classmen and rushed into the living-room, where they were received with loud cheers, slapped on the back, and passed around the room, each upper-classman shaking hands with them so vigorously that their hands hurt for an hour afterward. What pleasant pain! Each new arrival was similarly received, but the excitement did not last long. Both the freshmen and the upper-classmen were too tired to keep the enthusiasm at the proper pitch. At nine o'clock the freshmen were sent home with orders to report the next evening at eight.

Carl and Hugh, proudly conscious of the pledge buttons in the lapels of their coats, walked slowly across the campus, spent and weary, but exquisitely happy.

"They bid me on account of you," Carl said softly. "They did n't think they could get you unless they asked me, too."

"No," Hugh replied, "you 're wrong. They took you for yourself. They knew you would go where I did, and they were sure that I would go their way."

Hugh was quite right. The Nu Deltas had felt sure of both of them and had not rushed them harder because they were too busy to waste any time on certainties.

Carl stopped suddenly. "God, Hugh," he exclaimed. "Just suppose I had offered the Alpha Sigs that cash. God!"

"Are n't you glad you did n't?" Hugh asked happily.

"Glad? Glad? Boy, I 'm bug-house. And,"

he added softly, "I know the lad I've got to thank."

"Aw, go to hell."

The initiation season lasted two weeks, and the neophytes found that the dormitory initiations had been merely child's play. They had to account for every hour, and except for a brief time allowed every day for studying, they were kept busy making asses of themselves for the delectation of the upper-classmen.

In the Nu Delta house a freshman had to be on guard every hour of the day up to midnight. He was forced to dress himself in some outlandish costume, the more outlandish the better, and announce every one who entered or left the house. "Mr. Standish entering," he would bawl, or, "Mr. Kerwin leaving." If he bawled too loudly, he was paddled; if he did n't bawl loudly enough, he was paddled; and if there was no fault to be found with his bawling, he was paddled anyway. Every freshman had to supply his own paddle, a broad, stout oak affair sold at the coöperative store at a handsome profit.

If a freshman reported for duty one minute late, he was paddled; if he reported one minute early, he was paddled. There was no end to the paddling. "Assume the angle," an upper-classman would roar. The unfortunate freshman then hum-

bly bent forward, gripped his ankles with his hands
—and waited. The worst always happened. The
upper-classman brought the paddle down with a
resounding whack on the seat of the freshman's
trousers.

"Does it hurt?"

"Yes, sir."

Another resounding whack. *"What?"*

"No—no, sir."

"Oh, well, if it does n't hurt, I might as well give
you another one." And he gave him another one.

A freshman was paddled if he forgot to say
"sir" to an upper-classman; he was paddled if he
neglected to touch the floor with his fingers every
time he passed through a door in the fraternity
house; he was paddled if he laughed when an upper-
classman told a joke, and he was paddled if he
did n't laugh; he was paddled if he failed to return
from an errand in an inconceivably short time: he
was paddled for every and no reason, but mainly
because the upper-classmen, the sophomores particularly, got boundless delight out of doing the
paddling.

Every night a freshman stood on the roof of the
Nu Delta house and announced the time every fifteen seconds. "One minute and fifteen seconds
after nine, and all 's well in the halls of Nu Delta;
one minute and thirty seconds after nine, and all 's
well in the halls of Nu Delta; one minute and

forty-five seconds after nine, and all 's well in the halls of Nu Delta," and so on for an hour. Then he was relieved by another freshman, who took up the chant.

Nightly the freshmen had to entertain the upper-classmen, and if the entertainment was n't satis-factory, as it never was, the entertainers were pad-dled. They had to run races, shoving pennies across the floor with their noses. The winner was paddled for going too fast—"Did n't he have any sense of sportsmanship?"—and the loser was pad-dled for going too slow. Most of the freshmen lost skin off their noses and foreheads; all of them shivered at the sight of a paddle. By the end of the first week they were whispering to each other how many blisters they had on their buttocks.

It was a bitterly cold night in late February when the Nu Deltas took the freshmen for their "walk." They drove in automobiles fifteen miles into the country and then left the freshmen to walk back. It was four o'clock in the morning when the miser-able freshmen reached the campus, half frozen, unutterably weary, but thankful that the end of the initiation was at hand.

Hugh was thankful for another thing; the Nu Deltas did not brand. He had noticed several men in the swimming-pool with tiny Greek letters branded on their chests or thighs. The branded ones seemed proud of their permanent insignia, but the idea of a fraternity branding its members like beef-cattle was repugnant to Hugh. He told Carl that he was darn glad the Nu Deltas were above that sort of thing, and, surprisingly, Carl agreed with him.

The next night they were formally initiated. The Nu Delta house seemed strangely quiet; levity was strictly prohibited. The freshmen were given white robes such as the upper-classmen were wearing, the president excepted, who wore a really handsome robe of blue and silver.

Then they marched up-stairs to the "goat room." Once there, the president mounted a dais; a "brother" stood on each side of him. Hugh was so much impressed by the ritual, the black hangings of the room, the fraternity seal over the dais, the ornate chandelier, the long speeches of the president and his assistants, that he failed to notice that many of the brothers were openly bored.

Eventually each freshman was led forward by an upper-classman. He knelt on the lowest step of the dais and repeated after the president the oath of allegiance. Then one of the assisting brothers whispered to him the password and taught him the "grip," a secret and elaborate method of shaking hands, while the other pinned the jeweled pin to his vest.

When each freshman had been received into the fraternity, the entire chapter marched in twos down-stairs, singing the fraternity song. The initiation was over; Carl and Hugh were Nu Delts.

The whole ceremony had moved Hugh deeply, so deeply that he had hardly been able to repeat the oath after the president. He thought the ritual very beautiful, more beautiful even than the Easter service at church. He left the Nu Delta house that night feeling a deeper loyalty for the fraternity than he had words to express. He and Carl walked back to Surrey 19 in silence. Neither was capable of speech, though both of them wanted to give expression to their emotion in some way.

They reached their room.

"Well," said Hugh shyly, "I guess I 'll go to bed."

"Me, too." Then Carl moved hesitatingly to where Hugh was standing. He held out his hand and grinned, but his eyes were serious.

"Good night—brother."

Their hands met in the sacred grip.

"Good night—brother."

CHAPTER XIII

TO Hugh the remainder of the term was simply a fight to get an opportunity to study. The old saying, "if study interferes with college, cut out study," did not appeal to him. He honestly wanted to do good work, but he found that the chance to do it was rare. Some one always seemed to be in his room eager to talk; there was the fraternity meeting to attend every Monday night; early in the term there was at least one hockey or basketball game a week; later there were track meets, baseball games, and tennis matches; he had to attend Glee Club rehearsals twice a week; he ran every afternoon either in the gymnasium or on the cinder path; some one always seduced him into going to the movies; he was constantly being drawn into bull sessions; there was an occasional concert: and besides all these distractions, there was a fraternity dance, the excitement of Prom, a trip to three cities with the Glee Club, and finally a week's vacation at home at Easter.

Worst of all, none of his instructors was inspiring. He had been assigned to a new section in Latin, and in losing Alling he lost the one really enjoyable teacher he had had. The others were conscientious, more or less competent, but there was little enthusiasm in their teaching, nothing to make a freshman eager either to attend their classes or to study the lessons they assigned. They did not make the acquiring of knowledge a thrilling experience; they made it a duty—and Hugh found that duty exceedingly irksome.

He attended neither the fraternity dance nor the Prom. He had looked forward enthusiastically to the "house dance," but after he had, along with the other men in his delegation, cleaned the house from garret to basement, he suddenly took to his bed with grippe. He groaned with despair when Carl gave him glowing accounts of the dance and the "janes." Carl for once, however, was circumspect; he did not tell Hugh all that happened. He would have been hard put to explain his own reticence, but although he thought "the jane who got pie-eyed" had been enormously funny, he decided not to tell Hugh about her or the pie-eyed brothers.

No freshman was allowed to attend the Prom, but along with the other men who were n't "dragging women" Hugh walked the streets and watched the girls. There was a tea-dance at the fraternity house during Prom week. Hugh said that he got a great kick out of it, but, as a matter of fact, he remained only a short time; there was a hectic qual-

ity to both the girls and the talk that confused him.
For some reason he did n't like the atmosphere; and
he did n't know why.   His excuse to the brothers
and to himself for leaving early was that he was in
training and not supposed to dance.

Track above all things was absorbing his interest.   He could hardly think of anything else.
He lay awake nights dreaming of the race he would
run against Raleigh.   Sanford had three dual track
meets a year, but the first two were with small colleges and considered of little importance.   Only
a point winner in the Raleigh meet was granted his
letter.

Hugh won the hundred in the sophomore-fresh-
man meet and in a meet with the Raleigh freshmen, so that he was given his class numerals.
He did nothing, however, in the Raleigh meet; he
was much too nervous to run well, breaking three
times at the mark.   He was set back two yards
and was never able to regain them.   For a time he
was bitterly despondent, but he soon cheered up
when he thought of the three years ahead of him.

Spring brought first rain and slush and then the
"sings."   There was a fine stretch of lawn in the
center of the campus, and on clear nights the students gathered there for a sing, one class on each
side of the lawn.   First the seniors sang a college
song, then the juniors, then the sophomores, and
then the freshmen.   After each song, the other

classes cheered the singers, except when the sophomores and freshmen sang: they always "razzed"
each other.   Hugh led the freshmen, and he never
failed to get a thrill out of singing a clear note and
hearing his classmates take it up.

After each class had sung three or four songs,
the boys gathered in the center of the lawn, sang
the college hymn, gave a cheer, and the sing was
over.

On such nights, however, the singing really continued for hours.   The Glee Club often sang from
the Union steps; groups of boys wandered arm in
arm around the campus singing; on every fraternity steps there were youths strumming banjos and
others "harmonizing": here, there, everywhere
young voices were lifted in song—not joyous nor
jazzy but plaintive and sentimental. Adeline's
sweetness was extolled by unsure barytones and
"whisky" tenors; and the charms of Rosie O'Grady
were chanted in "close harmony" in every corner
of the campus:

> "Sweet Rosie O'Grady,
>   She's my pretty rose;
>   She's my pretty lady,
>   As every one knows.
>   And when we are married,
>   Oh, how happy we'll be,
>   For I love sweet Rosie O'Grady
>   And Rosie O'Grady loves me."

Hugh loved those nights: the shadows of the
elms, the soft spring moonlight, the twanging banjos, the happy singing. He would never, so long
as he lived, hear "Rosie O'Grady" without surren-
dering to a tender, sentimental mood; that song
would always mean the campus and singing youth.

Suddenly examinations threw their baleful influence over the campus again. Once more the excitement, but not so great this time, the cramming,
the rumors of examinations "getting out," the seminars, the tutoring sections, the nervousness, the
fear.

Hugh, however, was surer of himself than he
had been the first term, and although he had no
reason to be proud of the grades he received, he
was not particularly ashamed of them.

He and Carl left the same day but by different
trains. They had agreed to room together again
in Surrey 19; so they did n't feel that the parting
for the summer was very important.

"You 'll write, won't you, old man?"

"Sure, Hugh—surest thing you know. Say, it
don't seem possible that our freshman year 's over
already. Why, hell, Hugh, we 're sophomores."

"So we are! What do you know about that?"
Hugh's eyes shone. "Gosh!"

Carl looked at his watch. "Hell, I 've got to
beat it." He picked up his suit-case, dropped it,
shook hands vigorously with Hugh, snatched up his

suit-case, and was off with a final, "Good-by, Hugh, old boy," sounding behind him.

Hugh settled back into a chair.   He had half an hour to wait.

"A sophomore. . . . Gosh!"

CHAPTER XIV

HUGH spent the summer at home, working on the farm, reading a little, and occasionally visiting a lake summer resort a few miles away. Helen had left Merrytown to attend a secretarial school in a neighboring city, and Hugh was genuinely glad to find her gone when he returned from college. Helen was becoming not only a bore but a problem. Besides, he met a girl at Corley Lake, the summer resort, whom he found much more fascinating. For a month or two he thought that he was in love with Janet Harton. Night after night he drove to Corley Lake in his father's car, sometimes dancing with Janet in the pavilion, sometimes canoeing with her on the lake, sometimes taking her for long rides in the car, but often merely wandering through the pines with her or sitting on the shore of the lake and staring at the rippling water.

Janet was small and delicate; she seemed almost fragile. She did everything daintily—like a little girl playing tea-party. Her hands and feet were exquisitely small, her features childlike and indefinite, except her little coral mouth, which was as

clearly outlined with color as a doll's and as mobile
as a fluttering leaf. She had wide blue eyes and
hair that was truly golden. Strangely, she had not
bobbed it but wore it bound into a shining coil
around her head.

Hugh wrote a poem to her. It began thus:

> Maiden with the clear blue eyes,
> Lady with the golden hair,
> Exquisite child, serenely wise,
> Sweetly tender, morning fair.

He wasn't sure that it was a very good poem;
there was something reminiscent about the first
line, and he was dubious about "morning fair."
He had, however, studied German for a year in
high school, and he guessed that if *morgenschön*
was all right in German it was all right in English,
too.

They rarely talked. Hugh was content to sit
for hours with the delicate child nestling in his arm,
her hand lying passive and cool in his. She made
him feel very strong and protective. Nights, he
dreamed of doing brave deeds for her, of saving
her from terrible dangers. At first her vague,
fleeting kisses thrilled him, but as the weeks went
by and his passion grew, he found them strangely
unsatisfying.

When she cuddled her lovely head in the hollow

of his shoulder, he would lean forward and whisper: "Kiss me, Janet. Kiss me." Obediently
she would turn her face upward, her little mouth
pursed into a coral bud, but if he held her too
tightly or prolonged the kiss, she pushed him away
or turned her face.   Then he felt repelled, chilled.
She kissed him much as she kissed her mother every
night, and he wanted—well, he did n't quite know
what he did want except that he did n't want to be
kissed *that* way.

Finally he protested. "What's the matter,
Janet?" he asked gently.   "Don't you love me?"

"Of course," she answered calmly in her small
flute-like voice; "of course I love you, but you are
so rough.   You must n't kiss me hard like that; it
is n't nice."

Nice!   Hugh felt as if she had slapped his face.
Then he knew that she did n't understand at all.
He tried to excuse her by telling himself that she
was just a child—she was within a year of his own
age—and that she would love him the way he did
her when she grew older; but down in his heart
he sensed the fact that she was n't capable of love,
that she merely wanted to be petted and caressed
as a child did.   The shadows and the moonlight
did not move her as they did him, and she thought
that he was silly when he said that he could hear
a song in the night breeze.   She had said that his
poem was very pretty.   That was all.   Well,

maybe it was n't a very good poem, but it had—well, it had—it had something in it that was n't just pretty.

He began to visit the lake less often and to wish that September and the opening of college would arrive. When the day finally came to return, he was almost as much excited as he had been the year before. Gosh! it would be good to see Carl again. The bum had written only once. Yeah, and Pudge Jamieson, too, and Larry Stillwell, and Bill Freeman, and—yes, by golly! Merton Billings. He 'd be glad to see old Fat Billings. He wondered if Merton was as fat as ever and as pure. And all the brothers at the Nu Delta house. He 'd been too busy to get really acquainted with them last year; but this year, by gosh, he 'd get to know all of them. It certainly would be great to be back and be a sophomore and make the little fresh stand around.

He did n't carry his suit-case up the hill this time; he checked it and sent a freshman for it later. When he arrived at Surrey 19 Carl was already there—and he was kneeling before a trunk when Hugh walked into the room. Both of them instantly remembered the identical scene of the year before.

Carl jumped to his feet. "Hullo—who are you?" he demanded, his face beaming.

Hugh pretended to be frightened and shy.

"I 'm Hugh Carver. I—I guess I 'm going to room with you."

"You sure are!" yelled Carl, jumping over the trunk and landing on Hugh. "God! I 'm glad to see you. Put it there." They shook hands and stared at each other with shining eyes.

Then they began to talk, interrupting each other, gesticulating, occasionally slapping each other violently on the back or knee, shouting with laughter as one of them told of a summer experience that struck them as funny. They were both so glad to get back to college, so glad to see each other, that they were almost hysterical. And when they left Surrey 19 arm in arm on their way to the Nu Delta house "to see the brothers," their cup of bliss was full to the brim and running over.

"Criminy, the ol' campus sure does look good," said Hugh ecstatically. "Watch the frosh work." He was suddenly reminded of something. "Hey, freshman!" he yelled at a big, red-faced youngster who was to be full-back on the football team a year hence.

The freshman came on a run. "Yes—yes, sir?"

"Here 's a check. Take it down to the station and get my suit-case. Take it up to Surrey Nineteen and put it in the room. The door 's open. Hurry up now; I 'm going to want it pretty soon."

"Yes, sir. I 'll hurry." And the freshman was off running.

Hugh and Carl grinned at each other, linked arms again, and continued their way across the campus. When they entered the Nu Delta house a shout went up. "Hi, Carl! Hi, Hugh! Glad to see you back. Didya have a good summer? Put it there, ol' kid"—and they shook hands, gripping each other's forearm at the same time.

Hugh tried hard to become a typical sophomore and failed rather badly. He retained much of the shyness and diffidence that gives the freshman his charm, and he did not succeed very well in acquiring the swagger, the cocky, patronizing manner, the raucous self-assurance that characterize the true sophomore.

He found, too, that he couldn't lord it over the freshmen very well, and at times he was nothing less than a renegade to his class. He was constantly giving freshmen correct information about their problems, and during the dormitory initiations he more than once publicly objected to some "stunt" that seemed to him needlessly insulting to the initiates. Because he was an athlete, his opinion was respected, and quite unintentionally he won several good friends among the freshmen. His objections had all been spontaneous, and he was rather sorry about them afterward. He felt that he must be soft, that he ought to be able to stand anything that anybody else could. Further, he felt that there must be something wrong with his sense of humor; things that struck lots of his classmates as funny seemed merely disgusting to him.

He wanted very much to tell Carl about Janet, but for several weeks the opportunity did not present itself. There was too much excitement about the campus; the mood of the place was all wrong, and Hugh, although he did n't know it, was very sensitive to moods and atmosphere.

Finally one night in October he and Carl were seated in their big chairs before the fire. They had been walking that afternoon, and Hugh had been swept outside of himself by the brilliance of the autumn foliage. He was emotionally and physically tired, feeling that vague, melancholy happiness that comes after an intense but pleasant experience. Carl leaned back to the center-table and switched off the study light.

"Pleasanter with just the firelight," he said quietly. He, too, had something that he wanted to tell, and the less light the better.

Hugh sighed and relaxed comfortably into his chair. The shadows were thick and mysterious behind them; the flames leaped merrily in the fireplace. Both boys sat silent, staring into the fire. Finally Hugh spoke.

"I met a girl this summer, Carl," he said softly.
"Yeah?"
"Yeah. Little peach. Awf'lly pretty. Dainty,

you know. Awf'lly dainty—like a little kid. You know."

Carl had slumped down into his chair. He was smoking his pipe and staring pensively at the flames. "Un-huh. Go on."

"Well, I fell pretty hard. She was so—er, dainty. She always reminded me of a little girl playing lady. She had golden hair and blue eyes, the bluest eyes I 've ever seen; oh, lots bluer than mine, lots bluer. And little bits of hands and feet."

Carl continued to puff his pipe and stare at the fire. "Pet?" he asked dreamily.

"Un-huh. Yeah, she petted—but she was kinda funny—cold, you know, and kinda scared. Gee, Carl, I was crazy about her. I—I even wrote her a poem. I guess it was n't very good, but I don't think she knew what it was about. I guess I 'm off her now, though. She 's too cold. I don't want a girl to fall over me—my last girl did that— but, golly, Carl, Janet did n't understand. I don't think she knows anything about love."

"Some of 'em don't," Carl remarked philosophically, slipping deeper into his chair. "They just pet."

"That 's the way she was. She liked me to hold her and kiss her just as long as I acted like a big brother, but, criminy, when I felt that soft little thing in my arms, I did n't feel like a big brother;

I loved her like hell. . . . She was awfully sweet," he added regretfully; "I wish she was n't so cold."

"Hard luck, old man," said Carl consolingly, "hard luck. Guess you picked an iceberg."

For a few minutes the room was quiet except for the crackling of the fire, which was beginning to burn low. The shadows were creeping up on the boys; the flames were less merry.

Carl took his pipe out of his mouth and drawled softly, "I had better luck."

Hugh pricked up his ears. "You have n't really fallen in love, have you?" he demanded eagerly. Carl had often said that he would never fall in love, that he was "too wise" to women.

"No, I did n't fall in love; nothing like that. I met a bunch of janes down at Bar Harbor. Some of them I 'd known before, but I met some new ones, too. Had a damn good time. Some of those janes certainly could neck, and they were ready for it any time. Gee, if the old lady had n't been there, I 'd 'a' been potted about half the time. As it was, I drank enough gin and Scotch to float a battle-ship. Well, the old lady had to go to New York on account of some business; so I went down to Christmas Cove to visit some people I know there. Christmas Cove 's a nice place; not so high-hat as Bar Harbor, but still it 's a nice place."

Hugh felt that Carl was leaving the main track,

and he hastened to shunt him back. "Sure," he said in cheerful agreement; "sure it is—but what happened?"

"What happened? Oh—oh, yes!" Carl brought himself back to the present with an obvious effort. "Sure, I 'll tell you what happened. Well, there was a girl there named Elaine Marston. She was n't staying with the folks I was, but they knew her, so I saw a lot of her. See?"

"Sure." Hugh wished he would hurry up. Carl did n't usually wander all over when telling a story. This must be something special.

"Well, I saw lots of her. Lots. Pretty girl, nice family and everything, but she liked her booze and she liked to pet. Awful hot kid. Well, one night we went to a dance, and between dances we had a lot of gin I had brought with me. Good stuff, too. I bought it off a guy who brought it down from Canada himself. Where was I? Oh, yes, at the dance. We both got pie-eyed; I was all liquored up, and I guess she was, too. After the dance was over, I dared her to walk over to South Bristol—that 's just across the island, you know—and then walk back again. Well, we had n't gone far when we decided to sit down. We were both kinda dizzy from the gin. You have to go through the woods, you know, and it 's dark as hell in there at night. . . . We sat down among some ferns and I began to pet her. Don't know why—just did. . . . Oh, hell! what's the use of going into details? You can guess what happened."

Hugh sat suddenly erect. "You did n't—"

Carl stood up and stretched. "Yeah," he yawned, "I did it. Lots of times afterwards."

Hugh was dazed. He did n't know what to think. For an instant he was shocked, and then he was envious. "Wonder if Janet would have gone the whole way," flitted across his mind. He instantly dismissed the question; he felt that it was n't fair to Janet. But Carl? Gosh!

Carl yawned again. "Great stuff," he said nonchalantly. "Sleepy as hell. Guess I'll hit the hay." He eyed Hugh suspiciously. "You are n't shocked, are you? You don't think I'm a moral leper or anything like that?" He attempted to be light but was n't altogether successful.

"Of course not." Hugh denied the suggestion vehemently, and yet down in his heart he felt a keen disappointment. He hardly knew why he was disappointed, but he was. "Going to bed?" he asked as casually as he could.

"Yeah. Good night."

"Good night, old man."

Each boy went to his own bedroom, Hugh to go to bed and think Carl's story over. It thrilled him, and he envied Carl, and yet—and yet he wished Carl had n't done it. It made him and Carl different—sorta not the same; no that was n't it.

He did n't know just what the trouble was, but there was a sharp sting of disillusionment that hurt. He would have been more confused had he known what was happening in Carl's room.

Carl had walked into his own bedroom, lighted the light, and closed the door. Then he walked to the dresser and stared at himself in the mirror, stared a long time as if the face were somehow new to him.

There was a picture of the "old lady" on the dresser. It caught his eye, and he flinched. It seemed to look at him reproachfully. He thought of his mother, and he thought of how he had bluffed Hugh. He had cried after his first experience with the girl.

He looked again into the mirror. "You goddamn hypocrite," he said softly; "you goddamn hypocrite." His lip curled in contempt at his image.

He began to undress rapidly. The eyes of the "old lady" in the picture seemed to follow him around the room. The thought of her haunted him. Desperately, he switched out the light.

Once in bed, he rolled over on his stomach and buried his face in the pillow. "God!" he whispered. "God!"

CHAPTER XV

SANFORD defeated Raleigh this year in football, and for a time the college was wild with excitement and delight. Most of the free lumber in Haydensville was burned in a triumphant bonfire, and many of the undergraduates celebrated so joyously with their winnings that they looked sadly bedraggled for several days afterward.

The victory was discussed until the boys were thoroughly sick of it, and then they settled down to a normal life, studying; playing pool, billiards, and cards; going to the movies, reading a little, and holding bull sessions.

Hugh attended many bull sessions. Some of them he found interesting, but many of them were merely orgies of filthy talk, the participants vying with one another in telling the dirtiest stories; and although Hugh was not a prig, he was offended by a dirty story that was told merely for the sake of its dirt. Pudge Jamieson's stories were smutty, but they were funny, too, and he could send Hugh into paroxysms of laughter any time that he chose.

One night in late November Hugh was in Gordon Ross's room in Surrey along with four others.   Ross was a senior, a quiet man with gray eyes, rather heavy features, and soft brown hair. He was considerably older than the others, having worked for several years before he came to college. He listened to the stories that were being told, occasionally smiled, but more often studied the group curiously.

The talk became exceedingly nasty, and Hugh was about to leave in disgust when the discussion suddenly turned serious.

"Do you know," said George Winsor abruptly, "I wonder why we hold these smut sessions.   I sit here and laugh like a fool and am ashamed of myself half the time.   And this is n't the only smut session that 's going on right now.   I bet there 's thirty at least going on around the campus.   Why are we always getting into little groups and cover-ing each other with filth?   College men are sup-posed to be gentlemen, and we talk like a lot of gutter-pups."   Winsor was a sophomore, a fine student, and thoroughly popular.   He looked like an unkempt Airedale.   His clothes, even when new, never looked neat, and his rusty hair refused to lie flat.   He had an eager, quick way about him, and his brown eyes were very bright and lively.

"Yes, that 's what I want to know," Hugh chimed in, forgetting all about his desire to leave. "I 'm always sitting in on bull sessions, but I think they 're rotten.   About every so often I make up my mind that I won't take part in another one, and before I know it somebody's telling me the latest and I'm listening for all I'm worth."

"That's easy," Melville Burbank answered. He was a junior with a brilliant record. "You're merely sublimating your sex instincts, that's all. If you played around with cheap women more, you wouldn't be thinking about sex all the time and talking smut."

"You're crazy!" It was Keith Nutter talking, a sophomore notorious for his dissipations. "Hell, I'm out with bags all the time, as you damn well know. My sex instincts don't need sublimating, or whatever you call it, and I talk smut as much as anybody—more than some."

"Perhaps you're just naturally dirty," Burbank said, his voice edged with sarcasm. He didn't like Nutter. The boy seemed gross to him.

"Go to hell! I'm no dirtier than anybody else." Nutter was not only angry but frankly hurt. "The only difference between me and the rest of you guys is that I admit that I chase around with rats, and the rest of you do it on the sly. I'm no hypocrite."

"Oh, come off, Keith," Gordon Ross said quietly; "you're not fair. I admit that lots of the fellows are chasing around with rats on the sly, but lots of them aren't, too. More fellows go straight around this college than you think. I know a number that have never touched a woman. They just hate to admit they 're pure, that 's all; and you take their bluff for the real thing."

"You 've got to show me." Nutter was almost sullen. "I admit that I 'm no angel, but I don't believe that I 'm a damn bit worse than the average. Besides, what 's wrong about it, anyhow? It 's just as natural as eating, and I don't see where there is anything worse about it."

George Winsor stood up and leaned against the mantel. He ran his fingers through his hair until it stood grotesquely on end. "Oh, that 's the old argument. I 've heard it debated in a hundred bull sessions. One fellow says it 's all wrong, and another fellow says it 's all right, and you never get anywhere. I want somebody to tell me what 's wrong about it and what 's right. God knows you don't find out in your classes. They have Doc Conners give those smut talks to us in our freshman year, and a devil of a lot of good they do. A bunch of fellows faint and have to be lugged out, and the Doc gives you some sickening details about venereal diseases, and that 's as far as you get. Now, I 'm all messed up about this sex business, and I 'll admit that I 'm thinking about it all the time, too. Some fellows say it 's all right to have a woman, and some fellows say it 's all wrong, but I notice none of them have any use for a woman who is n't straight."

All of the boys were sitting in easy-chairs except

Donald Ferguson, who was lying on the couch and listening in silence. He was a handsome youth with Scotch blue eyes and sandy hair. Women were instantly attracted by his good looks, splendid physique, slow smile, and quiet drawl.

He spoke for the first time. "The old single-standard fight," he said, propping his head on his hand. "I don't see any sense in scrapping about that any more. We've got a single standard now. The girls go just as fast as the fellows."

"Oh, that's not so," Hugh exclaimed. "Girls don't go as far as fellows."

Ferguson smiled pleasantly at Hugh and drawled; "Shut up, innocent; you don't know anything about it. I tell you the old double standard has gone all to hell."

"You're exaggerating, Don, just to get Hugh excited," Ross said in his quiet way. "There are plenty of decent girls. Just because a lot of them pet on all occasions isn't any reason to say that they aren't straight. I'm older than you fellows, and I guess I've had a lot more experience than most of you. I've had to make my own way since I was a kid, and I've bumped up against a lot of rough customers. I worked in a lumber camp for a year, and after you've been with a gang like that for a while, you'll understand the difference between them and college fellows. Those boys are bad eggs. They just haven't any morals, that's all. They turn into beasts every pay night; and bad as some of our college parties are, they are n't a circumstance to a lumber town on pay night."

"That 's no argument," George Winsor said excitedly, taking his pipe out of his mouth and gesticulating with it. "Just because a lumberjack is a beast is no reason that a college man is all right because he 's less of a beast. I tell you I get sick of my own thoughts, and I get sick of the college when I hear about some things that are done. I keep straight, and I don't know why I do. I despise about half the fellows that chase around with rats, and sometimes I envy them like hell. Well, what 's the sense in me keeping straight? What 's the sense in anybody keeping straight? Fellows that don't seem to get along just as well as those that do. What do you think, Mel? You 've been reading Havelock Ellis and a lot of ducks like that."

Burbank tossed a cigarette butt into the fire and gazed into the flames for a minute before speaking, his homely face serious and troubled. "I don't know what to think," he replied slowly. "Ellis tells about some things that make you fairly sick. So does Forel. The human race can be awfully rotten. I 've been thinking about it a lot, and I 'm all mixed up. Sometimes life just does n't seem worth living to me, what with the filth and the slums and the greed and everything. I 've been taking a course in sociology, and some of the things that Prof Davis has been telling us make you wonder why the world goes on at all. Some poet has a line somewhere about man's inhumanity to man, and I find myself thinking about that all the time. The world's rotten as hell, and I don't see how anything can be done about it. I don't think sometimes that it's worth living in. I can understand why people commit suicide." He spoke softly, gazing into the fire.

Hugh had given him rapt attention. Suddenly he spoke up, forgetting his resolve not to say anything more after Ferguson had called him "innocent." "I think you're wrong, Mel," he said positively. "I was reading a book the other day called 'Lavengro.' It's all about Gipsies. Well, this fellow Lavengro was all busted up and depressed; he's just about made up his mind to commit suicide when he meets a friend of his, a Gipsy. He tells the Gipsy that he's going to bump himself off, that he doesn't see anything in life to live for. Then the Gipsy answers him. Gee, it hit me square in the eye, and I memorized it on the spot. I think I can say it. He says: 'There's night and day, brother, both sweet things; sun, moon, and stars, brother, all sweet things; there's likewise a wind on the heath. Life is very sweet, brother; who would wish to die?' I think that's beautiful," he added simply, "and I think it's true, too."

"Good for you, Hugh," Ross said quietly.

Hugh blushed with pleasure, but he was taken back by Nutter's vigorous rejoinder. "Bunk!" he exclaimed. "Hooey! The sun, moon, and stars, and all that stuff sounds pretty, but it is n't life. Life's earning a living, and working like hell, and women, and pleasure. The 'Rubaiyat' 's the only poem—if you're going to quote poetry. That's the only poem I ever saw that had any sense to it.

> "Come, Beloved, fill the Cup that clears
> To-day of past Regrets and future Fears.
> To-morrow? Why, To-morrow I may be
> Myself with Yesterday's seven thousand Years.

You bet. You never can tell when you're going to be bumped off, and so you might just as well have a good time while you can. You damn well don't know what's coming after you kick the bucket."

"Good stuff, the 'Rubaiyat,' " said Ferguson lazily. He was lying on his back staring at the ceiling. "I bet I've read it a hundred times. When they turn down an empty glass for me, it's going to be *empty*. I don't know what I'm here for or where I'm going or why. 'Into this world and why not knowing,' and so on. My folks sent me to Sunday-school and brought me up to be a good little boy. I believed just about everything they told me until I came to college. Now I know they told me a lot of damned lies. And I've talked with a lot of fellows who 've had the same experience. . . . Anybody got a butt?''

Burbank, who was nearest to him, passed him a package of cigarettes. Ferguson extracted one, lighted it, blew smoke at the ceiling, and then quietly continued, drawling lazily: "Most fellows don't tell their folks anything, and there 's no reason why they should, either. Our folks lie to us from the time we are babies. They lie to us about birth and God and life. My folks never told me the truth about anything. When I came to college I was n't very innocent about women, but I was about everything else. I believed that God made the world in six days the way the Bible says, and that some day the world was coming to an end and that we 'd all be pulled up to heaven where Christ would give us the once-over. Then he 'd ship some of us to hell and give the good ones harps. Well, since I 've found out that all that 's hooey I don't believe in much of anything."

"I suppose you are talking about evolution," said Ross. "Well, Prof Humbert says that evolutions has n't anything to do with the Bible— He says that science is science and that religion is religion and that the two don't mix. He says that he holds by evolution but that that does n't make Christ's philosophy bad."

"No," Burbank agreed, "it does n't make it bad; but that is n't the point. I 've read the Bible, which I bet is more than the rest of you can say, and I 've read the Sermon on the Mount a dozen times. It 's darn good sense, but what good does it do? The world will never practise Christ's philosophy. The Bible says, 'Man is born to trouble as the sparks fly upward,' and, believe me, that 's damn true. If people would be pure and good, then Christ's philosophy would work, but they are n't pure and good; they are n't made pure and good, they 're made selfish and bad: they 're made, mind you, *made* full of evil and lust. I tell you it 's all wrong. I 've been reading and reading, and the more I read the more I 'm convinced that we 're all rotten—and .that if there is a god he made us rotten."

"You 're wrong!" They all turned toward Winsor, who was still standing by the fireplace; even Ferguson rolled over and looked at the excited boy. "You 're wrong," he repeated, "all wrong. I admit all that 's been said about parents. They do cheat us just as Don said. I never tell my folks anything that really matters, and I don't know any other fellows that do, either. I suppose there are some, but I don't know them. And I admit that there is sin and vice, but I don't admit that Christ's philosophy is useless. I 've read the Sermon on the Mount, too. That 's about all of the Bible that I have read, but I 've read that; and I tell you you 're all wrong. There is enough good in man

to make that philosophy practical. Why, there is
more kindness and goodness around than we know
about. We see the evil, and we know we have lusts
and—and things, but we do good, too. And Hugh
was right when he talked a while ago about the
beauty in the world. There 's lots of it, lots and
lots of it. There 's beautiful poetry and beautiful
music and beautiful scenery; and there are people
who appreciate all of it. I tell you that in spite of
everything life *is* worth living. And I believe in
Christ's philosophy, too. I don't know whether
He is the son of God or not—I think that He must
be—but that does n't make any difference. Look
at the wonderful influence He has had."

"Rot," said Burbank calmly, "absolute rot.
There has never been a good deed done in His
name; just the Inquisition and the what-do-you-call-
'ems in Russia. Oh, yes, pogroms—and wars and
robbing people. Christianity is just a name; there
is n't any such thing. And most of the professional
Christians that I 've seen are damn fools. I tell
you, George, it 's all wrong. We 're all in the dark,
and I don't believe the profs know any more about
it than we do."

"Oh, yes, they do," Hugh exclaimed; "they must.
Think of all the studying they 've done."

"Bah." Burbank was contemptuous. "They 've
read a lot of books, that 's all. Most of them
never had an idea in their lives. Oh, I know that

some of them think; if they did n't, I 'd leave college to-morrow. It 's men like Davis and Maxwell and Henley and Jimpson who keep me here. But most of the profs can't do anything more than spout a few facts that they 've got out of books. No, they don't know any more about it than we do. We don't know why we 're here or where we 're going or what we ought to do while we are here. And we get into groups and tell smutty stories and talk about women and religion, and we don't know any more than when we started. Think of all the talk that goes on around this college about sex. There 's no end to it. Some of the fellows say positively there 's no sense in staying straight; and a few, damn few, admit that they think a fellow ought to leave women alone, but most of them are in a muddle."

He rose and stretched. "I 've got to be going— a philosophy quiz to-morrow." He smiled. "I don't agree with Nutter, and I don't agree with George, and I don't agree with you, Don; and the worst of it is that I don't agree with myself. You fellows can bull about this some more if you want to; I 've got to study."

"No, they can't," said Ross. "Not here, anyway. I 've got to study, too. The whole of you 'll have to get out."

The boys rose and stretched. Ferguson rolled lazily off the couch. "Well," he said with a yawn, "this has been very edifying.   I 've heard it all before in a hundred bull sessions, and I suppose I 'll hear it all again.   I don't know why I 've hung around.   There 's a little dame that I 've got to write a letter to, and, believe me, she 's a damn sight more interesting than all your bull."   He strolled out of the door, drawling a slow "good night" over his shoulder.

Hugh went to his room and thought over the talk. He was miserably confused.   Like Ferguson he had believed everything that his father and mother —and the minister—had told him, and he found himself beginning to discard their ideas.   There did n't seem to be any ideas to put in the place of those he discarded.   Until Carl's recent confidence he had believed firmly in chastity, but he discovered, once the first shock had worn off, that he liked Carl the unchaste just as much as he had Carl the chaste. Carl seemed neither better nor worse for his experience.

He was lashed by desire; he was burning with curiosity—and yet, and yet something held him back.   Something—he hardly knew what it was— made him avoid any woman who had a reputation for moral laxity.   He shrank from such a woman —and desired her so intensely that he was ashamed.

Life was suddenly becoming very complicated, more complicated, it seemed, every day.   With other undergraduates he discussed women and religion endlessly, but he never reached any satisfactory conclusions. He wished that he knew some professor that he could talk to. Surely some of them must know the answers to his riddles. . . .

CHAPTER XVI

HUGH was n't troubled only by religion and sex; the whole college was disturbing his peace of mind: all of his illusions were being ruthlessly shattered. He had supposed that all professors were wise men, that their knowledge was almost limitless, and he was finding that many of the undergraduates were frankly con-contemptuous of the majority of their teachers and that he himself was finding inspiration from only a few of them. He went to his classes because he felt that he had to, but in most of them he was confused or bored. He learned more in the bull sessions than he did in the class-room, and men like Ross and Burbank were teaching him more than his instructors.

Further, Nu Delta was proving a keen disappointment. More and more he found himself thinking of Malcolm Graham's talk to him during the rushing season of his freshman year. He often wished that Graham were still in college so that he could go to him for advice. The fraternity was not the brotherhood that he had dreamed about; it was composed of several cliques warring with each other, never coalescing into a single group except to contest the control of a student activity with some other fraternity. There were a few "brothers" that Hugh liked, but most of them were not his kind at all. Many of them were athletes taken into the fraternity because they were athletes and for no other reason, and although Hugh liked two of the athletes—they were really splendid fellows—he was forced to admit that three of them were hardly better than thugs, cheap muckers with fine bodies. Then there were the snobs, usually prep school men with more money than they could handle wisely, utterly contemptuous of any man not belonging to a fraternity or of one belonging to any of the lesser fraternities. These were the "smooth boys," interested primarily in clothes and "parties," passing their courses by the aid of tutors or fraternity brothers who happened to study.

Hugh felt that he ought to like all of his fraternity brothers, but, try as he would, he disliked the majority of them. Early in his sophomore year he knew that he ought to have "gone" Delta Sigma Delta, that that fraternity contained a group of men whom he liked and respected, most of them, at least. They were n't prominent in student activities, but they were earnest lads as a whole, trying hard to get something out of college.

The Nu Delta meetings every Monday night were a revelation to him. The brothers were openly bored; they paid little or no attention to the

business before them. The president was constantly calling for order and not getting it. 'During the rushing season in the second term, interest
picked up. Freshmen were being discussed.
Four questions were inevitably asked. Did the
freshman have money? Was he an athlete? Had
he gone to a prep school? What was his family
like?

Hugh had been very much attracted by a lad
named Parker. He was a charming youngster with
a good mind and beautiful manners. In general,
only bad manners were *au fait* at Sanford; so
Parker was naturally conspicuous. Hugh proposed
his name for membership to Nu Delta.

"He's a harp," said a brother scornfully. "At
any rate, he's a Catholic."

That settled that. Only Protestants were
eligible to Nu Delta at Sanford, although the fraternity had no national rule prohibiting members
of other religions.

The snobbery of the fraternity cut Hugh deeply.
He was a friendly lad who had never been taught
prejudice. He even made friends with a Jewish
youth and was severely censured by three fraternity
brothers for that friendship. He was especially
taken to task by Bob Tucker, the president.

"Look here, Hugh," Tucker said sternly,
"you've got to draw the line somewhere. I suppose
Einstein is a good fellow and all that, but you've

been running around with him a lot. You've even brought him here several times. Of course, you can have anybody in your room you want, but we don't want any Jews around the house. I don't see why you had to pick him up, anyway. There's plenty of Christians in college."

"He's a first-class fellow," Hugh replied stubbornly, "and I like him. I don't see why we have to be so high-hat about Jews and Catholics. Most of the fraternities take in Catholics, and the Phi Thetas take in Jews; at least, they've got two. They bid Einstein, but he turned them down; his folks don't want him to join a fraternity. And Chubby Elson told me that the Theta Kappas wanted him awfully, but they have a local rule against Jews."

"That doesn't make any difference," Tucker said sharply. "We don't want him around here. Because some of the fraternities are so damn broad-minded isn't any reason that we ought to be. I don't see that their broad-mindedness is getting them anything. We rate about ten times as much as the Phi Thetas or the Theta Kappas, and the reason we do is that we are so much more exclusive."

Hugh wanted to mention the three Nu Delta thugs, but he wisely restrained himself. "All right," he said stubbornly, "I won't bring Einstein around here again, and I won't bring Parker either, but I'll see just as much of them as I want to. My

friends are my friends, and if the fraternity
does n't like them, it can leave them alone. I
pledged loyalty to the fraternity, but I 'll be damned
if I pledged my life to it." He got up and started
for the door, his blue eyes dark with anger. "I
hate snobs," he said viciously, and departed.

After rushing season was over, he rarely entered
that fraternity house, chumming mostly with Carl,
but finding friends in other fraternities or among
non-fraternity men. He was depressed and gloomy,
although his grades for the first term had been
respectable. Nothing seemed very much worth
while, not even making his letter on the track. He
was gradually taking to cigarettes, and he had even
had a nip or two out of a flask that Carl had
brought to the room. He had read the
"Rubaiyat," and it made a great impression on him.
He and Carl often discussed the poem, and more
and more Hugh was beginning to believe in Omar's
philosophy. At least, he could n't answer the arguments presented in Fitzgerald's beautiful quatrains.
The poem both depressed and thrilled him. After
reading it, he felt desperate—and ready for anything, convinced that the only wise course was to
take the cash and let the credit go. He was much
too young to hear the rumble of the distant drum.
Sometimes he was sure that there was n't a drum,
anyway.

He was particularly blue one afternoon when

Carl rushed into the room and urged him to go to
Hastings, a town five miles from Haydensville.

"Jim Pearson 's outside with his car," Carl said
excitedly, "and he 'll take us down. He 's got to
come right back—he 's only going for some booze—
but we need n't come back if we don't want to.
We 'll have a drink and give Hastings the once-
over. How 's to come along?"

"All right," Hugh agreed indifferently and began
to pull on his baa-baa coat. "I 'm with you. A shot
of gin might jazz me up a little."

Once in Hastings, Pearson drove to a private
residence at the edge of the town. The boys got
out of the car and filed around to the back door,
which was opened to their knock by a young man
with a hatchet face and hard blue eyes.

"Hello, Mr. Pearson," he said with an effort to
be pleasant. "Want some gin?"

"Yes, and some Scotch, too, Pete—if you have it.
I 'll take two quarts of Scotch and one of gin."

"All right." Pete led the way down into the
cellar, switching on an electric light when he reached
the foot of the stairs. There was a small bar in
the rear of the dingy, underground room, a table or
two, and dozens of small boxes stacked against the
wall.

It was Hugh's first visit to a bootlegger's den,
and he was keenly interested. He had a high-ball
along with Carl and Pearson; then took another

when Carl offered to stand treat. Pearson bought his three quarts of liquor, paid Pete, and departed alone, Carl and Hugh having decided to have another drink or two before they returned to Haydensville. After a second high-ball Hugh did not care how many he drank and was rather peevish when Carl insisted that he stop with a third. Pete charged them eight dollars for their drinks, which they cheerfully paid, and then warily climbed the stairs and stumbled out into the cold winter air.

"Brr," said Carl, buttoning his coat up to his chin; "it's cold as hell."

"So 't is," Hugh agreed; "so 't is. So 't is. That's pretty. So 't is, so 't is, so 't is. Is n't that pretty, Carl?"

"Awful pretty. Say it again."

"So 't is. So 't ish. So—so—so. What wush it, Carl?"

"So 't is."

"Oh, yes. So 't ish."

They walked slowly, arm in arm, toward the business section of Hastings, pausing now and then to laugh joyously over something that appealed to them as inordinately funny. Once it was a tree, another time a farmer in a sleigh, and a third time a Ford. Hugh insisted, after laughing until he wept, that the Ford was the "funniest goddamned thing" he'd ever seen. Carl agreed with him.

They were both pretty thoroughly drunk by the

time they reached the center of the town, where they intended getting the bus back to Haydensville. Two girls passed them and smiled invitingly.

"Oh, what peaches," Carl exclaimed.

"Jush—jush—jush swell," Hugh said with great positiveness, hanging on to Carl's arm. "They 're the shwellest Janes I 've ever sheen."

The girls, who were a few feet ahead, turned and smiled again.

"Let 's pick them up," Carl whispered loudly.

"Shure," and Hugh started unsteadily to increase his pace.

The girls were professional prostitutes who visited Hastings twice a year "to get the Sanford trade." They were crude specimens, revealing their profession to the most casual observer. If Hugh had been sober they would have sickened him, but he was n't sober; he was joyously drunk and the girls looked very desirable.

"Hello, girls," Carl said expansively, taking hold of one girl's arm. "Busy?"

"Bish-bishy?" Hugh repeated valiantly.

The older "girl" smiled, revealing five gold teeth.

"Of course not," she replied in a hard, flat voice. "Not too busy for you boys, anyway. Come along with us and we 'll make this a big afternoon."

"Sure," Carl agreed.

"Sh-shure," Hugh stuttered. He reached forward to take the arm of the girl who had spoken, but at the same instant some one caught him by the wrist and held him still.

Harry Slade, the star football player and this year's captain, happened to be in Hastings; he was, in fact, seeking these very girls. He had intended to pass on when he saw two men with them, but as soon as he recognized Hugh he paused and then impulsively strode forward.

"Here, Carver," he said sharply. "What are you doing?"

"None—none of you da-damn business," Hugh replied angrily, trying to shake his wrist free. "Leggo of me or—or I'll—I'll—"

"You won't do anything," Slade interrupted. "You're going home with me."

"Who in hell are you?" one of the girls asked viciously. "Mind your own damn business."

"You mind yours, sister, or you'll get into a peck of trouble. This kid's going with me—and don't forget that. Come on, Carver."

Hugh was still vainly trying to twist his wrist free and was muttering, "Leggo, leggo o' me."

Slade jerked him across the sidewalk. Carl followed expostulating. "Get the hell out of here, Peters," Slade said angrily, "or I'll knock your fool block off. You chase off with those rats if you want to, but you leave Carver with me if you know what's good for you." He shoved Carl away, and

Carl was sober enough to know that Slade meant what he said. Each girl took him by an arm, and he walked off down the street between them, almost instantly forgetting Hugh.

Fortunately the street was nearly deserted, and no one had witnessed the little drama. Hugh began to sob drunkenly. Slade grasped his shoulders and shook him until his head waggled. "Now, shut up!" Slade commanded sharply. He took Hugh by the arm and started down the street with him, Hugh still muttering, "Leggo, leggo o' me."

Slade walked him the whole five miles back to Haydensville, and before they were half way home Hugh's head began to clear. For a time he felt a little sick, but the nausea passed, and when they reached the campus he was quite sober. Not a word was spoken until Hugh unlocked the door of Surrey 19. Then Slade said: "Go wash your face and head in cold water. Souse yourself good and then come back; I want to have a talk with you."

Hugh obeyed orders, but with poor grace. He was angry and confused, angry because his liberty had been interfered with, and confused because Slade had never paid more than passing attention to him—and for a year and a half Slade had been his god.

Slade was one of those superb natural athletes who make history for many colleges. He was big,

powerfully built, and moved as easily as a dancer.
His features were good enough, but his brown eyes
were dull and his jaw heavy rather than strong.
Hugh had often heard that Slade dissipated
violently, but he did not believe the rumors; he
was positive that Slade could not be the athlete he
was if he dissipated.   He had been thrilled every
time Slade had spoken to him—the big man of the
college, the one Sanford man who had ever made
All American, as Slade had this year.

When he returned to his room from the bath-
room, Slade was sitting in a big chair smoking a
cigarette.   Hugh walked into his bedroom, combed
his dripping hair, and then came into the study, still
angry but feeling a little sheepish and very curious.

"Well, what is it?" he demanded, sitting down.

"Do you know who those women were?"

"No.   Who are they?"

"They 're Bessie Haines and Emma Gleeson; at
least, that 's what they call themselves, and they 're
rotten bags."

Hugh had a little quiver of fright, but he felt
that he ought to defend himself.

"Well, what of it?" he asked sullenly.   "I don't
see as you had any right to pull me away.   You
never paid any attention before to me.   Why this
sudden interest?   How come you 're so anxious to
guard my purity?"

Slade was embarrassed.   He threw his cigarette

into the fireplace and immediately lighted another
one. Then he looked at his shoes and muttered,
"I 'm a pretty bad egg myself."

"So I 've heard." Hugh was frankly sarcastic.

"Well, I am." Slade looked up defiantly. "I
guess it 's up to me to explain—and I don't know
how to do it. I 'm a dumbbell. I can't talk
decently. I flunked English One three times, you
know." He hesitated a moment and then blurted
out, "I was looking for those bags myself."

"What?" Hugh leaned forward and stared at
him, bewildered and dumfounded. *"You* were
looking for them?"

"Yeah . . . You see, I 'm a bad egg—always
been a bad one with women, ever since I was a kid.
Gotta have one about every so often. . . . I—I 'm
not much."

"But what made you stop me?" Hugh pressed
his hand to his temple. His head was aching, and
he could make nothing out of Slade's talk.

"Because—because . . . Oh, hell, Carver, I
don't know how to explain it. I 'm twenty-four and
you 're about nineteen, and I know a lot that you
don't. I was brought up in South Boston and I ran
with a gang. There was n't anything rotten that
we did n't do. . . . I 've been watching you.
You 're different."

"How different?" Hugh demanded. "I want
women just as much as you do."

"That is n't it." Slade ran his fingers through his thick black hair and scowled fiercely at the fireplace. "That is n't it at all. You 're—you 're awfully clean and decent. I 've been watching you lots—oh, for a year. You 're—you 're different," he finished lamely.

Hugh was beginning to understand. "Do you mean," he asked slowly, "that you want me to keep straight—that—that, well—that you like me that way better?" He was really asking Slade if he admired him, and Slade got his meaning perfectly. To Hugh the idea was preposterous. Why, Slade had made every society on the campus; he had been given every honor that the students could heap on him—and he envied Hugh, an almost unknown sophomore. Why, it was ridiculous.

"Yes, that 's what I mean; that 's what I was trying to get at." For a minute Slade hesitated; he was n't used to giving expression to his confused emotions, and he did n't know how to go about it. "I 'd—I 'd like to be like you; that 's it. I—I did n't want you to be like me. . . . Those women are awful bags. Anything might happen."

"Why did n't you stop Carl Peters, too, then?"

"Peters knows his way about. He can take care of himself. You 're different, though. . . . You 've never been drunk before, have you?"

"No. No, I never have." Hugh's irritation was all gone. He was touched, deeply touched, by

Slade's clumsy admiration, and he felt weak, emotionally exhausted after his little spree. "It's awfully good of you to—to think of me that way. I'm—I'm glad you stopped me."

Slade stood up. He felt that he had better be going. He could n't tell Hugh how much he liked and admired him, how much he envied him. He was altogether sentimental about the boy, entirely devoted to him. He had wanted to talk to Hugh more than Hugh had wanted to talk to him, but he had never felt that he had anything to offer that could possibly interest Hugh. It was a strange situation; the hero had put the hero worshiper on a high, white marble pedestal.

He moved toward the door. "So long," he said as casually as he could.

Hugh jumped up and rushed to him. "I'm awfully grateful to you, Harry," he said impulsively. "It was damn white of you. I—I don't know how to thank you." He held out his hand.

Slade gripped it for a moment, and then, muttering another "So long," passed out of the door.

Hugh was more confused than ever and grew steadily more confused as the days passed. He could n't understand why Slade, frankly unchaste himself, should consider his chastity so important. He was genuinely glad that Slade had rescued him, genuinely grateful, but his confusion about all things sexual was more confounded. The strangest thing was that when he told Carl about Slade's talk, Carl seemed to understand perfectly, though he never offered a satisfactory explanation.

"I know how he feels," Carl said, "and I'm awfully glad he butted in and pulled you away. I'd hate to see you messing around with bags like that myself, and if I had n't been drunk I would n't have let you. I'm more grateful to him than you are. Gee! I'd never have forgiven myself," he concluded fervently.

Just when the incident was beginning to occupy less of Hugh's thoughts, it was suddenly brought back with a crash. He came home from the gymnasium one afternoon to find Carl seated at his desk writing. He looked up when Hugh came in, tore the paper into fragments, and tossed them into the waste-basket.

"Guess I'd better tell you," he said briefly. "I was just writing a note to you."

"To me? Why?"

Carl pointed to his suit-case standing by the center-table.

"That's why."

"Going away on a party?"

"My trunk left an hour ago. I'm going away for good." Carl's voice was husky, and he spoke with an obvious effort.

Hugh walked quickly to the desk. "Why, old

man, what's the matter? Anything wrong with your mother? You're not sick, are you?"

Carl laughed, briefly, bitterly. "Yes, I'm sick all right. I'm sick."

Hugh, worried, looked at him seriously. "Why, what's the matter? I didn't know that you weren't feeling well."

Carl looked at the rug and muttered, "You remember those rats we picked up in Hastings?"

"Yes?"

"Well, I know of seven fellows they've sent home."

"What!" Hugh cried, his eyes wide with horror. "You don't mean that you—that you—"

"I mean exactly that," Carl replied in a low, flat voice. He rose and moved to the other side of the room. "I mean exactly that; and Doc Conners agrees with me," he added sarcastically. Then more softly, "He's got to tell the dean. That's why I'm going home."

Hugh was swept simultaneously by revulsion and sympathy. "God, I'm sorry," he exclaimed. "Oh, Carl, I'm so damn sorry."

Carl was standing by Hugh's desk, his hands clenched, his lips compressed. "Keep my junk," he said unevenly, "and sell anything you want to if you live in the house next year."

"But you'll be back?"

"No, I won't come back—I won't come back."
He was having a hard time to keep back the tears
and bit his trembling lip mercilessly. "Oh, Hugh,"
he suddenly cried, "what will my mother say?"

Hugh was deeply distressed, but he was startled
by that "my mother." It was the first time he had
ever heard Carl speak of his mother except as the
"old lady."

"She will understand," he said soothingly.

"How can she? How can she? God, Hugh,
God!" He buried his face in his hands and wept
bitterly. Hugh put his arm around his shoulder
and tried to comfort him, and in a few minutes Carl
was in control of himself again. He dried his eyes
with his handkerchief.

"What a fish I am!" he said, trying to grin. "A
goddamn fish." He looked at his watch. "Hell,
I 've got to be going if I 'm going to make the five
fifteen." He picked up his suit-case and held out
his free hand. "There 's something I want to say
to you, Hugh, but I guess I 'll write it. Please
don't come to the train with me." He gripped
Hugh's hand hard for an instant and then was out
of the door and down the hall before Hugh had
time to say anything.

Two days afterward the letter came. The customary "Dear brother" and "Fraternally yours"
were omitted.

Dear Hugh:

I 've thought of letters yards long but I 'm not going to write them. I just want to say that you are the finest thing that ever happened to me outside of my mother, and I respect you more than any fellow I 've ever known. I 'm ashamed because I started you drinking and I hope you 'll stop it. I feel toward you the way Harry Slade does, only more I guess. You 've done an awful lot for me.

I want to ask a favor of you. Please leave women alone. Keep straight, please. You don't know how much I want you to do that.

Thanks for all you 've done for me.

CARL.

Hugh's eyes filled with tears when he read that letter. Carl seemed a tragic figure to him, and he missed him dreadfully. Poor old Carl! What hell it must have been to tell his mother! "And he wants me to keep straight. By God, I will. . . . I 'll try to, anyhow."

CHAPTER XVII

HUGH'S depression was not continuous by any means. He was much too young and too healthy not to find life an enjoyable experience most of the time. Disillusionment followed disillusionment, each one painful and dispiriting in itself, but they came at long enough intervals for him to find a great deal of pleasure in between.

Also, for the first time since he had been transferred from Alling's section in Latin, he was taking genuine interest in a course. Having decided to major in English, he found that he was required to take a composition course the second half of his sophomore year. His instructor was Professor Henley, known as Jimmie Henley among the students, a man in his middle thirties, spare, neat in his dress, sharp with his tongue, apt to say what he thought in terms so plain that not even the stupidest undergraduate could fail to understand him. His hazel-brown eyes were capable of a friendly twinkle, but they had a way of darkening suddenly and snapping that kept his students constantly on the alert. There was little of the professor about him but a great deal of the teacher.

185

Hugh went to his first conference with him not entirely easy in his mind. Henley had a reputation for "tearing themes to pieces and making a fellow feel like a poor fish." Hugh had written his themes hastily, as he had during his freshman year, and he was afraid that Henley might discover evidences of that haste.

Henley was leaning back in his swivel chair, his feet on the desk, a brier pipe in his mouth, as Hugh entered the cubbyhole of an office. Down came the feet with a bang.

"Hello, Carver," Henley said cheerfully. "Come in and sit down while I go through your themes." He motioned to a chair by the desk. Hugh muttered a shy "hello" and sat down, watching Henley expectantly and rather uncomfortably.

Henley picked up three themes. Then he turned his keen eyes on Hugh. "I 've already read these. Lazy cuss, are n't you?" he asked amiably.

Hugh flushed. "I—I suppose so."

"You know that you are; no supposing to it." He slapped the desk lightly with the themes. "First drafts, are n't they?"

"Yes, sir." Hugh felt his cheeks getting warmer.

Henley smiled. "Thanks for not lying. If you had lied, this conference would have ended right now. Oh, I would n't have told you that I thought you were lying; I would simply have made a few polite but entirely insincere comments about your work and let you go. Now I am going to talk to you frankly and honestly."

"I wish you would," Hugh murmured, but he was n't at all sure that he wished anything of the sort.

Henley knocked the ashes out of his pipe into a metal tray, refilled it, lighted it, and then puffed meditatively, gazing at Hugh with kind but speculative eyes.

"I think you have ability," he began slowly. "You evidently write with great fluency and considerable accuracy, and I can find poetic touches here and there that please me. But you are careless, abominably careless, lazy. Whatever virtues there are in your themes come from a natural gift, not from any effort you made to say the thing in the best way. Now, I 'm not going to spend any time discussing these themes in detail; they are n't worth it."

He pointed his pipe at Hugh. "The point is exactly this," he said sternly. "I 'll never spend any time discussing your themes so long as you turn in hasty, shoddy work. I can see right now that you can get a C in this course without trying. If that 's all you want, all right, I 'll give it to you— and let it go at that. The Lord knows that I have enough to do without wasting time on lazy youngsters who have n't sense enough to develop their gifts. If you continue to turn in themes like these,

I'll give you C's or D's on them and let you dig your own shallow grave by yourself. But if you want to try to write as well as you can, I'll give you all the help in my power. Not one minute can you have so long as you don't try, but you can have hours if you do try. Furthermore, you will find writing a pleasure if you write as well as you can, but you won't get any sport just scribbling off themes because you have to."

He paused to toss the three themes across the desk to Hugh, who was watching him with astonishment. No instructor had ever talked to him that way before.

"You can rewrite these themes if you want to," Henley went on. "I haven't graded them, and I'll reserve the grades for the rewritten themes; and if I find that you have made a real effort, I'll discuss them in detail with you. What do you say?"

"I'd like to rewrite them," Hugh said softly. "I know they are rotten."

"No, they aren't rotten. I've got dozens that are worse. That isn't the point. They aren't nearly so good as you can make them, and only your best work is acceptable to me. Now show me what you can do with them, and then we'll tear them to shreds in regular fashion." He turned to his desk and smiled at Hugh, who, understanding that the conference was over, stood up and reached for the themes. "I 'll be interested in seeing what you can do with those," Henley concluded. "Every one of them has a good idea. Go to it—and get them back in a week."

"Yes, sir. Thanks very much."

"Right-o. Good-by."

"Good-by, sir," and Hugh left the office determined to rewrite those themes so that "they 'd knock Jimmie Henley's eye out." They did n't do exactly that, but they did interest him, and he spent an hour and a half discussing them with Hugh.

That was merely the first of a series of long conferences. Sometimes Henley and Hugh discussed writing, but often they talked about other subjects, not as instructor and student but as two men who respected each other's mind. Before the term was out Henley had invited Hugh to his home for dinner and to meet Mrs. Henley. Hugh was enormously flattered and, for some reason, stimulated to do better work. He found his talks with Henley really exciting, and he expressed his opinions to him as freely and almost as positively as he did to his classmates. He told his friends that Jimmie Henley was human, not like most profs. And he worked at his writing as he had never worked at anything, running excepted, since he had been in college.

The students never knew what to expect from Henley in the class-room. Sometimes he read

themes and criticized them; sometimes he discussed
books that he had been reading; sometimes he read
poetry, not because contemporary poetry was part
of the course but because he happened to feel like
reading it that morning; sometimes he discoursed
on the art of writing; and sometimes he talked
about anything that happened to be occupying his
mind. He made his class-room an open forum,
and the students felt free to interrupt him at any
time* and to disagree with him. Usually they did
disagree with him and afterward wrote violent
themes to prove that he was wrong. That was
exactly what Henley wanted them to do, and the
more he could stir them up the better satisfied he
was.

One morning, however, he talked without inter-
ruption. He did n't want to be interrupted, and
the boys were so taken back by his statements that
they could find no words to say anything.

The bell rang. Henley called the roll, stuck his
class-book into his coat pocket, placed his watch on
the desk; then leaned back and looked the class over.

"Your themes are making me sick," he began,
"nauseated. I have a fairly strong stomach, but
there is just so much that I can stand—and you have
passed the limit. There is hardly a man in this
class who has n't written at least one theme on the
glory that is Sanford. As you know, I am a Sanford man myself, and I have my share of affection

for the college, but you have reached an ecstasy of
chauvinism that makes Chauvin's affection for Napoleon seem almost like contempt.

"In the last batch of themes I got five telling me
of the perfection of Sanford: Sanford is the
greatest college in the country; Sanford has the best
athletes, the finest equipment, the most erudite
faculty, the most perfect location, the most loyal
alumni, the strongest spirit—the most superlative
everything. Nonsense! Rot! Bunk! Sanford
has n't anything of the sort, and I who love it say
so. Sanford is a good little college, but it is n't a
Harvard, a Yale, or a Princeton, or, for that matter, a Dartmouth or Brown; and those colleges still
have perfection ahead of them. Sanford has made
a place for itself in the sun, but it will never find a
bigger place so long as its sons do nothing but chant
its praises and condemn any one as disloyal who
happens to mention its very numerous faults.

"Well, I 'm going to mention some of those
faults, not all of them by any means, just those that
any intelligent undergraduate ought to be able to
see for himself.

"In the first place, this is supposed to be an
educational institution; it is endowed for that purpose and it advertises itself as such. And you men
say that you come here to get an education. But
what do you really do? You resist education with
all your might and main, digging your heels into the

gravel of your own ignorance and fighting any attempt to teach you anything every inch of the way. What's worse, you are n't content with your own ignorance; you insist that every one else be ignorant, too. Suppose a man attempts to acquire culture, as some of them do. What happens? He is branded as wet. He is a social leper.

"Wet! What currency that bit of slang has—and what awful power. It took me a long time to find out what the word meant, but after long research I think that I know. A man is wet ·if he is n't a 'regular guy'; he is wet if he is n't 'smooth'; he is wet if he has intellectual interests and lets the mob discover them; and, strangely enough, he is wet by the same token if he is utterly stupid. He is wet if he does n't show at least a tendency to dissipate, but he is n't wet if he dissipates to excess. A man will be branded as wet for any of these reasons, and once he is so branded, he might as well leave college; if he does n't, he will have a lonely and hard row to hoe. It is a rare undergraduate who can stand the open contempt of his fellows."

He paused, obviously ordering his thoughts before continuing. The boys waited expectantly. Some of them were angry, some amused, a few in agreement, and all of them intensely interested.

Henley leaned back in his chair. "What horrible little conformers you are," he began sarcastically, "and how you loathe any one who does n't conform! You dress both your bodies and your minds to some set model. Just at present you are making your hair foul with some sort of perfumed axle-grease; nine tenths of you part it in the middle. It makes no difference whether the style is becoming to you or not; you slick it down and part it in the middle. Last year nobody did it; the chances are that next year nobody will do it, but anybody who does n't do it right now is in danger of being called wet."

Hugh had a moment of satisfaction. He did not pomade his hair, and he parted it on the side as he had when he came to college. True, he had tried the new fashion, but after scanning himself carefully in the mirror, he decided that he looked like a "blond wop"—and washed his hair. He was guilty, however, of the next crime mentioned.

"The same thing is true of clothes," Henley was saying. "Last year every one wore four-button suits and very severe trousers. This year every one is wearing Norfolk jackets and bell-bottomed trousers, absurd things that flop around the shoes, and some of them all but trail on the ground. Now, any one who can't afford the latest creation or who declines to wear it is promptly called wet.

"And, as I said before, you insist on the same standardization of your minds. Just now it is not *au fait* to like poetry; a man who does is exceedingly wet, indeed; he is effeminate, a sissy. As a matter of fact, most of you like poetry very much. You never give me such good attention as when I read poetry. What's more, some of you are writing the disgraceful stuff. But what happens when a man does submit a poem as a theme? He writes at the bottom of the page, 'Please do not read this in class.' Some of you write that because you don't think that the poem is very good, but most of you are afraid of the contempt of your classmates. I know of any number of men in this college who read vast quantities of poetry, but always on the sly. Just think of that! Men pay thousands of dollars and give four years of their lives supposedly to acquire culture and then have to sneak off into a corner to read poetry.

"Who are your college gods? The brilliant men who are thinking and learning, the men with ideals and aspirations? Not by a long shot. They are the athletes. Some of the athletes happen to be as intelligent and as eager to learn as anybody else, but a fair number are here simply because they are paid to come to play football or baseball or what not. And they are worshiped, bowed down to, cheered, and adored. The brilliant men, unless they happen to be very 'smooth' in the bargain, are considered wet and are ostracized.

"Such is the college that you write themes about to tell me that it is perfect. The college is made up of men who worship mediocrity; that is their ideal except in athletics. The condition of the football field is a thousand times more important to the undergraduates and the alumni than the number of books in the library or the quality of the faculty. The fraternities will fight each other to pledge an athlete, but I have yet to see them raise any dust over a man who was merely intelligent.

"I tell you that you have false standards, false ideals, and that you have a false loyalty to the college. The college can stand criticism; it will thrive and grow on it—but it won't grow on blind adoration. I tell you further that you are as standardized as Fords and about as ornamental. Fords are useful for ordinary work; so are you—and unless some of you wake up and, as you would say, 'get hep to yourselves,' you are never going to be anything more than human Fords.

"You pride yourselves on being the cream of the earth, the noblest work of God. You are told so constantly. You are the intellectual aristocracy of America, the men who are going to lead the masses to a brighter and broader vision of life. Merciful heavens preserve us! You swagger around utterly contemptuous of the man who has n't gone to college. You talk magnificently about democracy, but you scorn the non-college man—and you try pathetically to imitate Yale and Princeton. And I suppose Yale and Princeton are trying to imitate Fifth Avenue and Newport. Democracy! Rot!

This college is n't democratic. Certain fraternities condescend to other fraternities, and those
fraternities barely deign even to condescend to the
non-fraternity men. You say hello to everybody
on the campus and think that you are democratic.
Don't fool yourselves, and don't try to fool me. If
you want to write some themes about Sanford that
have some sense and truth in them, some honest
observation, go ahead; but don't pass in any more
chauvinistic bunk. I 'm sick of it."

He put his watch in his pocket and stood up.
"You may belong to the intellectual aristocracy of
the country, but I doubt it; you may lead the masses
to a 'bigger and better' life, but I doubt it; you may
be the cream of the earth, but I doubt it. All I 've
got to say is this: if you 're the cream of the earth,
God help the skimmed milk." He stepped down
from the rostrum and briskly left the room.

For an instant the boys sat silent, and then suddenly there was a rustle of excitement. Some of
them laughed, some of them swore softly, and most
of them began to talk. They pulled on their baa-
baa coats and left the room chattering.

"He certainly has the dope," said Pudge Jamieson. "We 're a lot of low-brows pretending to be
intellectual high-hats. We 're intellectual hypo-
crites; that 's what we are."

"How do you get that way?" Ferdy Hillman,
who was walking with Hugh and Pudge, demanded

angrily. "We may not be so hot, but we 're a damn
sight better than these guys that work in offices and
mills. Jimmie Henley gives me a pain. He shoots
off his gab as if he knew everything. He 's got to
show me where other colleges have anything on
Sanford. He 's a hell of a Sanford man, he is."

They were walking slowly down the stairs.
George Winsor caught up with them.

"What did you think of it, George?" Hugh
asked.

Winsor grinned. "He gave me some awful body
blows," he said, chuckling. "Cripes, I felt most of
the time that he was talking only to me. I 'm sore
all over. What did you think of it? Jimmie 's a
live wire, all right."

"I don't know what to think," Hugh replied
soberly. "He 's knocked all the props from under
me. I 've got to think it over."

He did think it over, and the more he thought
the more he was inclined to believe that Henley was
right. Boy-like, he carried Henley's statements to
their final conclusion and decided that the college
was a colossal failure. He wrote a theme and said
so.

"You 're wrong, Hugh," Henley said when he
read the theme. "Sanford has real virtues, a
bushel of them. You 'll discover them all right
before you graduate."

CHAPTER XVIII

SANFORD'S virtues were hard for Hugh to find, and they grew more inconspicuous as the term advanced. For the time being nothing seemed worth while: he was disgusted with himself, the undergraduates, and the fraternity; he felt that the college had bilked him. Often he thought of the talk he had had with his father before he left for college. Sometimes that talk seemed funny, entirely idiotic, but sometimes it infuriated him. What right had his father to send him off to college with such fool ideas in his head? Nu Delta, the perfect brotherhood! Bull! How did his father get that way, anyhow? Hugh had yet to learn that nearly every chapter changes character at least once a decade and that Nu Delta thirty years earlier had been an entirely different organization from what it was at present. At times he felt that his father had deliberately deceived him, but in quieter moments he knew better; then he realized that his father was a dreamer and an innocent, a delicately minded man who had never really known anything about Sanford College or the world either. Hugh often felt older and wiser than his father; and in many ways he was.

In March he angered his fraternity brothers again by refusing a part in the annual musical comedy, which was staged by the Dramatic Society during Prom week. Hugh's tenor singing voice and rather small features made him an excellent possibility for a woman's part. But he was not a good actor, and he knew it. His attempts at acting in a high-school play had resulted in a flat failure, and he had no intention of publicly making a fool of himself again. Besides, he did not like the idea of appearing on the stage as a girl; the mere idea was offensive to him. Therefore, when the Society offered him a part he declined it.

Bob Tucker took him severely to task. "What do you mean, Hugh," he demanded, "by turning down the Dramat? Here you 've got a chance for a lead, and you turn up your nose at it as if you were God Almighty. It seems to me that you are getting gosh-awful high-hat lately. You run around with a bunch of thoroughly wet ones; you never come to fraternity meetings if you can help it; you are n't half training down at the track; and now you give the Dramat the air just as if an activity or two was n't anything in your young life."

"The Dramat is n't anything to me," Hugh replied, trying to keep his temper. Tucker's arrogance always made him angry. "I can't act worth a damn. Never could. I tried once in a play at home and made a poor fish of myself, and

you can bet your bottom dollar that I 'm not going
to again."

"Bunk!" Tucker ejaculated contemptuously.
"Hooey! Anybody can act good enough for the
Dramat. I tell you right now that you 're turning
the fraternity down; you 're playing us dirt. What
have you done in college? Not a goddamn thing
except make the Glee Club. I don't care about
track. I suppose you did your best last year,
though I know damn well that you are n't doing it
this year. What would become of the fraternity
if all of us parked ourselves on our tails and gave
the activities the air the way you do? You 're
throwing us down, and we don't like it."

"Well, I 'm not going out for the Dramat,"
Hugh mumbled sullenly; "you can just bet on that.
I 'll admit that I have n't trained the way I ought
to, but I have made the Glee Club, and I have
promised to join the Banjo Club, and I am still on
the track squad, and that 's more than half the fellows in this fraternity can say. Most of 'em don't
do anything but go on parties and raise hell generally. How come you 're picking on me? Why
don't you ride some of them for a while? I don't
see where they 're so hot."

"Never mind the other fellows." Tucker's black
eyes flashed angrily. He was one of the "hell-rais-
ers" himself, good looking, always beautifully
dressed, and proud of the fact that he was "rated

the smoothest man on the campus." His "smooth-
ness" had made him prominent in activities—that
and his estimate of himself. He took it for granted
that he would be prominent, and the students accepted him at his own valuation; and powerful Nu
Delta had been behind him, always able to swing
votes when votes were needed.

"Never mind the other fellows," he repeated.
"They 're none of your party. You 've got talents,
and you re not making use of them. You could be
as popular as the devil if you wanted to, but you
go chasing around with kikes and micks."

Hugh was very angry and a little absurd in his
youthful pomposity. "I suppose you refer to
Parker and Einstein—my one mick friend, although
he is n't Irish, and my one Jewish friend. Well, I
shall stick to them and see just as much of them as
I like. I 've told you that before, and you might
as well get me straight right now: I 'm going to
run with whoever I want. The fraternity cannot
dictate to me about my friends. You told me you
did n't want Parker and Einstein around the house.
I don't bring them around. I don't see as how
you 've got a right to ask anything more."

"I don't suppose you realize that everything you
do reflects on the fraternity," Tucker retorted,
slightly pompous himself.

"I suppose it does, but I can't see that I have
done anything that is going to ruin the name of Nu

Delta. I don't get potted regularly or chase around
with filthy bags or flunk n.y courses or crib my way
through; and I could mention some men in this house
who do all those things." Hugh was thoroughly
angry and no longer in possession of his best judgment. "If you don't like the way I act, you can
have my pin any time you say." He stood up, his
blue eyes almost black with rage, his cheeks flushed,
his mouth a thin white line.

Tucker realized that he had gone too far. "Oh,
don't get sore, Hugh," he said soothingly. "I
didn't mean it the way you are taking it. Of
course, we don't want you to turn in your pin. We
all like you. We just want you to come around
more and be one of the fellows, more of a regular
guy. We feel that you can bring a lot of honor to
the fraternity if you want to, and we've been kinda
sore because you've been giving activities the
go-by."

"How about my studies?" Hugh retorted. "I
suppose you want me to give them the air. Well,
I did the first term, and I made a record that I was
ashamed of. I promised my folks that I'd do better; and I'm going to. I give an hour or two a
day to track and several hours a week to the Glee
Club, and now I'm going to have to give several
more to the Banjo Club. That's all I can give at
present, and that's all I'm going to give. I know
perfectly well that some fellows can go out for a

bunch of activities and make Phi Bete, too; but they 're sharks and I 'm not. Don't worry, either; I won't disgrace the fraternity by making Phi Bete," he concluded sarcastically.

"Oh, calm down, Hugh, and forget what I said," Tucker pleaded, thoroughly sorry that he had started the argument. "You go ahead and do what you think right and we 'll stand by you." He stood up and put his hand on Hugh's shoulder. "No hard feelings, are there, old man?"

Kindness always melted Hugh; no matter how angry he was, he could not resist it. "No," he said softly; "no hard feelings. I 'm sorry I lost my temper."

Tucker patted his shoulder. "Oh, that 's all right. I guess I kinda lost mine, too. You 'll be around to the meeting to-morrow night, won't you? Better come. Paying fines don't get you anywhere."

"Sure, I 'll come."

He went but took no part in the discussion, nor did he frequent the fraternity house any more than he had previously. More and more he realized that he had "gone with the wrong crowd," and more and more he thought of what Graham had said to him in his freshman year about how a man was in hell if he joined the wrong fraternity. "I was the wise bird," he told himself caustically; "I was the guy who knew all about it. Graham saw

what would happen, and I did n't have sense enough
to take his advice. Hell, I never even thought
about what he told me. I knew that I would be in
heaven if Nu Delta gave me a bid. Heaven! Well,
I 'm glad that they were too high-hat for Norry
Parker and that he went with the right bunch."

Norville Parker was Hugh's Catholic friend, and
the more he saw of the freshman the better he liked
him. Parker had received several bids from fraternities, and he followed the advice Hugh had
given him. "If Delta Sigma Delta bids you, go
there," Hugh had said positively. "They 're the
bunch you belong with. Apparently the Kappa
Zetes are going to bid you, too. You go Delta Sig
if you get the chance." Hugh envied Parker the
really beautiful fraternity life he was leading.
"Why in God's name," he demanded of himself regularly, "did n't I have sense enough to take Graham's
advice?"

When spring came, the two boys took long walks
into the country, both of them loving the new beauty
of the spring and happy in perfect companionship.
Hugh missed Carl badly, and he wanted to ask
Parker to room with him the remainder of the
term. He felt, however, that the fraternity would
object, and he wanted no further trouble with Nu
Delta. As a matter of fact, the fraternity would
have said nothing, but Hugh had become hypersen-

sitive and expected his "brothers" to find fault with
his every move.   He had no intention of deserting
Parker, but he could not help feeling that rooming
with him would be a gratuitous insult to the fraternity.

Parker—every one called him Norry—was a
slender, delicate lad with dreamy gray eyes and silky
brown hair that, unless he brushed it back severely,
fell in soft curls on his extraordinarily white forehead.   Except for a slightly aquiline nose and a
firm jaw, he was almost effeminate in appearance,
his mouth was so sensitive, his hands so white and
slender, his manner so gentle.   He had a slow,
winning smile, a quiet, low voice.   He was a dreamer
and a mystic, a youth who could see fairies dancing in the shadows; and he told Hugh what he
saw.

"I see things," he said to Hugh one moonlight
night as they strolled through the woods; "I see
things, lovely little creatures flitting around among
the trees: I mean I see them when I 'm alone.
I like to lie on my back in the meadows and look
at the clouds and imagine myself sitting on a big
fellow and sailing and sailing away to heaven.   It 's
wonderful.   I feel that way when I play my fiddle."
He played the violin beautifully and had promptly
been made soloist for the Musical Clubs.   "I—I
can't explain.   Sometimes when I finish playing, I

find my eyes full of tears. I feel as if I had been to some wonderful place, and I don't want to come back.

"I guess I'm not like other fellows. I cry over poetry, not because it makes me sad. It's not that. It's just so beautiful. Why, when I first read Shelley's 'Cloud' I was almost sick I was so happy. I could hardly stand it. And when I hear beautiful music I cry, too. Why, when I listen to Kreisler, I sometimes want to beg him to stop; it hurts and makes me so happy that—that I just can't stand it," he finished lamely.

"I know," Hugh said. "I know how it is. I feel that way sometimes, too, but not as much as you, I guess. I don't cry. I never really cry, but I want to once in a while. I—I write poetry sometimes," he confessed awkwardly, "but I guess it's not very good. Jimmie Henley says it isn't so bad for a sophomore, but I'm afraid that he's just stringing me along, trying to encourage me, you know. But there are times when I've said a little bit right, just a little bit, but I've known that it was right—and then I feel the way you do."

"I've written lots of poetry," Norry said simply, "but it's no good; it's never any good." He paused between two big trees and pointed upward. "Look, look up there. See those black branches and that patch of sky between them and those stars. I want to picture that—and I can't; and I

want to picture the trees the way they look now so
fluffy with tiny new leaves, but I miss it a million
miles. . . . But I can get it in music," he added
more brightly. "Grieg says it. Music is the most
wonderful thing in the world. I wish I could be a
great violinist. I can't, though. I'm not a genius,
and I'm not strong enough. I can't practise very
long."

They continued walking in silence for a few minutes, and then Norry said: "I'm awfully happy
here at college, and I did n't expect to be, either. I
knew that I was kinda different from other fellows,
not so strong; and I don't like ugly things or smutty
stories or anything like that. I think women are
lovely, and I hate to hear fellows tell dirty stories
about them. I'm no fool, Hugh; I know about the
things that happen, but I don't want to hear about
them. Things that are dirty and ugly make me feel
sick.

"Well, I was afraid the fellows would razz me.
But they don't. They don't at all. The fellows
over at the Delta Sig house are wonderful to me.
They don't think I'm wet. They don't razz me
for not going on wild parties, though I know that
some of the fellows are pretty gay themselves.
They ask me to fiddle for them nearly every evening,
and they sit and listen very, very quietly just as
long as I'll play. I'm glad you told me to go
Delta Sig."

Norry made Hugh feel very old and a little crude and hard. He realized that there was something rare, almost exquisite, about the boy, and that he lived largely in a beautiful world of his own imagination. It would have surprised Norry if any one had told him that his fraternity brothers stood in awe of him, that they thought he was a genius. Some of them were built out of pretty common clay, but they felt the almost unearthly purity of the boy they had made a brother; and the hardest of them, the crudest, silently elected himself the guardian of that purity.

CHAPTER XIX

HUGH found real happiness in Norry Parker's companionship, and such men as Burbank and Winsor were giving him a more robust but no less pleasant friendship. They were earnest youths, eager and alive, curious about the world, reading, discussing all sorts of topics vigorously, and yet far more of the earth earthy than Parker, who was so mystical and dreamy that constant association with him would have been something of a strain.

For a time life seemed to settle down into a pleasant groove of studies that took not too much time, movies, concerts, an occasional play by the Dramatic Society, perhaps a slumming party to a dance in Hastings Saturday nights, bull sessions, long talks with Henley in his office or at his home, running on the track, and some reading.

For a week or two life was lifted out of the groove by a professor's daughter. Burbank introduced Hugh to her, and at first he was attracted by her calm dignity. He called three times and then gave her up in despair. Her dignity hid an utterly blank mind. She was as uninteresting as her father, and he had the reputation, well deserved, of being the dullest lecturer on the campus.

Only one event disturbed the pleasant calm of Hugh's life after his argument with Tucker. He did not attend Prom because he knew no girl whom he cared to ask; he failed again to make his letter and took his failure philosophically; and he received a note from Janet Harton telling him that she was engaged to "the most wonderful man in the world" —and he did n't give a hoot if she was.

Just after Easter vacation the Nu Deltas gave their annual house dance. Hugh looked forward to it with considerable pleasure. True, he was not "dragging a woman," but several of the brothers were going "stag"; so he felt completely at ease.

The freshmen were put to work cleaning the house, the curtains were sent to the laundry, bedroom closets and dresser drawers were emptied of anything the girls might find too interesting, and an enormously expensive orchestra was imported from New York. Finally a number of young alumni, the four patronesses, and the girls appeared.

Getting dressed for the dance was a real event in Hugh's life. He had worn evening clothes only a few times before, but those occasions, fraternity banquets and glee club concerts, were, he felt, relatively unimportant. The dance, however, was different, and he felt that he must look his best, his very "smoothest." He was a rare undergraduate;

he owned everything necessary to wear to an evening
function—at least, everything an undergraduate
considered necessary.   He did not own a dress-
suit, and he would have had no use for it if he had;
only Tuxedos were worn.

He dressed with great care, tying and retying
his tie until it was knotted perfectly.   When at last
he drew on his jacket, he looked himself over in the
mirror with considerable satisfaction.   He knew
that he was dressed right.

It hardly entered his mind that he was an exceedingly good-looking young man.   Vanity was not one
of his faults.   But he had good reason to be pleased
with the image he was examining for any sartorial
defects.   He had brushed his sandy brown hair until it shone; his shave had left his slender cheeks
almost as smooth as a girl's; his blue eyes were very
bright and clear; and the black suit emphasized
his blond cleanness: it was a wholesome-looking, attractive youth who finally pulled on his top-coat and
started happily across the campus for the Nu Delta
house.

The dance was just starting when he arrived.
The patronesses were in the library, a small room
off the living-room.   Hugh learned later that six
men had been delegated to keep the patronesses in
the library and adequately entertained.   The men
worked in shifts, and although the dance lasted
until three the next morning, not a patroness got

a chance to wander unchaperoned around the house.

The living-room of the Nu Delta house was so large that it was unnecessary to use the dining-room for a dance. Therefore, most of the big chairs and divans had been moved into the dining-room—and the dining-room was dark.

Hugh permitted himself to be presented to the patronesses, mumbled a few polite words, and then joined the stag line, waiting for a chance to cut in. Presently a couple moved slowly by, so slowly that they did not seem to move at all. The girl was Hester Sheville, and Hugh had been introduced to her in the afternoon. Despite rather uneven features and red hair, she was almost pretty; and in her green evening gown, which was cut daringly low, she was flashing and attractive.

Hugh stepped forward and tapped her partner on the shoulder. The brother released her with a grimace at Hugh, and Hester, without a word, put her right hand in Hugh's left and slipped her left arm around his neck. They danced in silence for a time, bodies pressed close together, swaying in place, hardly advancing. Presently, however, Hester drew her head back and spoke.

"Hot stuff, is n't it?" she asked lazily.

Hugh was startled. Her breath was redolent of whisky.

"Sure is," he replied and executed a difficult step, the girl following him without the slightest difficulty.

She danced remarkably, but he was glad when he was tapped on the shoulder and another brother claimed Hester. The whisky breath had repelled him.

As the evening wore on he danced with a good many girls who had whisky breaths. One girl clung to him as they danced and whispered, "Hold me up, kid; I 'm ginned." He had to rush a third, a dainty blond child, to the porch railing. She was n't a pretty sight as she vomited into the garden; nor did Hugh find her gasped comment, "The seas are rough to-night," amusing. Another girl went sound asleep in a chair and had to be carried up-stairs and put to bed.

A number of the brothers were hilarious; a few had drunk too much and were sick; one had a "crying jag." There were men there, however, who were not drinking at all, and they were making gallant efforts to keep the sober girls away from the less sober girls and the inebriated brothers.

Hugh was not drinking. The idea of drinking at a dance was offensive to him; he thought it insulting to the girls. The fact that some of the girls were drinking horrified him. He did n't mind their smoking—well, not very much; but drinking? That was going altogether too far.

About midnight he danced again with Hester Sheville, not because he wanted to but because she had insisted. He had been standing gloomily in the doorway watching the bacchanalian scene, listening to the tom-tom of the drums when she came up to him.

"I wanta dance," she said huskily. "I wanta dance with you—you—you blond beast." Seeing no way to decline to dance with the half-drunk girl, he put his arm around her and started off. Hester's tongue was no longer in control, but her feet followed his unerringly. When the music stopped, she whispered, "Take me—ta-take me to th' th' dining-room." Wonderingly, Hugh led her across the hall. He had not been in the dining-room since the dance started, and he was amazed and shocked to find half a dozen couples in the big chairs or on the divans in close embrace. He paused, but Hester led him to an empty chair, shoved him clumsily down into it, and then flopped down on his lap.

"Le 's—le 's pet," she whispered. " I wanna pet "

Again Hugh smelled the whisky fumes as she put her hot mouth to his and kissed him hungrily. He was angry, angry and humiliated. He tried to get up, to force the girl off of his lap, but she clung tenaciously to him, striving insistently to kiss him on the mouth. Finally Hugh's anger got the better of his manners; he stood up, the girl hanging to his neck, literally tore her arms off of him, took her by the waist and set her down firmly in the chair.

"Sit there," he said softly, viciously; "sit there."

She began to cry, and he walked rapidly out of the dining-room, his cheeks flaming and his eyes flashing; and the embracing couples paid no attention to him at all. He had to pass the door of the library to get his top-coat—he made up his mind to get out of the "goddamned house"—and was walking quickly by the door when one of the patronesses called to him.

"Oh, Mr. Carver. Will you come here a minute?"

"Surely, Mrs. Reynolds." He entered the library and waited before the dowager.

"I left my wrap up-stairs—in Mr. Merrill's room, I think it is. I am getting a little chilly. Won't you get it for me?"

"Of course. It's in Merrill's room?"

"I think it is. It's right at the head of the stairs. The wrap's blue with white fur."

Hugh ran up the stairs, opened Merrill's door, switched on the lights, and immediately spotted the wrap lying over the back of a chair. He picked it up and was about to leave the room when a noise behind him attracted his attention. He turned and saw a man and a girl lying on the bed watching him.

Hugh stared blankly at them, his mouth half open.

"Get th' hell out of here," the man said roughly.

For an instant Hugh continued to stare; then he whirled about, walked out of the room, slammed the door behind him, and hurried down the stairs. He delivered the wrap to Mrs. Reynolds, and two minutes later he was out of the house walking, almost running, across the campus to Surrey Hall. Once there, he tore off his top-coat, his jacket, his collar and tie, and threw himself down into a chair.

So this was college! This was the fraternity— that goddamned rat house! That was what he had pledged allegiance to, was it? Those were his brothers, were they? Brothers! Brothers!

He fairly leaped out of his chair and began to pace the floor. College! Gentlemen! A lot of muckers chasing around with a bunch of rats; that's what they were. Great thing—fraternities. No doubt about it, they were a great institution.

He paused in his mental tirade, suddenly conscious of the fact that he wasn't fair. Some of the fraternities, he knew, would never stand for any such performance as he had witnessed that evening; most of them, he was sure, wouldn't. It was just the Nu Deltas and one or two others; well, maybe three or four. So that's what he had joined, was it?

He thought of Hester Sheville, of her whisky breath, her lascivious pawing—and his hands clenched. "Filthy little rat," he said aloud, "the stinkin', rotten rat."

Then he remembered that there had been girls there who had n't drunk anything, girls who somehow managed to move through the whole orgy calm and sweet. His anger mounted. It was a hell of a way to treat a decent girl, to ask her to a dance with a lot of drunkards and soused rats.

He was warm with anger. Reckless of the buttons, he tore off his waistcoat and threw it on a chair. The jeweled fraternity pin by the pocket caught his eye. He stared at it for a moment and then slowly unpinned it. He let it lie in his hand and addressed it aloud, hardly aware of the fact that he was speaking at all.

"So that 's what you stand for, is it? For snobs and politicians and muckers. Well, I don't want any more of you—not—one—damn—bit—more—of—you."

He tossed the pin indifferently upon the centertable, making up his mind that he would resign from the fraternity the next day.

When the next day came he found, however, that his anger had somewhat abated. He was still indignant, but he did n't have the courage to go through with his resignation. Such an action, he knew, would mean a great deal of publicity, publicity impossible to avoid. The fraternity would announce its acceptance of his resignation in "The Sanford Daily News"; and then he would either have to lie or start a scandal.

As the days went by and he thought more and more about the dance, he began to doubt his indignation. Was n't he after all a prude to get so hot? Was n't he perhaps a prig, a sissy? At times he thought that he was; at other times he was sure that he was n't. He could be permanently sure of only one thing, that he was a cynic.

CHAPTER XX

HUGH avoided the Nu Delta house for the remainder of the term and spent more time on his studies than he had since he had entered college. The result was, of course, that he made a good record, and the A that Henley gave him in English delighted him so much that he almost forgot his fraternity troubles. Not quite, however. During the first few weeks of the vacation he often thought of talking to his father about Nu Delta, but he could not find the courage to destroy his father's illusions. He found, too, that he couldn't talk to his mother about things that he had seen and learned at college. Like most of his friends, he felt that "the folks wouldn't understand."

He spent the first two months at home working on the farm, but when Norry Parker invited him to visit him for a month on Long Island Sound, Hugh accepted the invitation and departed for the Parker summer cottage in high feather. He was eager to see Norry again, but he was even more eager to see New York. He had just celebrated his twentieth birthday, and he considered it disgraceful that he had never visited the "Big City," as New York was always known at Sanford.

Norry met him at Grand Central, a livelier and more robust Norry than Hugh had ever seen. The boy actually seemed like a boy and not a sprite; his cheeks were tanned almost brown, and his gray eyes danced with excitement when he spotted Hugh in the crowd.

"Gee, Hugh, I 'm glad to see you," he exclaimed, shaking Hugh's hand joyously. "I 'm tickled to death that you could come."

"So am I," said Hugh heartily, really happy to see Norry looking so well, and thrilled to be in New York. "Gosh, you look fine. I hardly know you. Where 'd you get all the pep?"

"Swimming and sailing. This is the first summer I 've been well enough to swim all I want to. Oh, it 's pretty down where we are. You 'll love the nights, Hugh. The Sound is wonderful."

"I 'll bet. Well, where do we go from here? Say, this is certainly a whale of a station, is n't it? It makes me feel like a hick."

"Oh, you 'll get over that soon enough," Norry, the seasoned New Yorker, assured him easily. "We 're going right out to the cottage. It 's too hot to-day to run around the city, but we 'll come in soon and you can give it the once-over." He took Hugh's arm and led him out of the station.

It had never entered Hugh's mind that Norry's

father might be rich. He had noticed that Norry's clothes were very well tailored, and Norry had told him that his violin was a Cremona, but the boy was not lavish with money and never talked about it at all. Hugh was therefore surprised and a little startled to see Norry walk up to an expensive limousine with a uniformed chauffeur at the wheel. He wondered if the Parkers were n't too high-hat for him?

"We'll go right home, Martin," Norry said to the chauffeur. "Get in, Hugh."

The Parker cottage was a short distance from New Rochelle. It was a beautiful place, hardly in the style of a Newport "cottage" but roomy and very comfortable. It was not far from the water, and the Parkers owned their own boat-house.

Mrs. Parker was on the veranda when the car drew up at the steps.

"Hello, Mother," Norry called.

She got up and ran lightly down the steps, her hand held out in welcome to Hugh.

"I know that you are Hugh Carver," she said in a beautifully modulated voice, "and I am really delighted to meet you. Norry has talked so much about you that I should have felt cheated if you had n't come."

Hugh's fears immediately departed. "I should have myself," he replied. "It was awfully good of you to invite me."

After meeting Norry's father and mother, Hugh understood the boy better. Mrs. Parker was both charming and pretty, a delightful woman who played the piano with professional skill. Mr. Parker was an artist, a portrait-painter, and he got prices for his pictures that staggered Hugh when Norry mentioned them casually. He was a quiet, grave man with gray eyes like his son's.

When he had a minute alone with Hugh, he said to him with simple sincerity: "You have been very kind to Norry, and we are grateful. He is a strange, poetic lad who needs the kind of understanding friendship you have given him. We should have been deeply disappointed if you had n't been able to visit us."

The expressions of gratitude embarrassed Hugh, but they made him feel sure of his welcome; and once he was sure of that he began to enjoy himself as he never had before. Before the month was out, he had made many visits to New York and was able to talk about both the Ritz and Macdougal Alley with elaborate casualness when he returned to college. He and Norry went swimming nearly every day and spent hours sailing on the Sound.

Norry introduced him to the many girls who had summer homes near the Parker cottage. They were a new type to him, boarding-school products, sure of themselves, "finished" with a high polish that glittered effectively, daringly frank both in their speech and their actions, beautiful dancers, good swimmers, full of "dirt," as they called gossip, and as offhand with men as they were with each other. Within a week Hugh got over his prejudice against women's smoking. Nearly every woman he met, including Mrs. Parker, smoked, and every girl carried her cigarette-case.

Most of the girls treated Norry as if he were a very nice small boy, but they adopted a different attitude toward Hugh. They flirted with him, perfected his "petting" technique, occasionally treated him to a drink, and made no pretense of hiding his attraction for them.

At first Hugh was startled and a little repelled, but he soon grew to like the frankness, the petting, and the liquor; and he was having a much too exciting time to pause often for criticism of himself or anybody else. It was during the last week of his visit that he fell in love.

He and Norry were standing near the float watching a number of swimmers. Suddenly Hugh was attracted by a girl he had never seen before. She wore a red one-piece bathing-suit that revealed every curve of her slender, boyish figure.

She noticed Norry and threw up her arm in greeting.

"Who is she?" Hugh demanded eagerly.

"Cynthia Day. She's just back from visiting friends in Maine. She's an awfully good swimmer.

Watch her." The girl poised for an instant on the edge of the float and then dived gracefully into the water, striking out with a powerful overhand stroke for another float a quarter of a mile out in the Sound. The boys watched her red cap as she rounded the float and started back, swimming easily and expertly. When she reached the beach, she ran out of the water, rubbed her hands over her face, and then strolled over to Norry.

Her hair was concealed by a red bathing-cap, but Hugh guessed that it was brown; at any rate, her eyes were brown and very large. She had an impudent little nose and full red lips.

" 'Lo, Norry," she said, holding out her hand. "How 's the infant?"

"Oh, I 'm fine. This is my friend Hugh Carver."

"I 've heard about you," she said as they shook hands. "I only got back last night, but everybody seems to be digging dirt about Norry's friend. Three of my friends are enemies on account of you, and one of 'em says she 's going in swimming some day and forget to come back if you don't give her a little more time."

Hugh blushed, but he had learned a few things in the past weeks.

"I wish they would tell me about it," he said with a fair assumption of ease. "Why did n't you come back sooner?" He was pleased with that speech. He would n't have dared it a month before.

The brown eyes smiled at him. "Because I did n't know you were here. You have n't got a cigarette about you, have you? Norry's useless when it comes to smokes."

Hugh did have a package of cigarettes. She took one, put it in her mouth, and waited for Hugh to light it for her. When he did, she gazed curiously over the flame at him. She puffed the cigarette for a moment and then said, "You look like a good egg. Let's talk." She threw herself down on the sand, and the boys sat down beside her.

From that moment Hugh was lost. For the remaining days of the visit he spent every possible moment with Cynthia, fascinated by her chatter, thrilled by the touch of her hand. She made no objection when he offered shyly to kiss her; she quietly put her arms around his neck and turned her face up to his—and her kisses set him aflame.

For once, he did not want to return to college, and when he arrived in Haydensville he felt none of his usual enthusiasm. The initiation of the freshmen amused him only slightly, and the football games did not seem so important as they had the two previous years. A letter from Cynthia was the most important thing in the world, and she wrote good letters, chatty, gay, and affectionate.

Custom made it necessary for him to room in the fraternity house. It was an unwritten law of Nu

Delta that all members live in the house their last two years, and Hugh hardly dared to contest the law. There were four men in the chapter whom he thoroughly liked and with whom he would have been glad to room, but they all had made their arrangements by the time he spoke to them; so he was forced to accept Paul Vinton's invitation to room with him.

Vinton was a cheerful youth with too much money and not enough sense. He wanted desperately to be thought a good fellow, a "regular guy," and he was willing to buy popularity if necessary by standing treat to any one every chance he got. He was known all over the campus as a "prize sucker."

He bored Hugh excessively by his confidences and almost offensive generosity. He always had a supply of Scotch whisky on hand, and he offered it to him so constantly that Hugh drank too much because it was easier and pleasanter to drink than to refuse.

Tucker had graduated, and the new president, Leonard Gates, was an altogether different sort of man. There had been a fight in the fraternity over his election. The "regular guys" opposed him and offered one of their own number as a candidate. Gates, however, was prominent in campus activities and had his own following in the house; as a result, he was elected by a slight margin.

He won Hugh's loyalty at the first fraternity

meeting after he took the chair. "Some things are going to be changed in this house," he said sternly, "or I will bring influence to bear that will change them." Every one knew that he referred to the national president of the fraternity. "There will be no more drunken brawls in this house such as we had at the last house dance. Any one who brings a cheap woman into this house at a dance will hear from it. Both my fiancée and my sister were at the last dance. I do not intend that they shall be insulted again. This is not a bawdy-house, and I want some of you to remember that."

He tried very hard to pass a rule, such as many of the fraternities had, that no one could bring liquor into the house and that there should be no gambling. He failed, however. The brothers took his scolding about the dance because most of them were heartily ashamed of that occasion; but they announced that they did not intend to have the chapter turned into the S. C. A., which was the Sanford Christian Association. It would have been well for Hugh if the law had been passed. Vinton's insistent generosity was rapidly turning him into a steady drinker. He did not get drunk, but he was taking down more high-balls than were good for him.

Outside of his drinking, however, he was leading a virtuous and, on the whole, an industrious life. He was too much in love with Cynthia Day to let his mind dwell on other women, and he had become sufficiently interested in his studies to like them for their own sake.

A change had come over the campus. It was inexplicable but highly significant. There had been evidences of it the year before, but now it became so evident that even some of the members of the faculty were aware of it. Intolerance seemed to be dying, and the word "wet" was heard less often. The undergraduates were forsaking their old gods. The wave of materialism was swept back by an inrushing tide of idealism. Students suddenly ceased to concentrate in economics and filled the English and philosophy classes to overflowing.

No one was able really to explain the causes for the change, but it was there and welcome. The "Sanford Literary Magazine," which had been slowly perishing for several years, became almost as popular as the "Cap and Bells," the comic magazine, which coined money by publishing risqué jokes and pictures of slightly dressed women. A poetry magazine daringly made its appearance on the campus and, to the surprise of its editors, was received so cordially that they were able to pay the printer's bill.

It became the fashion to read. Instructors in English were continually being asked what the best new books were or if such and such a book was all that it was "cracked up to be." If the instructor had n't read the book, he was treated to a look of contempt that sent him hastening to the library.

Of course, not all of the undergraduates took to reading and thinking; the millennium had not arrived, but the intelligent majority began to read and discuss books openly, and the intelligent majority ruled the campus.

Hugh was one of the most enthusiastic of the readers. He was taking a course in nineteenth-century poetry with Blake, the head of the English department. His other instructors either bored him or left him cold, but Blake turned each class hour into a thrilling experience. He was a handsome man with gray hair, dark eyes, and a magnificent voice. He taught poetry almost entirely by reading it, only occasionally interpolating an explanatory remark, and he read beautifully. His reading was dramatic, almost tricky; but it made the poems live for his students, and they reveled in his classes.

Hugh's junior year was made almost beautiful by that poetry course and by his adoration for Cynthia. He was writing verses constantly—and he found "Cynthia" an exceedingly troublesome word; it seemed as if nothing would rime with it. At times he thought of taking to free verse, but the results of his efforts did not satisfy him. He always had the feeling that he had merely chopped up some rather bad prose; and he was invariably right.   Cynthia wrote him that she loved the poems he sent her because they were so passionate.   He blushed when he read her praise.   It disturbed him. He wished that she had used a different word.

CHAPTER XXI

FOR the first term Hugh slid comfortably down a well oiled groove of routine. He went to the movies regularly, wrote as regularly to Cynthia and thought about her even more, read enormous quantities of poetry, "bulled" with his friends, attended all the athletic contests, played cards occasionally, and received his daily liquor from Vinton. He no longer protested when Vinton offered him a drink; he accepted it as a matter of course, and he had almost completely forgotten that "smoking was n't good for a runner." He had just about decided that he was n't a runner, anyway.

One evening in early spring he met George Winsor as he was crossing the campus.

"Hello, George. Where are you going?"

"Over to Ted Allen's room. Big poker party to-night. Don't you want to sit in?"

"You told me last week that you had sworn off poker. How come you 're playing again so soon?" Hugh strolled lazily along with Winsor.

"Not poker, Hugh—craps. I 've sworn off craps for good, and maybe I 'll swear off poker after to-night. I 'm nearly a hundred berries to the good right now, and I can afford to play if I want to."

"I'm a little ahead myself," said Hugh. "I don't play very often, though, except in the house when the fellows insist. I can't shoot craps at all, and I get tired of cards after a couple of hours."

"I'm a damn fool to play," Winsor asserted positively, "a plain damn fool. I ought n't to waste my time at it, but I'm a regular fiend for the game. I get a great kick out of it. How's to sit in with us? There's only going to be half a dozen fellows. Two-bit limit."

"Yeah, it'll start with a two-bit limit, but after an hour deuces 'll be wild all over the place and the sky will be the limit. I've sat in those games before."

Winsor laughed. "Guess you're right, but what's the odds? Better shoot a few hands."

"Well, all right, but I can't stay later than eleven. I've got a quiz in eccy to-morrow, and I've got to bone up on it some time to-night."

"I've got that quiz, too. I'll leave with you at eleven."

Winsor and Hugh entered the dormitory and climbed the stairs. Allen's door was open, and several undergraduates were lolling around the room, smoking and chatting. They welcomed the newcomers with shouts of "Hi, Hugh," and "Hi, George."

Allen had a large round table in the center of

his study, and the boys soon had it cleared for action. Allen tossed the cards upon the table, produced several ash-trays, and then carefully locked the door.

"Keep an ear open for Mac," he admonished his friends. "He's warned me twice now." "Mac" was the night-watchman, and he had a way of dropping in unexpectedly on gambling parties. "Here are the chips. You count 'em out, George. Two-bit limit."

The boys drew up chairs to the table, lighted cigarettes or pipes, and began the game. Hugh had been right; the "two-bit limit" was soon lifted, and Allen urged his guests to go as far as they liked.

There were ugly rumors about Allen around the campus. He was good looking, belonged to a fraternity in high standing, wore excellent clothes, and did fairly well in his studies; but the rumors persisted. There were students who insisted that he had n't the conscience of a snake, and a good many of them hinted that no honest man ever had such consistently good luck at cards and dice.

The other boys soon got heated and talkative, but Allen said little besides announcing his bids. His blue eyes remained coldly expressionless whether he won or lost the hand; his crisp, curly brown hair remained neatly combed and untouched by a nervous hand; his lips parted occasionally in a quiet smile:

he was the perfect gambler, never excited, always in absolute control of himself.

Hugh marveled at the control as the evening wore on. He was excited, and, try as he would, he could not keep his excitement from showing. Luck, however, was with him; by ten o'clock he was seventy-five dollars ahead, and most of it was Allen's money.

Hugh passed by three hands in succession, unwilling to take any chances. He had decided to "play close," never betting unless he held something worth putting his money on.

Allen dealt the fourth hand. "Ante up," he said quietly. The five other men followed his lead in tossing chips into the center of the table. He looked at his hand. "Two blue ones if you want to stay in." Winsor and two of the men threw down their cards, but Hugh and a lad named Mandel each shoved two blue chips into the pot.

Hugh had three queens and an ace. "One card," he said to Allen. Allen tossed him the card, and Hugh's heart leaped when he saw that it was an ace.

"Two cards, Ted," Mandel requested, nervously crushing his cigarette in an ash-tray. He picked up the cards one at a time, lifting each slowly by one corner, and peeking at it as if he were afraid that a sudden full view would blast him to eternity. His face did not change expression as he added the cards to the three that he held in his hand.

"I'm sitting pretty," Allen remarked casually, picking up the five cards that he had laid down before he dealt.

The betting began, Hugh nervous, openly excited, Mandel stonily calm, Allen completely at ease. At first the bets were for a dollar, but they gradually rose to five. Mandel threw down his cards.

"Fight it out," he said morosely. "I've thrown away twenty-five bucks, and I'll be damned if I'm going to throw away any more to see your four-flushes."

Allen lifted a pile of chips and let them fall lightly, clicking a rapid staccato. "It'll cost you ten dollars to see my hand, Hugh," he said quietly.

"It'll cost you twenty if you want to see mine," Hugh responded, tossing the equivalent to thirty dollars into the pot. He watched Allen eagerly, but Allen's face remained quite impassive as he raised Hugh another ten.

The four boys who weren't playing leaned forward, pipes or cigarettes in their mouths, their stomachs pressed against the table, their eyes narrowed and excited. The air was a stench of stale smoke; the silence between bets was electric.

The betting continued, Hugh sure that Allen was bluffing, but Allen never failed to raise him ten dollars on every bet. Finally Hugh had a hundred dollars in the pot and dared not risk more on his hand.

"I think you 're bluffing, goddamn it," he said, his voice shrill and nervous. "I 'll call you. Show your stinkin' hand."

"Oh, not so stinkin'," Allen replied lightly. "I 've got four of a kind, all of 'em kings. Let 's see your three deuces."

He tossed down his hand, and Hugh slumped in his chair at the sight of the four kings. He shoved the pile of chips toward Allen. "Take the pot, damn you. Of all the bastard luck. Look!" He slapped down his cards angrily. "A full house, queens up. Christ!" He burst into a flood of obscenity, the other boys listening sympathetically, all except Allen who was carefully stacking the chips.

In a few minutes Hugh's anger died. He remembered that he was only about twenty-five dollars behind and that he had an hour in which to recover them. His face became set and hard; his hands lost their jerky eagerness. He played carefully, never daring to enter a big pot, never betting for more than his hands were worth.

As the bets grew larger, the room grew quieter. Every one was smoking constantly; the air was heavy with smoke, and the stench grew more and more foul. Outside of a soft, "I raise you twenty," or, even, "Fifty bucks if you want to see my hand," a muttered oath or a request to buy chips, there was hardly a word said. The excitement was so intense that it hurt; the expletives smelled of the docks.

At times there was more than five hundred dollars in a pot, and five times out of seven when the pot was big, Allen won it. Win or lose, he continued cool and calm, at times smoking a pipe, other times puffing nonchalantly at a cigarette.

The acrid smoke cut Hugh's eyes; they smarted and pained, but he continued to light cigarette after cigarette, drawing the smoke deep into his lungs, hardly aware of the fact that they hurt.

He won and lost, won and lost, but gradually he won back the twenty-five dollars and a little more. The college clock struck eleven. He knew that he ought to go, but he wondered if he could quit with honor when he was ahead.

"I ought to go," he said hesitatingly. "I told George when I said that I 'd sit in that I 'd have to leave at eleven. I 've got an eccy quiz to-morrow that I 've got to study for."

"Oh, don't leave now," one of the men said excitedly. "Why, hell, man, the game 's just getting warm."

"I know," Hugh agreed, "and I hate like hell to quit, but I 've really got to beat it. Besides, the stakes are too big for me. I can't afford a game like this."

"You can afford it as well as I can," Mandel said irritably. "I 'm over two hundred berries in the hole right now, and you can goddamn well bet that I 'm not going to leave until I get them back."

"Well, I 'm a hundred and fifty to the bad," Winsor announced miserably, "but I 've got to go. If I don't hit that eccy, I 'm going to be out of luck." He shoved back his chair. "I hate like hell to leave; but I promised Hugh that I 'd leave with him at eleven, and I 've got to do it."

Allen had been quite indifferent when Hugh said that he was leaving. Hugh was obviously small money, and Allen had no time to waste on chicken-feed, but Winsor was a different matter.

"You don't want to go, George, when you 're in the hole. Better stick around. Maybe you 'll win it back. Your luck can't be bad all night."

"You 're right," said Winsor, stretching mightily. "It can't be bad all night, but I can't hang around all night to watch it change. You 're welcome to the hundred and fifty, Ted, but some night soon I 'm coming over and take it away from you."

Allen laughed. "Any time you say, George."

Hugh and Winsor settled their accounts, then stood up, aching and weary, their muscles cramped from three hours of sitting and nervous tension. They said brief good nights, unlocked the door—they heard Allen lock it behind them—and left their disgruntled friends, glad to be out of the noisome odor of the room.

"God, what luck!" Winsor exclaimed as they started down the hall. "I 'm off Allen for good. That boy wins big pots too regularly and always

loses the little ones.   I bet he 's a cold-deck artist
or something."

"He 's something all right," Hugh agreed.
"Cripes, I feel dirty and stinko.   I feel as if I 'd
been in a den."

"You have been.   Say, what 's that?"   They
had almost traversed the length of the long hall
when Winsor stopped suddenly, taking Hugh by the
arm.   A door was open, and they could hear somebody reading.

"What 's what?" Hugh asked, a little startled by
the suddenness of Winsor's question.

"Listen.   That poem.   I 've heard it somewhere
before.   What is it?"

Hugh listened a moment and then said: "Oh,
that 's the poem Prof Blake read us the other day—
you know, 'Marpessa.'   It 's about the shepherd,
Apollo, and *Marpessa.*   It 's great stuff.   Listen."

They remained standing in the deserted hall,
the voice coming clearly to them through the open
doorway.   "It 's Freddy Fowler," Winsor whispered.   "He can sure read."

The reading stopped, and they heard Fowler say
to some one, presumably his room-mate: "This is
the part that I like best.   Get it."   Then he read
Idas's plea to *Marpessa:*

> " 'After such argument what can I plead?
> Or what pale promise make?   Yet since it is

In women to pity rather than to aspire,
A little I will speak.   I love thee then
Not only for thy body packed with sweet
Of all this world, that cup of brimming June,
That jar of violet wine set in the air,
That palest rose sweet in the night of life;
Nor for that stirring bosom all besieged
By drowsing lovers, or thy perilous hair;
Nor for that face that might indeed provoke
Invasion of old cities; no, nor all
Thy freshness stealing on me like strange sleep.' "

Winsor's hand tightened on Hugh's arm, and the two boys stood almost rigid listening to the young voice, which was trembling with emotion, rich with passion:

" 'Not only for this do I love thee, but
Because Infinity upon thee broods;
And thou are full of whispers and of shadows.
Thou meanest what the sea has striven to say
So long, and yearned up the cliffs to tell;
Thou art what all the winds have uttered not,
What the still night suggesteth to the heart.
Thy voice is like to music heard ere birth,
Some spirit lute touched on a spirit sea;
Thy face remembered is from other worlds,
It has been died for, though I know not when,
It has been sung of, though I know not where.' "

"God," Winsor whispered, "that's beautiful."
"Hush.   This is the best part."

" 'It has the strangeness of the luring West,
And of sad sea-horizons; beside thee
I am aware of other times and lands,
Of birth far back, of lives in many stars.
O beauty lone and like a candle clear
In this dark country of the world! Thou art
My woe, my early light, my music dying.' "

Hugh and Winsor remained silent while the young voice went on reading *Marpessa's* reply, her gentle refusal of the god and her proud acceptance of the mortal. Finally they heard the last words:

"When she had spoken, Idas with one cry
Held her, and there was silence; while the god
In anger disappeared. Then slowly they,
He looking downward, and she gazing up,
Into the evening green wandered away."

When the voice paused, the poem done, the two boys walked slowly down the hall, down the steps, and out into the cool night air. Neither said a word until they were half-way across the campus. Then Winsor spoke softly:

"God! Was n't that beautiful?"

"Yes—beautiful." Hugh's voice was hardly more than a whisper. "Beautiful. . . . It—it— oh, it makes me—kinda ashamed."

"Me, too. Poker when we can have that! We 're awful fools, Hugh."

"Yes—awful fools."

CHAPTER XXII

PROM came early in May, and Hugh looked forward to it joyously, partly because it would be his first Prom and partly because Cynthia was coming. Cynthia! He thought of her constantly, dreamed of her, wrote poems about her and to her. At times his longing for her swelled into an ecstasy of desire that racked and tore him. He was lost in love, his moods sweeping him from lyric happiness to black despair. He wrote to her several times a week, and between letters he took long walks composing dithyrambic epistles that fortunately were never written.

When he received her letter saying that she would come to Prom, he yelled like a lunatic, pounded the astonished Vinton on the back, and raced down-stairs to the living-room.

"She 's coming!" he shouted.

There were several men in the room, and they all turned and looked at him, some of them grinning broadly.

"What th' hell, Hugh?" Leonard Gates asked amiably. "Who 's coming? Who 's she?"

Hugh blushed and shuffled his feet. He knew that he had laid himself open to a "royal razzing," but he proceeded to bluff himself out of the dilemma.

"She? Oh, yes, she. Well, she is she. Altogether divine, Len." He was trying hard to be casual and flippant, but his eyes were dancing and his lips trembled with smiles.

Gates grinned at him. "A poor bluff, old man —a darn poor bluff. You're in love, *pauvre enfant,* and I'm afraid that you're in a very bad way. Come on, tell us the lady's name, her pedigree, and list of charms."

Hugh grinned back at Gates. "Chase yourself," he said gaily. "I won't tell you a blamed thing about her."

"You'd better," said Jim Saunders from the depths of a leather chair. "Is she the jane whose picture adorns your desk?"

"Yeah," Hugh admitted. "How do you like her?"

"Very fair, very fair." Saunders was magnificently lofty. "I've seen better, of course, but I've seen worse, too. Not bad—um, not very bad."

The "razzing" had started, and Hugh lost his nerve.

"Jim, you can go to hell," he said definitely, prepared to rush up-stairs before Saunders could reply. "You don't know a queen when you see one. Why, Cynthia—"

"Cynthia!" four of the boys shouted. "So her name 's Cynthia. That 's—"

But Hugh was half-way up-stairs, embarrassed and delighted.

The girls arrived on Thursday, the train which brought most of them reaching Haydensville early in the afternoon. Hugh paced up and down the station, trying to keep up a pretense of a conversation with two or three others. He gave the wrong reply twice and then decided to say nothing more. He listened with his whole body for the first whistle of the train, and so great was the chatter of the hundreds of waiting youths that he never heard it. Suddenly the engine rounded a curve, and a minute later the train stopped before the station. Immediately the boys began to mill around the platform like cattle about to stampede, standing on their toes to look over the heads of their comrades, shoving, shouting, dancing in their impatience.

Girls began to descend the steps of the cars. The stampede broke. A youth would see "his girl" and start through the crowd for her. Dozens spotted their girls at the same time and tried to run through the crowd. They bumped into one another, laughed joyously, bumped into somebody else, and finally reached the girl.

When Hugh eventually saw Cynthia standing on a car platform near him, he shouted to her and held his hand high in greeting. She saw him and waved back, at the same time starting down the steps.

She had a little scarlet hat pulled down over her curly brown hair, and she wore a simple blue traveling-suit that set off her slender figure perfectly. Her eyes seemed bigger and browner than ever, her nose more impudently tilted, her mouth more supremely irresistible. Her cheeks were daintly rouged, her eyebrows plucked into a thin arch. She was New York from her small pumps to the expensively simple scarlet hat.

Hugh dashed several people aside and grabbed her hand, squeezing it unmercifully.

"Oh, gee, Cynthia, I 'm glad to see you. I thought the darn train was never going to get here. How are you? Gee, you 're looking great, wonderful. Where 's your suit-case?" He fairly stuttered in his excitement, his words toppling over each other.

"I 'm full of pep. You look wonderful. There 's my suit-case, the big black one. Give the porter two bits or something. I have n't any change."

Hugh tipped the porter, picked up the suit-case with one hand, and took Cynthia by the arm with the other, carefully piloting her through the noisy, surging crowd of boys and girls, all of them talking at top speed and in high, excited voices.

Once Hugh and Cynthia were off the platform they could talk without shouting.

"We 've got to walk up the hill," Hugh explained

miserably. "I could n't get a car for love nor money. I 'm awfully sorry."

Cynthia did a dance-step and petted his arm happily. "What do I care? I 'm so—so damn glad to see you, Hugh. You look nicer 'n ever—just as clean and washed and sweet. Ooooh, look at him blush! Stop it or I 'll have to kiss you right here. Stop it, I say."

But Hugh went right on blushing. "Go ahead," he said bravely. "I wish you would."

Cynthia laughed. "Like fun you do. You 'd die of embarrassment. But your mouth is an awful temptation. You have the sweetest mouth, Hugh. It 's so damn kissable."

She continued to banter him until they reached the fraternity house. "Where do I live?" she demanded. "In your room, I hope."

"Yep. I 'm staying down in Keller Hall with Norry Parker. His room-mate 's sick in the hospital; so he 's got room for me. Norry 's going to see you later."

"Right-o. What do we do when I get six pounds of dirt washed off and some powder on my nose?"

"Well, we 're having a tea-dance here at the house at four-thirty; but we 've got an hour till then, and I thought we 'd take a walk. I want to show you the college."

After Cynthia had repaired the damages of travel and had been introduced to Hugh's fraternity

brothers and their girls, she and Hugh departed for
a tour of the campus. The lawns were so green
that the grass seemed to be bursting with color;
the elms waved tiny new leaves in a faint breeze;
the walls of the buildings were speckled with green
patches of ivy. Cynthia was properly awed by the
chapel and enthusiastic over the other buildings.
She assured Hugh that Sanford men looked awfully
smooth in their knickers and white flannels; in fact,
she said the whole college seemed jake to her.

They wandered past the lake and into the woods
as if by common consent. Once they were out of
sight of passers-by, Hugh paused and turned to Cynthia. Without a word she stepped into his arms
and lifted her face to his. Hugh's heart seemed
to stop; he was so hungry for that kiss, he had
waited so long for it.

When he finally took his lips from hers, Cynthia
whispered softly, "You're such a good egg, Hugh
honey, such a damn good egg."

Hugh could say nothing; he just held her close,
his mind swimming dizzily, his whole being atingle.
For a long time he held her, kissing her, now tenderly, now almost brutally, lost in a thrill of passion.

Finally she whispered faintly: "No more,
Hugh. Not now, dear."

Hugh released her reluctantly. "I love you so
damned hard, Cynthia," he said huskily. "I—I
can't keep my hands off of you."

"I know," she replied. "But we 've got to go back. Wait a minute, though. I must look like the devil." She straightened her hat, powdered her nose, and then tucked her arm in his.

After the tea-dance and dinner, Hugh left her to dress for the Dramatic Society musical comedy that was to be performed that evening. He returned to Norry Parker's room and prepared to put on his Tuxedo.

"You look as if somebody had left you a million dollars," Norry said to Hugh. "I don't think I ever saw anybody look so happy. You—you shine."

Hugh laughed. "I am happy, Norry, happy as hell. I 'm so happy I ache. Oh, God, Cynthia 's wonderful. I 'm crazy about her, Norry—plumb crazy."

Norry had known Cynthia for years, and despite his ingenuousness, he had noticed some of her characteristics.

"I never expected you to fall in love with Cynthia, Hugh," he said in his gentle way. "I 'm awfully surprised."

Hugh was humming a strain from "Say it with Music" while he undressed. He pulled off his trousers and then turned to Norry, who was sitting on the bed. "What did you say? You said something, did n't you?"

Norry smiled. For some quite inexplicable reason, he suddenly felt older than Hugh.

"Yes, I said something. I said that I never expected you to fall in love with Cynthia."

Hugh paused in taking off his socks. "Why not?" he demanded. "She 's wonderful."

"You 're so different."

"How different? We understand each other perfectly. Of course, we only saw each other for a week when I was down at your place, but we understood each other from the first. I was crazy about her as soon as I saw her."

Norry was troubled. "I don't think I can explain exactly," he said slowly. "Cynthia runs with a fast crowd, and she smokes and drinks—and you 're—well, you 're idealistic."

Hugh pulled off his underclothes and laughed as he stuck his feet into slippers and drew on a bathrobe. "Of course, she does. All the girls do now. She 's just as idealistic as I am."

He wrapped the bath-robe around him and departed for the showers, singing gaily:

"Say it with music,
Beautiful music;
Somehow they 'd rather be kissed
To the strains of Chopin or Liszt.
A melody mellow played on a cello
Helps Mister Cupid along—
So say it with a beautiful song."

Shortly he returned, still singing the same song, his voice full and happy. He continued to sing as he dressed, paying no attention to Norry, completely lost in his own Elysian thoughts.

To Hugh and Cynthia the musical comedy was a complete success, although the music, written by an undergraduate, was strangely reminiscent of several recent Broadway song successes, and the plot of the comedy got lost after the first ten minutes and was never recovered until the last two. It was amusing to watch men try to act like women, and two of the "ladies" of the chorus were patently drunk. *Cleopatra,* the leading lady, was a wrestler and looked it, his biceps swelling magnificently every time he raised his arms to embrace the comic *Antony.* It was glorious nonsense badly enough done to be really funny. Hugh and Cynthia, along with the rest of the audience, laughed joyously—and held hands.

After the play was over, they returned to the Nu Delta house and danced until two in the morning. During one dance Cynthia whispered to him, "Hugh, get me a drink or I 'll pass out."

Hugh, forgetting his indignation of the year before, went in search of Vinton and deprived that young man of a pint of gin without a scruple. He and Cynthia then sneaked behind the house and did away with the liquor. Other couples were drinking, all of them surreptitiously, Leonard Gates having

laid down the law in no uncertain manner, and all
of the brothers were a little afraid of Gates.

Cynthia slept until noon the next day, and Hugh
went to his classes.   In the afternoon they attended
a baseball game, and then returned to the fraternity
house for another tea-dance.   The Prom was to be
that night.   Hugh assured Cynthia that it was going to be a "wet party," and that Vinton had sold
him a good supply of Scotch.

The campus was rife with stories: this was the
wettest Prom on record, the girls were drinking as
much as the men, some of the fraternities had made
the sky the limit, the dormitories were being in-
vaded by couples in the small hours of the night,
and so on.   Hugh heard numerous stories but paid
no attention to them.   He was supremely happy,
and that was all that mattered.   True, several men
had advised him to bring plenty of liquor along to
the Prom if he wanted to have a good time, and he
was careful to act on their advice, especially as
Cynthia had assured him that she would dance until doomsday if he kept her "well oiled with hooch."

The gymnasium was gaily decorated for the Prom,
the walls hidden with greenery, the rafters twined
with the college colors and almost lost behind hundreds of small Japanese lanterns.   The fraternity
booths were made of fir boughs, and the orchestra
platform in the middle of the floor looked like a
small forest of saplings.

The girls were beautiful in the soft glow of the lanterns, their arms and shoulders smooth and white; the men were trim and neat in their Tuxedos, the dark suits emphasizing the brilliant colors of the girls' gowns.

It was soon apparent that some of the couples had got at least half "oiled" before the dance began, and before an hour had passed many more couples gave evidence of imbibing more freely than wisely. Occasionally a hysterical laugh burst shrilly above the pounding of the drums and the moaning of the saxophones. A couple would stagger awkwardly against another couple and then continue unevenly on an uncertain way.

The stags seemed to be the worst offenders. Many of them were joyously drunk, dashing dizzily across the floor to find a partner, and once having taken her from a friend, dragging her about, happily unconscious of anything but the girl and the insistent rhythm of the music.

The musicians played as if in a frenzy, the drums pound-pounding a terrible tom-tom, the saxophones moaning and wailing, the violins singing sensuously, shrilly as if in pain, an exquisite searing pain.

Boom, boom, boom, boom. "Stumbling all around, stumbling all around, stumbling all around so funny—" Close-packed the couples moved slowly about the gymnasium, body pressed tight to body, swaying in place—boom, boom, boom, boom

—"Stumbling here and there, stumbling every-where—" Six dowagers, the chaperons, sat in a corner, gossiped, and idly watched the young couples. . . . A man suddenly released his girl and raced clumsily for the door, one hand pressed to his mouth, the other stretched uncertainly in front of him.

Always the drums beating their terrible tom-tom, their primitive, blood-maddening tom-tom. . . . Boom, boom, boom, boom— "I like it just a little bit, just a little bit, quite a little bit." The music ceased, and some of the couples disentangled them-selves; others waited in frank embrace for the orchestra to begin the encore. . . . A boy slumped in a chair, his head in his hands. His partner sought two friends. They helped the boy out of the gymnasium.

The orchestra leader lifted his bow. The stags waited in a broken line, looking for certain girls. The music began, turning a song with comic words into something weirdly sensuous—strange syncopa-tions, uneven, startling drum-beats—a mad tom-tom. The couples pressed close together again, swaying, barely moving in place—boom, boom, boom, boom— "Second-hand hats, second-hand clothes— That's why they call me second-hand Rose. . . ." The saxophones sang the melody with passionate despair; the violins played tricks with a broken heart; the clarinets rose shrill in pain;

the drums beat on—boom, boom, boom, boom. . . .
A boy and girl sought a dark corner. He shielded
her with his body while she took a drink from a
flask. Then he turned his face to the corner and
drank. A moment later they were back on the
floor, holding each other tight, drunkenly swaying . . . Finally the last strains, a wail of agony—
"Ev-'ry one knows that I'm just Sec-ond-hand
Rose—from Sec-ond Av-en-ue."

The couples moved slowly off the floor, the
pounding of the drums still in their ears and in their
blood; some of them sought the fraternity booths;
some of the girls retired to their dressing-room,
perhaps to have another drink; many of the men
went outside for a smoke and to tip a flask upward.
Through the noise, the sex-madness, the half-
drunken dancers, moved men and women quite
sober, the men vainly trying to shield the women
from contact with any one who was drunk. There
was an angry light in those men's eyes, but most of
them said nothing, merely kept close to their part-
ners, ready to defend them from any too assertive
friend.

Again the music, again the tom-tom of the drums.
On and on for hours. A man "passed out cold"
and had to be carried from the gymnasium. A girl
got a "laughing jag" and shrieked with idiotic
laughter until her partner managed to lead her protesting off the floor. On and on, the constant

rhythmic wailing of the fiddles, syncopated passion
screaming with lust, the drums, horribly primitive;
drunken embraces. . . . "Oh, those Wabash Blues
—I know I got my dues— A lone-some soul
am I—I feel that I could die . . ." Blues, sobbing, despairing blues. . . . Orgiastic music—
beautiful, hideous! "Can-dle light that gleams—
Haunts me in my dreams . . ." The drums
boom, boom, boom, booming— "I'll pack
my walking shoes, to lose—those Wa-bash
Blues . . ."

Hour after hour—on and on. Flushed faces,
breaths hot with passion and whisky . . . Pretty
girls, cool and sober, dancing with men who held
them with drunken lasciviousness; sober men hating
the whisky breaths of the girls . . . On and on, the
drunken carnival to maddening music—the passion,
the lust.

Both Hugh and Cynthia were drinking, and by
midnight both of them were drunk, too drunk any
longer to think clearly. As they danced, Hugh was
aware of nothing but Cynthia's body, her firm
young body close to his. His blood beat with the
pounding of the drums. He held her tighter and
tighter—the gymnasium, the other couples, a swaying mist before his eyes.

When the dance ended, Cynthia whispered
huskily, "Ta-take me somewhere, Hugh."

Strangely enough, he got the significance of her

words at once. His blood raced, and he staggered so crazily that Cynthia had to hold him by the arm.

"Sure—sure; I 'll—I 'll ta-take you some-somewhere. I—I, too, Cyntheea."

They walked unevenly out of the gymnasium, down the steps, and through the crowd of smokers standing outside. Hardly aware of what he was doing, Hugh led Cynthia to Keller Hall, which was not more than fifty yards distant.

He took a flask out of his pocket. "Jush one more drink," he said thickly and emptied the bottle. Then, holding Cynthia desperately by the arm, he opened the door of Keller Hall and stumbled with her up the stairs to Norry Parker's room. Fortunately the hallways were deserted, and no one saw them. The door was unlocked, and Hugh, after searching blindly for the switch, finally clicked on the lights and mechanically closed the door behind him.

He was very dizzy. He wanted another drink—and he wanted Cynthia. He put his arms around her and pulled her drunkenly to him. The door of one of the bedrooms opened, and Norry Parker stood watching them. He had spent the evening at the home of a musical professor and had returned to his room only a few minutes before. His face went white when he saw the embracing couple.

"Hugh!" he said sharply.

Hugh and Cynthia, still clinging to each other,

looked at him. Slowly Cynthia took her arms
from around Hugh's neck and forced herself from
his embrace. Norry disappeared into his room
and came out a minute later with his coat on; he had
just begun to undress when he had heard a noise in
the study.

"I'll see you home, Cynthia," he said quietly.
He took her arm and led her out of the room—and
locked the door behind him. Hugh stared at them
blankly, swaying slightly, completely befuddled.
Cynthia went with Norry willingly enough, leaning
heavily on his arm and occasionally sniffing.

When he returned to his room, Hugh was sitting
on the floor staring at a photograph of Norry's
mother. He had been staring at it for ten minutes,
holding it first at arm's length and then drawing it
closer and closer to him. No matter where he held
it, he could not see what it was—and he was determined to see it.

Norry walked up to him and reached for the
photograph.

"Give me that," he said curtly. "Take your
hands off my mother's picture."

"It's not," Hugh exclaimed angrily; "it's not.
It's my musher, my own mu-musher—my, my own
dear musher. Oh, oh!"

He slumped down in a heap and began to sob
bitterly, muttering, "Musher, musher, musher."

Norry was angry. The whole scene was revolting to him. His best friend was a disgusting sight, apparently not much better than a gibbering idiot. And Hugh had shamefully abused his hospitality. Norry was no longer gentle and boyish; he was bitterly disillusioned.

"Get up," he said briefly. "Get up and go to bed."

"Tha 's my musher. You said it was n't my— my musher." Hugh looked up, his face wet with maudlin tears.

Norry leaned over and snatched the picture from him. "Take your dirty hands off of that," he snapped. "Get up and go to bed."

"Tha 's my musher." Hugh was gently persistent.

"It 's not your mother. You make me sick. Go to bed." Norry tugged at Hugh's arm impotently; Hugh simply sat limp, a dead weight.

Norry's gray eyes narrowed. He took a glass, filled it with cold water in the bedroom, and then deliberately dashed the water into Hugh's face. Then he repeated the performance.

Hugh shook his head and rubbed his hands wonderingly over his face. "I 'm no good," he said almost clearly. "I 'm no good."

"You certainly are n't. Come on; get up and go to bed." Again Norry tugged at his arm, and this time Hugh, clinging clumsily to the edge of the table by which he was sitting, staggered to his feet.

"I 'm a blot," he declared mournfully; "I 'm no good, Norry. I 'm an—an excreeshence, an ex-cree-shence, tha 's what I am."

"Something of the sort," Norry agreed in disgust. "Here, let me take off your coat."

"Leave my coat alone." He pulled himself away from Norry. "I 'm no good. I 'm an ex-cree-shence. I 'm goin' t' commit suicide; tha 's what I 'm goin' t' do. Nobody 'll care 'cept my musher, and she would n't either if she knew me. Oh, oh, I wish I did n't use a shafety-razor. I 'll tell you what to do, Norry." He clung pleadingly to Norry's arm and begged with passionate in-tensity. "You go over to Harry King's room. He 's got a re-re—a pistol. You get it for me and I 'll put it right here—" he touched his temple awkwardly—"and I 'll—I 'll blow my damn brains out. I 'm a blot, Norry; I 'm an ex-cree-shence."

Norry shook him. "Shut up. You 've got to go to bed. You 're drunk."

"I 'm sick. I 'm an ex-cree-shence." The room was whizzing rapidly around Hugh, and he clung hysterically to Norry. Finally he permitted him-self to be led into the bedroom and undressed, still moaning that he was an "ex-cree-shence."

The bed pitched. He lay on his right side, clutching the covers in terror. He turned over on his back. Still the bed swung up and down sicken-ingly. Then he twisted over to his left side, and the bed suddenly swung into rest, almost stable. In a few minutes he was sound asleep.

He cut chapel and his two classes the next morning, one at nine and the other at ten o'clock; in fact, it was nearly eleven when he awoke. His head was splitting with pain, his tongue was furry, and his mouth tasted like bilge-water. He made wry faces, passed his thick tongue around his dry mouth —oh, so damnably dry!—and pressed the palms of his hands to his pounding temples. He craved a drink of cold water, but he was afraid to get out of bed. He felt pathetically weak and dizzy.

Norry walked into the room and stood quietly looking at him.

"Get me a drink, Norry, please," Hugh begged. "I'm parched." He rolled over. "Ouch! God, how my head aches!"

Norry brought him the drink, but nothing less than three glasses even began to satisfy Hugh. Then, still saying nothing, Norry put a cold compress on Hugh's hot forehead.

"Thanks, Norry old man. That's awfully damn good of you."

Norry walked out of the room, and Hugh quickly fell into a light sleep. An hour later he woke up, quite unaware of the fact that Norry had changed the cold compress three times. The nap had refreshed him. He still felt weak and faint; but his head no longer throbbed, and his throat was less dry.

"Norry," he called feebly.

"Yes?" Norry stood in the doorway. "Feeling better?"

"Yes, some. Come sit down on the bed. I want to talk to you. But get me another drink first, please. My mouth tastes like burnt rubber."

Norry gave him the drink and then sat down on the edge of the bed, silently waiting.

"I 'm awfully ashamed of myself, old man," Hugh began. "I—I don't know what to say. I can't remember much what happened. I remember bringing Cynthia up here and you coming in and then—well, I somehow can't remember anything after that. What did you do?"

"I took Cynthia home and then came back and put you to bed." Norry gazed at the floor and spoke softly.

"You took Cynthia home?"

"Of course."

Hugh stared at him in awe. "But if you 'd been seen with her in the dorm, you 'd have been fired from college."

"Nobody saw us. It 's all right."

Hugh wanted to cry. "Oh, Lord, Norry, you 're white," he exclaimed. "The whitest fellow that ever lived. You took that chance for me."

"That's all right." Norry was painfully embarrassed.

"And I'm such a rotter. You—you know what we came up here for?"

"I can guess." Norry's glance still rested on the floor. He spoke hardly above a whisper.

"Nothing happened. I swear it, Norry. I meant to—but—but you came—thank God! I was awfully soused. I guess you think I'm rotten, Norry. I suppose I am. I don't know how I could treat you this way. Are you awfully angry?"

"I was last night," Norry replied honestly, "but I'm not this morning. I'm just terribly disappointed. I understand, I guess; I'm human, too—but I'm disappointed. I can't forget the way you looked."

"Don't!" Hugh cried. "Please don't, Norry. I—I can't stand it if you talk that way. I'm so damned ashamed. Please forgive me."

Norry was very near to tears. "Of course, I forgive you," he whispered, "but I hope you won't do it again."

"I won't, Norry. I promise you. Oh, God, I'm no good. That's twice I've been stopped by an accident. I'll go straight now, though; I promise you."

Norry stood up. "It's nearly noon," he said more naturally. "Cynthia will be wondering where you are."

"Cynthia! Oh, Norry, how can I face her?"

"You 've got to," said the young moralist firmly.

"I suppose so," the sinner agreed, his voice miserably lugubrious. "God!"

After three cups of coffee, however, the task did not seem so impossible. Hugh entered the Nu Delta house with a fairly jaunty air and greeted the men and women easily enough. His heart skipped a beat when he saw Cynthia standing in the far corner of the living-room. She was wearing her scarlet hat and blue suit.

She saved him the embarrassment of opening the conversation. "Come into the library," she said softly. "I want to speak to you."

Wondering and rather frightened, he followed her.

"I 'm going home this afternoon," she began. "I 've got everything packed, and I 've told everybody that I don't feel very well."

"You are n't sick?" he asked, really worried.

"Of course not, but I had to say something. The train leaves in an hour or two, and I want to have a talk with you before I go."

"But hang it, Cynthia, think of what you 're missing. There 's a baseball game with Raleigh this afternoon, a tea-dance in the Union after that, the Musical Clubs concert this evening—I sing with the Glee club and Norry 's going to play a solo, and I 'm in the Banjo Club, too—and we are going to have a farewell dance at the house after the concert." Hugh pleaded earnestly; but somehow down in his heart he wished that she would n't stay.

"I know, but I 've got to go. Let 's go somewhere.out in the woods where we can talk without being disturbed."

Still protesting, he led her out of the house, across the campus, past the lake, and into the woods. Finally they sat down on a smooth rock.

"I 'm awfully sorry to bust up your party, Hugh," Cynthia began slowly, "but I 've been doing some thinking, and I 've just got to beat it." She paused a moment and then looked him square in the eyes. "Do you love me?"

For an instant Hugh's eyes dropped, and then he looked up and lied like a gentleman. "Yes," he said simply; "I love you, Cynthia."

She smiled almost wearily and shook her head. "You *are* a good egg, Hugh. It was white of you to say that, but I know that you don't love me. You did yesterday, but you don't now. Do you realize that you have n't asked to kiss me to-day?"

Hugh flushed and stammered: "I—I 've got an awful hang-over, Cynthia. I feel rotten."

"Yes, I know, but that is n't why you did n't want to kiss me. I know all about it. Listen, Hugh." She faced him bravely. "I 've been running with a fast crowd for three years, and I 've learned a lot about fellows; and most of 'em that I 've known were n't your kind. How old are you?"

"Twenty-one in a couple of months."

"I 'm twenty and lots wiser about some things than you are. I 've been crazy about you—I guess I am kinda yet—and I know that you thought you were in love with me. I wanted you to have hold of me all the time. That 's all that mattered. It was—was your body, Hugh. You 're sweet and fine, and I respect you, but I 'm not the kid for you to run around with. I 'm too fast. I woke up early this morning, and I 've done a lot of thinking since. You know what we came near doing last night? Well, that 's all we want each other for. We 're not in love."

A phrase from the bull sessions rushed into Hugh's mind. "You mean—sex attraction?" he asked in some embarrassment. He felt weak and tired. He seemed to be listening to Cynthia in a dream. Nothing was real—and everything was a little sad.

"Yes, that 's it—and, oh, Hugh, somehow I don't want that with you. We 're not the same kind at all. I used to think that when I got your letters. Sometimes I hardly understood them, but I 'd close my eyes and see you so strong and blond and clean, and I 'd imagine you were holding me tight—and—and then I was happy. I guess I did kinda love you, but we 've spoiled it." She wanted desperately to cry but bit her lip and held back her tears.

"I think I know what you mean, Cynthia," Hugh said softly. "I don't know much about love and sex attraction and that sort of thing, but I know that I was happier kissing you than I 've ever been in my life. I—I wish that last night had n't happened. I hate myself."

"You need n't. It was more my fault than yours. I 'm a pretty bad egg, I guess; and the booze and you holding me was too much. I hate myself, too. I 've spoiled the nicest thing that ever happened to me." She looked up at him, her eyes bright with tears. "I *did* love you, Hugh. I loved you as much as I could love any one."

Hugh put his arms around her and drew her to him. Then he bent his head and kissed her gently. There was no passion in his embrace, but there was infinite tenderness. He felt spiritually and physically weak, as if all his emotional resources had been quite spent.

"I think that I love you more than I ever did before," he whispered.

If he had shown any passion, if there had been any warmth in his kiss, Cynthia might have believed him, but she was aware only of his gentleness. She pushed him back and drew out of his arms.

"No," she said sharply; "you don't love me.

You 're just sorry for me. . . . You 're just kind."
Hugh had read "Marpessa" many times, and a line from it came to make her attitude clear:

> "thou wouldst grow kind;
> Most bitter to a woman that was loved."

"Oh, I don't know; I don't know," he said miserably. "Let 's not call everything off now, Cynthia. Let 's wait a while."

"No!" She stood up decisively. "No. I hate loose ends." She glanced at her tiny wrist-watch. "If I 'm going to make that train, I 've got to hurry. We 've got barely half an hour. Come, Hugh. Be a sport."

He stood up, his face white and weary, his blue eyes dull and sad.

"Just as you say, Cynthia," he said slowly. "But I 'm going to miss you like hell."

She did not reply but started silently for the path. He followed her, and they walked back to the fraternity house without saying a word, both busy with unhappy thoughts.

When they reached the fraternity, she got her suit-case, handed it to him, declined his offer of a taxi, and walked unhappily by his side down the hill that they had climbed so gaily two days before. Hugh had just time to get her ticket before the train started.

She paused a moment at the car steps and held out her hand. "Good-by, Hugh," she said softly, her lips trembling, her eyes full of tears.

"Good-by, Cynthia," he whispered. And then, foolishly, "Thanks for coming."

She did not smile but drew her hand from his and mounted the steps. An instant later she was inside the car and the train was moving.

Numbed and miserable, Hugh slowly climbed the hill and wandered back to Norry Parker's room. He was glad that Norry was n't there. He paced up and down the room a few minutes trying to think. Then he threw himself despairingly on a couch, face down. He wanted to cry; he had never wanted so much to cry—and he could n't. There were no tears—and he had lost something very precious. He thought it was love; it was only his dreams.

CHAPTER XXIII

FOR several days Hugh was tortured by doubt and indecision: there were times when he thought that he loved Cynthia, times when he was sure that he did n't; when he had just about made up his mind that he hated her, he found himself planning to follow her to New Rochelle; he tried to persuade himself that his conduct was no more reprehensible than that of his comrades, but shame invariably overwhelmed his arguments; there were hours when he ached for Cynthia, and hours when he loathed her for smashing something that had been beautiful. Most of all, he wanted comfort, advice, but he knew no one to whom he was willing to give his confidence. Somehow, he could n't admit his drunkenness to any one whose advice he valued. He called on Professor Henley twice, intending to make a clean breast of his transgressions. Henley, he knew, would not lecture him, but when he found himself facing him, he could not bring himself to confession; he was afraid of losing Henley's respect.

Finally, in desperation, he talked to Norry, not

because he thought Norry could help him but because he had to talk to somebody and Norry already knew the worst. They went walking far out into the country, idly discussing campus gossip or pausing to revel in the beauty of the night, the clear, clean sky, the pale moon, the fireflies sparkling suddenly over the meadows or even to the tree-tops. Weary from their long walk, they sat down on a stump, and Hugh let the dam of his emotion break.

"Norry," he began intensely, "I 'm in hell—in hell. It 's a week since Prom, and I have n't had a line from Cynthia. I have n't dared write to her."

"Why not?"

"She—she—oh, damn it!—she told me before she left that everything was all off. That 's why she left early. She said that we did n't love each other, that all we felt was sex attraction. I don't know whether she 's right or not, but I miss her like the devil. I—I feel empty, sort of hollow inside, as if everything had suddenly been poured out of me—and there 's nothing to take its place. I was full of Cynthia, you see, and now there 's no Cynthia. There 's nothing left but—oh, God, Norry, I 'm ashamed of myself. I feel—dirty." The last word was hardly audible.

Norry touched his arm. "I know, Hugh, and I 'm awfully sorry. I think, though, that Cynthia

was right. I know her better than you do. She 's
an awfully good kid but not your kind at all. I
think I feel as badly almost as you do about it."
He paused a moment and then said simply, "I was
so proud of you, Hugh."

"Don't!" Hugh exclaimed. "I want to kill myself when you say things like that."

"You don't understand. I know that you don't
understand. I 've been doing a lot of thinking
since Prom, too. I 've thought over a lot of things
that you 've said to me—about me, I mean. Why,
Hugh, you think I 'm not human. I don't believe
you think I have passions like the rest of you.
Well, I do, and sometimes it 's—it 's awful. I 'm
telling you that so you 'll understand that I know
how you feel. But love 's beautiful to me, Hugh,
the most wonderful thing in the world. I was in
love with a girl once—and I know. She did n't
give a hang for me; she thought I was a baby. I
suffered awfully; but I know that my love was
beautiful, as beautiful as—" He looked around
for a simile—"as to-night. I think it 's because of
that that I hate mugging and petting and that sort
of thing. I don't want beauty debased. I want
to fight when orchestras jazz famous arias. Well,
petting is jazzing love; and I hate it. Do you see
what I mean?"

Hugh looked at him wonderingly. He did n't
know this Norry at all. "Yes," he said slowly;

"yes, I see what you mean; I think I do, anyway. But what has it to do with me?"

"Well, I know most of the fellows pet and all that sort of thing, and they don't think anything about it. But you 're different; you love beautiful things as much as I do. You told me yourself that Jimmie Henley said last year that you were gifted. You can write and sing and run, but I 've just realized that you are n't proud of those things at all; you just take them for granted. And you 're ashamed that you write poetry. Some of your poems are good, but you have n't sent any of them to the poetry magazine. You don't want anybody to know that you write poetry. You 're trying to make yourself like fellows that are inferior to you."

Norry was piteously in earnest. His hero had crumbled into clay before his eyes, and he was trying to patch him together again preparatory to boosting him back upon his pedestal.

"Oh, cripes, Norry," Hugh said a little impatiently, "you exaggerate all my virtues; you always have. I 'm not half the fellow you think I am. I do love beautiful things, but I don't believe my poetry is any good." He paused a moment and then confessed mournfully: "I 'll admit, though, that I have been going downhill. I 'm going to do better from now on. You watch me."

They talked for hours, Norry embarrassing

Hugh with the frankness of his admiration. Norry's hero-worship had always embarrassed him, but he didn't like it when the worshiper began to criticize. He admitted the justness of the criticism, but it hurt him just the same. Perching on a pedestal had been uncomfortable but a little thrilling; sitting on the ground and gazing up at his perch was rather humiliating. The fall had bruised him; and Norry, with the best intentions in the world, was kicking the bruises.

Nevertheless, he felt better after the talk, determined to win back Norry's esteem and his own. He swore off smoking and drinking and stuck to his oath. He told Vinton that if he brought any more liquor to their room one of them was going to be carried out, and that he had a hunch that it would be Vinton. Vinton gazed at him with round eyes and believed him. After that he did his drinking elsewhere, confiding to his cronies that Carver was on the wagon and that he had got as religious as holy hell. "He won't let me drink in my own room," he wailed dolorously. And then with a sudden burst of clairvoyance, he added, "I guess his girl has given him the gate."

For weeks the campus buzzed with talk about the Prom. A dozen men who had been detected *flagrante delicto* were summarily expelled. Many others who had been equally guilty were in a constant state of mental goose-flesh. Would the next mail bring a summons from the dean? President Culver spoke sternly in chapel and hinted that there would be no Prom the coming year. Most of the men said that the Prom had been an "awful brawl," but there were some who insisted that it was no worse than the Proms held at other colleges, and recited startling tales in support of their argument.

Leonard Gates finally settled the whole matter for Hugh. There had been many discussions in the Nu Delta living-room about the Prom, and in one of them Gates ended the argument with a sane and thoughtful statement.

"The Prom was a brawl," he said seriously, "a drunken brawl. We all admit that. The fact that Proms at other colleges are brawls, too, does n't make ours any more respectable. If a Yale man happens to commit murder and gets away with it, that is no reason that a Harvard man or a Sanford man should commit murder, too. Some of you are arguing like babies. But some of you are going to the other extreme.

"You talk as if everybody at the Prom was lit. Well, I was n't lit, and as a matter of fact most of them were n't lit. Just use a little common sense. There were three hundred and fifty couples at the Prom. Now, not half of them even had a drink. Say that half did. That makes one hundred and seventy-five fellows. If fifty of those

fellows were really soused, I'll eat my hat, but
we'll say that there were fifty. Fifty were quite
enough to make the whole Prom look like a long-
shoreman's ball. You've got to take the music
into consideration, too. That orchestra could
certainly play jazz; it could play it too damn well.
Why, that music was enough to make a saint shed
his halo and shake a shimmy.

"What I'm getting to is this: there are over a
thousand fellows in college, and out of that thousand not more than fifty were really soused at the
Prom, and not more than a hundred and seventy-
five were even a little teed. To go around saying that Sanford men are a lot of muckers just because a small fraction of them acted like gutter-
pups is sheer bunk. The Prom *was* a drunken
brawl, but all Sanford men are n't drunkards—not
by a damn sight."

Hugh had to admit the force of Gates's reason-
ing, and he found comfort in it. He had been just
about ready to believe that all college men and Sanford men in particular were hardly better than common muckers. But in the end the comfort that he
got was small: he realized bitterly that he was one
of the minority that had disgraced his college; he
was one of the gutter-pups. The recognition of
that undeniable fact cut deep.

He was determined to redeem himself; he *had*
to, somehow. Living a life of perfect rectitude

was not enough; he had to do something that would win back his own respect and the respect of his fellows, which he thought, quite absurdly, that he had forfeited. So far as he could see, there was only one way that he could justify his existence at Sanford; that was to win one of the dashes in the Sanford-Raleigh meet. He clung to that idea with the tenacity of a fanatic.

He had nearly a month in which to train, and train he did as he never had before. His diet became a matter of the utmost importance; a rubdown was a holy rite, and the words of Jansen, the coach, divine gospel. He placed in both of the preliminary meets, but he knew that he could do better; he wasn't yet in condition.

When the day for the Raleigh-Sanford meet finally came, he did not feel any of the nervousness that had spelled defeat for him in his freshman year. He was stonily calm, silently determined. He was going to place in the hundred and win the two-twenty or die in the attempt. No golden dreams of breaking records excited him. Calvert of Raleigh was running the hundred consistently in ten seconds and had been credited with better time. Hugh had no hopes of defeating him in the hundred, but there was a chance in the two-twenty. Calvert was a short-distance man, the shorter the better. Two hundred and twenty yards was a little too far for him.

Calvert did not look like a runner. He was a good two inches shorter than Hugh, who lacked nearly that much of six feet. Calvert was heavily built—a dark, brawny chap, both quick and powerful. Hugh looked at him and for a moment hated him. Although he did not phrase it so—in fact, he did not phrase it at all—Calvert was his obstacle in his race for redemption.

Calvert won the hundred-yard dash in ten seconds flat, breaking the Sanford-Raleigh record. Hugh, running faster than he ever had in his life, barely managed to come in second ahead of his team-mate Murphy. The Sanford men cheered him lustily, but he hardly listened. He *had* to win the two-twenty.

At last the runners were called to the starting-line. They danced up and down the track flexing their muscles. Hugh was tense but more determined than nervous. Calvert pranced around easily; he seemed entirely recovered from his great effort in the hundred. Finally the starter called them to their marks. They tried their spikes in the starting-holes, scraped them out a bit more, made a few trial dashes, and finally knelt in line at the command of the starter.

Hugh expected Calvert to lead for the first hundred yards; but the last hundred, that was where Calvert would weaken. Calvert was sure to be ahead at the beginning—but after that!

"On your marks.

"Set."

The pistol cracked. The start was perfect; the five men leaped forward almost exactly together. For once Calvert had not beaten the others off the mark, but he immediately drew ahead. He was running powerfully, his legs rising and falling in exact rhythm, his spikes tearing into the cinder path. But Hugh and Murphy were pressing him close. At the end of the first hundred Calvert led by a yard. Hugh pounded on, Murphy falling behind him. The others were hopelessly outclassed. Hugh did not think; he did not hear a thousand men shouting hysterically, "Carver! Carver!" He saw nothing but Calvert a yard ahead of him. He knew nothing but that he had to make up that yard. Down the track they sped, their breath bursting from them, their hands clenched, their faces grotesquely distorted, their legs driving them splendidly on.

Hugh was gaining; that yard was closing. He sensed it rather than saw it. He saw nothing now, not even Calvert. Blinded with effort, his lungs aching, his heart pounding terribly, he fought on, mechanically keeping between the two white lines. Ten yards from the tape he was almost abreast of Calvert. He saw the tape through a red haze; he made a final valiant leap for it—but he never

touched it: Calvert's chest had broken it a tiny
fraction of a second before.

Hugh almost collapsed after the race. Two
men caught him and carried him, despite his pro-
tests, to the dressing-room. At first he was aware
only of his overwhelming weariness. Something
very important had happened. It was over, and
he was tired, infinitely tired. A rub-down refreshed
his muscles, but his spirit remained weary. For a
month he had thought of nothing but that race—
even Cynthia had become strangely insignificant in
comparison with it—and now that the race had
been run and lost, his whole spirit sagged and
drooped.

He was pounded on the back; his hand was
grasped and shaken until it ached; he was cheered
to an echo by the thrilled Sanford men; but still
his depression remained. He had won his letter,
he had run a magnificent race, all Sanford sang his
praise—Norry Parker had actually cried with excitement and delight—but he felt that he had
failed; he had not justified himself.

A few days later he entered Henley's office, intending to make only a brief visit. Henley con-
gratulated him. "You were wonderful, Hugh,"
he said enthusiastically. "The way that you
crawled up on him the last hundred yards was
thrilling. I shouted until I was hoarse. I never

saw any one fight more gamely. He's a faster man than you are, but you almost beat him. I congratulate you—excuse the word, please—on your guts."

Somehow Hugh could n't stand Henley's enthusiasm. Suddenly he blurted out the whole story, his drunkenness at the Prom, his split with Cynthia —he did not mention the visit to Norry's room— his determination to redeem himself, his feeling that if he had won that race he would at least have justified his existence at the college, and, finally, his sense of failure.

Henley listened sympathetically, amused and touched by the boy's naïve philosophy. He did not tell him that the race was relatively unimportant—he was sure that Hugh would find that out for himself—but he did bring him comfort.

"You did not fail, Hugh," he said gently; "you succeeded magnificently. As for serving your college, you can always serve it best by being yourself, being true to yourself, I mean, and that means being the very fine gentleman that you are." He paused a minute, aware that he must be less personal; Hugh was red to the hair and gazing unhappily at the floor.

"You must read Browning," he went on, "and learn about his success-in-failure philosophy. He maintains that it is better to strive for a million and miss it than to strive for a hundred and get it. 'A

man 's reach should exceed his grasp or what 's a
heaven for?' He says it in a dozen different ways.
It 's the man who tries bravely for something beyond his power that gets somewhere, the man who
really succeeds. Well, you tried for something
beyond your power—to beat Calvert, a really great
runner. You tried to your utmost; therefore, you
succeeded. I admire your sense of failure; it
means that you recognize an ideal. But I think
that you succeeded. You may not have quite
justified yourself to yourself, but you have proved
capable of enduring a hard test bravely. You have
no reason to be depressed, no reason to be
ashamed."

They talked for a long time, and finally Henley
confessed that he thought Cynthia had been wise
in taking herself out of Hugh's life.

"I can see," he said, "that you are n't telling me
quite all the story. I don't want you to, either. I
judge, however, from what you have said that you
went somewhere with her and that only complete
drunkenness saved you from disgracing both yourself and her. You need no lecture, I am sure; you
are sufficiently contrite. I have a feeling that she
was right about sexual attraction being paramount;
and I think that she is a very brave girl. I like
the way she went home, and I like the way she has
kept silent. Not many girls could or would do
that. It takes courage. From what you have

said, however, I imagine that she is not your kind; at least, that she is n't the kind that is good for you. You have suffered and are suffering, I know, but I am sure that some day you are going to be very grateful to that girl—for a good many reasons."

Hugh felt better after that talk, and the end of the term brought him a surprise that wiped out his depression and his sense of failure. He found, too, that his pain was growing less; the wound was healing. Perversely, he hated it for healing, and he poked it viciously to feel it throb. Agony had become sweet. It made life more intense, less beautiful, perhaps, but more wonderful, more real. Romantically, too, he felt that he must be true both to his love and to his sorrow, and his love was fading into a memory that was plaintively gray but shot with scarlet thrills—and his sorrow was bowing before the relentless excitement of his daily life.

The surprise that rehabilitated him in his own respect was his election to the Boulé, the senior council and governing board of the student body. It was the greatest honor that an undergraduate could receive, and Hugh had in no way expected it. When Nu Delta had first suggested to him that he be a candidate, he had demurred, saying that there were other men in his delegation better fitted to serve and with better chances of election.

Leonard Gates, however, felt otherwise; and before Hugh knew what had happened he was a candidate along with thirty other juniors, only twelve of whom could be elected.

He took no part in the campaigning, attended none of the caucuses, was hardly interested in the fraternity "combine" that promised to elect him. He did not believe that he could be elected; he saw no reason why he should be. As a matter of fact, as Gates and others well knew, his chances were more than good. Hugh was popular in his own right, and his great race in the Sanford-Raleigh meet had made him something of a hero for the time being. Furthermore, he was a member of both the Glee and Banjo Clubs, he had led his class in the spring sings for three years, and he had a respectable record in his studies.

The tapping took place in chapel the last week of classes. After the first hymn, the retiring members of the Boulé rose and marched down the aisle to where the juniors were sitting. The new members were tapped in the order of the number of votes that they had received, and the first man tapped, having received the largest number of votes, automatically became president of the Boulé for the coming year.

Hugh's interest naturally picked up the day of the election, and he began to have faint hopes that he would be the tenth or eleventh man. To his

enormous surprise he was tapped third, and he
marched down the aisle to the front seat reserved
for the new members with the applause of his fellows sweet in his ears.   It did n't seem possible;
he was one of the most popular and most respected
men in his class.   He could not understand it,
but he did n't particularly care to understand it;
the honor was enough.

Nu Delta tried to heap further honors on him,
but he declined them.   As a member of Boulé he
was naturally nominated for the presidency of the
chapter.   Quite properly, he felt that he was not
fitted for such a position; and he retired in favor
of John Lawrence, the only man in his delegation
really capable of controlling the brothers.   Lawrence was a man like Gates.   He would,
Hugh knew, carry on the constructive work that
Gates had so splendidly started.   Nu Delta was in
the throes of one of those changes so characteristic
of fraternities.

CHAPTER XXIV

HUGH spent his last college vacation at home, working on the farm, reading, occasionally dancing at Corley Lake, and thinking a great deal. He saw Janet Harton, now Janet Moffitt, several times at the lake and wondered how he could ever have adored her. She was still childlike, still dainty and pretty, but to Hugh she was merely a talking doll, and he felt a little sorry for her burly, rather stupid husband who lumbered about after her like a protecting watch-dog.

He met plenty of pretty girls at the lake, but, as he said, he was "off women for good." He was afraid of them; he had been severely burnt, and while the fire still fascinated him, it frightened him, too. Women, he was sure, were shallow creatures, dangerous to a man's peace of mind and self-respect. They were all right to dance with and pet a bit; but that was all, absolutely all.

He thought a lot about girls that summer and even more about his life after graduation from college. What was he going to do? Life stretched ahead of him for one year like a smooth,

flowered plain—and then the abyss. He felt prepared to do nothing at all, and he was not swept by
an overpowering desire to do anything in particular.
Writing had the greatest appeal for him, but
he doubted his ability. Teach? Perhaps. But
teaching meant graduate work. Well, he would
see what the next year at college would show. He
was going to take a course in composition with
Professor Henley, and if Henley thought his gifts
warranted it, he would ask his father for a year or
two of graduate work at Harvard.

College was pleasant that last year. It was
pleasant to wear a blue sweater with an orange S on
it; it was pleasant, too, to wear a small white hat
that had a blue B on the crown, the insignia of the
Boulé and a sign that he was a person to be respected and obeyed; it was pleasant to be spoken
to by the professors as one who had reached
something approaching manhood; life generally was pleasant, not so exciting as the three
preceding years but fuller and richer. Early
in the first term he was elected to Helmet, an honor
society that possessed a granite "tomb," a small
windowless building in which the members were
supposed to discuss questions of great importance
and practise secret rites of awe-inspiring wonder.
As a matter of fact, the monthly meetings were
nothing but "bull fests," or as one cynical member
put it, "We wear a gold helmet on our sweaters

and chew the fat once a month." True enough, but that gold helmet glittered enticingly in the eyes of every student who did not possess one.

For the first time Hugh's studies meant more to him than the undergraduate life. He had chosen his instructors carefully, having learned from three years of experience that the instructor was far more important than the title of the course. He had three classes in literature, one in music—partly because it was a "snap" and partly because he really wanted to know more about music—and his composition course with Henley, to him the most important of the lot.

He really studied, and at the end of the first term received three A's and two B's, a very creditable record. What was more important than his record, however, was the fact that he was really enjoying his work; he was intellectually awakened and hungry for learning.

Also, for the first time he really enjoyed the fraternity. Jack Lawrence was proving an able president, and Nu Delta pledged a freshman delegation of which Hugh was genuinely proud. There were plenty of men in the chapter whom he did not like or toward whom he was indifferent, but he had learned to ignore them and center his interest in those men whom he found congenial.

The first term was ideal, but the second became a maelstrom of doubt and trouble in which he whirled madly around trying to find some philosophy that would solve his difficulties.

When Norry returned to college after the Christmas vacation, he told Hugh that he had seen Cynthia. Naturally, Hugh was interested, and the mere mention of Cynthia's name was still enough to quicken his pulse.

"How did she look?" he asked eagerly.

"Awful."

"What! What's the matter? Is she sick?"

Norry shook his head. "No, I don't think she is exactly sick," he said gravely, "but something is the matter with her. You know, she has been going an awful pace, tearing around like crazy. I told you that, I know, when I came back in the fall. Well, she's kept it up, and I guess she's about all in. I couldn't understand it. Cynthia's always run with a fast bunch, but she's never had a bad name. She's beginning to get one now."

"No!" Hugh was honestly troubled. "What's the matter, anyway? Didn't you try to stop her?"

Norry smiled. "Of course not. Can you imagine me stopping Cynthia from doing anything she wanted to do? But I did have a talk with her. She got hold of me one night at the country club and pulled me off in a corner. She wanted to talk about you."

"Me?" Hugh's heart was beginning to pound. "What did she say?"

"She asked questions. She wanted to know everything about you. I guess she asked me a thousand questions. She wanted to know how you looked, how you were doing in your courses, where you were during vacation, if you had a girl—oh, everything; and finally she asked if you ever talked about her?"

"What did you say?" Hugh demanded breathlessly.

"I told her yes, of course. Gee, Hugh, I thought she was going to cry. We talked some more, all about you. She's crazy about you, Hugh; I'm sure of it. And I think that's why she's been hitting the high spots. I felt sorry as the devil for her. Poor kid. . . ."

"Gee, that's tough; that's damn tough. Did she send me any message?"

"No. I asked her if she wanted to send her love or anything, and she said she guessed not. I think she's having an awful time, Hugh."

That talk tore Hugh's peace of mind into quivering shreds. Cynthia was with him every waking minute, and with her a sense of guilt that would not down. He knew that if he wrote to her he might involve himself in a very difficult situation, but the temptation was stronger than his discretion. He wanted to know if Norry was right, and he knew that he would never have an hour's real comfort until he found out. Cynthia had told him that she was not in love with him; she had said definitely that their attraction for each other was merely sexual. Had she lied to him? Had she gone home in the middle of Prom week because she thought she ought to save him from herself? He couldn't decide, and he felt that he had to know. If Cynthia was unhappy and he was the cause of her unhappiness, he wanted, he assured himself, to "do the right thing," and he had very vague notions indeed of what the right thing might be.

Finally he wrote to her. The letter took him hours to write, but he flattered himself that it was very discreet; it implied nothing and demanded nothing.

Dear Cynthia:

I had a talk with Norry Parker recently that has troubled me a great deal. He said that you seemed both unwell and unhappy, and he felt that I was in some way responsible for your depression. Of course, we both know how ingenuous and romantic Norry is; he can find tragedy in a cut finger. I recognize that fact, but what he told me has given me no end of worry just the same.

Won't you please write to me just what is wrong—if anything really is and if I have anything to do with it. I shall continue to worry until I get your letter.

Most sincerely,
HUGH.

Weeks went by and no answer came. Hugh's

confusion increased. He thought of writing her another letter, but pride and common sense forbade. Then her letter came, and all of his props were kicked suddenly from under him.

Oh my dear, my dear [she wrote], I swore that I would n't answer your letter—and here I am doing it. I 've fought and fought and fought until I can't fight any longer; I 've held out as long as I can. Oh, Hugh my dearest, I love you. I can't help it—I do, I do. I 've tried so hard not to—and when I found that I could n't help it I swore that I would never let you know—because I knew that you did n't love me and that I am bad for you. I thought I loved you enough to give you up—and I might have succeeded if you had n't written to me.

Oh, Hugh dearest, I nearly fainted when I saw your letter. I hardly dared open it—I just looked and looked at your beloved handwriting. I cried when I did read it. I thought of the letters you used to write to me—and this one was so different—so cold and impersonal. It hurt me dreadfully.

I said that I would n't answer it—I swore that I would n't. And then I read your old letters—I 've kept every one of them—and looked at your picture—and to-night you just seemed to be here—I could see your sweet smile and feel your dear arms around me—and Hugh, my darling, I had to write—I *had* to.

My pride is all gone. I can't think any more. You are all that matters. Oh, Hugh dearest, I love you so damned hard.

CYNTHIA.

Two hours after the letter arrived it was followed by a telegram:

Don't pay any attention to my letter. I was crazy when I wrote it.

Hugh had sense enough to pay no attention to the telegram; he tossed it into the fireplace and re-read the letter. What could he do? What *should* he do? He was torn by doubt and confusion. He looked at her picture, and all his old longing for her returned. But he had learned to distrust that longing. He had got along for a year without her; he had almost ceased thinking of her when Norry brought her back to his mind. He *had* to answer her letter. What could he say? He paced the floor of his room, ran his hands through his hair, pounded his forehead; but no solution came. He took a long walk into the country and came back more confused than ever. He was flattered by her letter, moved by it; he tried to persuade himself that he loved her as she loved him—and he could not do it. His passion for her was no longer overpowering, and no amount of thinking could make it so. In the end he temporized. His letter was brief.

Dear Cynthia:
There is no need, I guess, to tell you that your letter swept me clean off my feet. I am still dizzy with con-

fusion. I don't know what to say, and I have decided that
it is best for me not to say anything until I know my own
mind. I could n't be fair either to you or myself otherwise.
And I want to be fair; I must be.

Give me time, please. It is because I care so much for
you that I ask it. Don't worry if you don't hear from me
for weeks. My silence won't mean that I have forgotten
you; it will mean that I am thinking of you.

Sincerely,
HUGH.

Her answer came promptly:

Hugh, my dear—

I was a fish to write that letter—and I know that I 'll
never forgive myself. But I could n't help it—I just
could n't help it. I am glad that you are keeping your head
because I 've lost mine entirely. Take all the time you like.
Do you hate me for losing my pride? I do.

Your stupid
CYNTHIA.

Weeks went by, and Hugh found no solution.
He damned college with all his heart and soul.
What good had it done him anyway? Here he
was with a serious problem on his hands and he
could n't solve it any better than he could have when
he was a freshman. Four years of studying and
lectures and examinations, and the first time he
bucked up against a bit of life he was licked.

Eventually he wrote to her and told her that he

was fonder of her than he was of any girl that he had ever known but that he did n't know whether he was in love with her or not. "I have learned to distrust my own emotions," he wrote, "and my own decisions. The more I think the more bewildered I become. I am afraid to ask you to marry me for fear that I 'll wreck both our lives, and I 'm afraid not to ask you for the same reason. Do you think that time will solve our problem? I don't know. I don't know anything."

She replied that she was willing to wait just so long as they continued to correspond; she said that she could no longer bear not to hear from him. So they wrote to each other, and the tangle of their relations became more hopelessly knotted. Cynthia never sent another letter so unguarded as her first, but she made no pretense of hiding her love.

As Hugh sank deeper and deeper into the bog of confusion and distress, his contempt for his college "education" increased. One night in May he expressed that contempt to a small group of seniors.

"College is bunk," said Hugh sternly, "pure bunk. They tell us that we learn to think. Rot! I have n't learned to think; a child can solve a simple human problem as well as I can. College has played hell with me. I came here four years ago a darned nice kid, if I do say so myself. I was chock-full of ideals and illusions. Well, college has smashed most of those ideals and knocked the illusions plumb to hell. I thought, for example, that all college men were gentlemen; well, most of them are n't. I thought that all of them were intelligent and hard students."

The group broke into loud laughter. "Me, too," said George Winsor when the noise had abated. "I thought that I was coming to a regular educational heaven, halls of learning and all that sort of thing. Why, it's a farce. Here I am sporting a Phi Bete key, an honor student if you please, and all that I really know as a result of my college 'education' is the fine points of football and how to play poker. I don't really know one damn thing about anything."

The other men were Jack Lawrence and Pudge Jamieson. Jack was an earnest chap, serious and hard working but without a trace of brilliance. He, too, wore a Phi Beta Kappa key, and so did Pudge. Hugh was the only one of the group who had not won that honor; the fact that he was the only one who had won a letter was hardly, he felt, complete justification. His legs no longer seemed more important than his brains; in fact, when he had sprained a tendon and been forced to drop track, he had been genuinely pleased.

Pudge was quite as plump as he had been as a freshman and quite as jovial, but he did not tell so many smutty stories. He still persisted in crossing his knees in spite of the difficulties involved.

When Winsor finished speaking, Pudge forced his legs into his favorite position for them and then twinkled at Winsor through his glasses.

"Right you are, George," he said in his quick way. "I wear a Phi Bete key, too. We both belong to the world's greatest intellectual fraternity, but what in hell do we know? We've all majored in English except Jack, and I'll bet any one of us can give the others an exam offhand that they can't pass. I'm going to law school. I hope to God that I learn something there. I certainly don't feel that I know anything now as a result of my four years of 'higher education.'"

"Well, if you fellows feel that way," said Hugh mournfully, "how do you suppose I feel? I made my first really good record last term, and that wasn't any world beater. I've learned how to gamble and smoke and drink and pet in college, but that's about all that I have learned. I'm not as fine as I was when I came here. I've been coarsened and cheapened; all of us have. I take things for granted that shocked me horribly once. I know that they ought to shock me now, but they don't. I've made some friends and I've had a wonderful time, but I certainly don't feel that I have got any other value out of college."

Winsor could not sit still and talk. He filled his pipe viciously, lighted it, and then jumped up and leaned against the mantel. "I admit everything

that 's been said, but I don't believe that it is altogether our fault." He was intensely in earnest, and
so were his listeners. "Look at the faculty.
When I came here I thought that they were all wise
men because they were on the faculty. Well, I 've
found out otherwise. Some of them know a lot
and can't teach, a few of them know a lot and can
teach, some of them know a little and can't teach,
and some of them don't know anything and can't
explain c-a-t. Why, look at Kempton. That
freshman, Larson, showed me a theme the other
day that Kempton had corrected. It was full of
errors that were n't marked, and it was nothing in
the world but drip. Even Larson knew that, but
he 's the foxy kid; he wrote the theme about Kempton. All right—Kempton gives him a B and tells
him that it is very amusing. Hell of a lot Larson 's
learning. Look at Kane in math. I had him
when I was a freshman."

"Me, too," Hugh chimed in.

" 'Nough said, then. Math 's dry enough, God
knows, but Kane makes it dryer. He 's a born
desiccator. He could make 'Hamlet' as dry as
calculus."

"Right-o," said Pudge. "But Mitchell could
make calculus as exciting as 'Hamlet.' It 's fifty
fifty."

"And they fired Mitchell." Jack Lawrence
spoke for the first time. "I have that straight.

The administration seems afraid of a man that can teach. They 've made Buchanan a full professor, and there is n't a man in college who can tell what he 's talking about. He 's written a couple of books that nobody reads, and that makes him a scholar. I was forced to take three courses with him. They were agony, and he never taught me a damn thing."

"Most of them don't teach you a damn thing," Winsor exclaimed, tapping his pipe on the mantel. "They either tell you something that you can find more easily in a book, or just confuse you with a lot of ponderous lectures that put you to sleep or drive you crazy if you try to understand them."

"There are just about a dozen men in this college worth listening to," Hugh put in, "and I 've got three of them this term. I 'm learning more than I did in my whole three first years. Let 's be fair, though. We 're blaming it all on the profs, and you know damn well that we don't study. All we try to do is to get by—I don't mean you Phi Betes; I mean all the rest of us—and if we can put anything over on the profs we are tickled pink. We 're like a lot of little kids in grammar-school. Just look at the cheating that goes on, the copying of themes, and the cribbing. It 's rotten!"

Winsor started to protest, but Hugh rushed on. "Oh, I know that the majority of the fellows don't consciously cheat; I 'm talking about the copying of

math problems and the using of trots and the para-
phrasing of 'Literary Digest' articles for themes and
all that sort of thing.   If more than half of the
fellows don't do that sort of thing some time or
other in college, I'll eat my hat.   And we all know
darned well that we are n't supposed to do it, but
the majority of fellows cheat in some way or other
before they graduate!

"We are n't so much.   Do you remember,
George, what Jimmie Henley said to us when we
were sophomores in English Thirty-six?   He laid
us out cold, said that we were as standardized as
Fords and that we were ashamed of anything intellectual.   Well, he was right.   Do you remember
how he ended by saying that if we were the cream
of the earth, he felt sorry for the skimmed milk—
or something like that?"

"Sure, I remember," Winsor replied, running his
fingers through his rusty hair.   "He certainly
pulled a heavy line that day.   He was right, too."

"I'll tell you what," exclaimed Pudge suddenly,
so suddenly that his crossed legs parted company
and his foot fell heavily to the floor.   "Let's put it
up to Henley in class to-morrow.   Let's ask him
straight out if he thinks college is worth while."

"He'll hedge," objected Lawrence.   "All the
profs do if you ask them anything like that."

Winsor laughed.   "You don't know Jimmie
Henley.   He won't hedge.   You've never had a

class with him, but Hugh and Pudge and I are all in English Fifty-three, and we 'll put it up to him. He 'll tell us what he thinks all right, and I hope to God that he says it is worth while. I 'd like to have somebody convince me that I 've got something out of these four years beside lower ideals. Hell, sometimes I think that we 're all damn fools. We worship athletics—no offense, Hugh—above everything else; we gamble and drink and talk like bums; and about every so often some fellow has to go home because a lovely lady has left him with bitter, bitter memories. I 'm with Henley. If we 're the cream of the earth—well, thank the Lord, we 're not."

"Who is," Lawrence asked earnestly.

"God knows."

CHAPTER XXV

ENGLISH 53 had only a dozen men in it;
so Henley conducted the course in a very
informal fashion. The men felt free to
bring up for discussion any topic that interested
them.

Nobody was surprised, therefore, when George
Winsor asked Henley to express his opinion of the
value of a college education. He reminded Henley
of what he had said two years before, and rapidly
gave a résumé of the discussion that resulted in the
question he was asking. "We'd like to know,
too," he concluded, grinning wickedly, "just whom
you consider the cream of the earth. You remember you said that if we were you felt sorry for
the skimmed milk."

Henley leaned back in his chair and laughed.
"Yes," he said, "I remember saying that. I did n't
think, though, that you would remember it for two
years. You seem to remember most of what I
said. I am truly astonished." He grinned back
at Winsor. "The swine seem to have eaten the
pearls."

The class laughed, but Winsor was not one to

refuse the gambit. "They were very indigestible,"
he said quickly.

"Good!" Henley exclaimed. "I wanted them to
give you a belly-ache, and I am delighted that you
still suffer."

"We do," Pudge Jamieson admitted, "but we'd
like to have a little mercy shown to us now. We've
spent four years here, and while we've enjoyed
them, we've just about made up our minds that
they have been all in all wasted years."

"No." Henley was decisive. His playful
manner entirely disappeared. "No, not wasted.
You have enjoyed them, you say. Splendid justification. You will continue to enjoy them as the
years grow between you and your college days.
All men are sentimental about college, and in that
sentimentality there is continuous pleasure.

"Your doubt delights me. Your feeling that
you haven't learned anything delights me, too. It
proves that you have learned a great deal. It is
only the ignoramus who thinks he is wise; the wise
man knows that he is an ignoramus. That's a
platitude, but it is none the less true. I have cold
comfort for you: the more you learn, the less con-
fident you will be of your own learning, the more
utterly ignorant you will feel. I have never known
so much as the day I graduated from high school.
I held my diploma and the knowledge of the ages

in my hand. I had never heard of Socrates, but I would have challenged him to a debate without the slightest fear.

"Since then I have grown more humble, so humble that there are times when I am ashamed to come into the class-room. What right have I to teach anybody anything? I mean that quite sincerely. Then I remember that, ignorant as I am, the undergraduates are more ignorant. I take heart and mount the rostrum ready to speak with the authority of a pundit."

He realized that he was sliding off on a tangent and paused to find a new attack. Pudge Jamieson helped him.

"I suppose that's all true," he said, "but it does n't explain why college is really worth while. The fact remains that most of us don't learn anything, that we are coarsened by college, and that we —well, we worship false gods."

Henley nodded in agreement. "It would be hard to deny your assertions," he acknowledged, "and I don't think that I am going to try to deny them. Of course, men grow coarser while they are in college, but that does n't mean that they would n't grow coarser if they were n't in college. It is n't college that coarsens a man and destroys his illusions; it is life. Don't think that you can grow to manhood and retain your pretty dreams.

You have become disillusioned about college. In the next few years you will suffer further disillusionment. That is the price of living.

"Every intelligent man with ideals eventually becomes a cynic. It is inevitable. He has standards, and, granted that he is intelligent, he cannot fail to see how far mankind falls below those standards. The result is cynicism, and if he is truly intelligent, the cynicism is kindly. Having learned that man is frail, he expects little of him; therefore, if he judges at all, his judgment is tempered either with humor or with mercy."

The dozen boys were sprawled lazily in their chairs, their feet resting on the rungs of the chairs before them, but their eyes were fastened keenly on Henley. All that he was saying was of the greatest importance to them. They found comfort in his words, but the comfort raised new doubts, new problems.

"How does that affect college?" Winsor asked.

"It affects it very decidedly," Henley replied. "You have n't become true cynics yet; you expect too much of college. You forget that the men who run the college and the men who attend it are at best human beings, and that means that very much cannot be expected of them. You do worship false gods. I find hope in the fact that you recognize the stuff of which your gods are made. I have great hopes for the American colleges, not because

I have any reason to believe that the faculties will
become wiser or that the administrations will lead
the students to true gods; not at all, but I do think
that the students themselves will find a way. They
have already abandoned Mammon; at least, the
most intelligent have, and I begin to see signs of
less adoration for athletics. Athletics, of course,
have their place, and some of the students are beginning to find that place. Certainly the alumni
have n't, and I don't believe that the administrative
officers have, either. Just so long as athletes
advertise the college, the administrations will coddle
them. The undergraduates, however, show signs
of frowning on professionalism, and the stupid
athlete is rapidly losing his prestige. An athlete
has to show something more than brawn to be a
hero among his fellows nowadays."

He paused, and Pudge spoke up. "Perhaps you
are right," he said, "but I doubt it. Athletics are
certainly far more important to us than anything
else, and the captain of the football team is always
the biggest man in college. But I don't care particularly about that. What I want to know is how
the colleges justify their existence. I don't see
that you have proved that they do."

"No, I have n't," Henley admitted, "and I don't
know that I can prove it. Of course, the colleges
are n't perfect, not by a long way, but as human institutions go, I think they justify their existence.

The four years spent at college by an intelligent boy—please notice that I say intelligent—are well spent indeed. They are gloriously worth while. You said that you have had a wonderful time. Not so wonderful as you think. It is a strange feeling that we have about our college years. We all believe that they are years of unalloyed happiness, and the further we leave them behind the more perfect they seem. As a matter of fact, few undergraduates are truly happy. They are going through a period of storm and stress; they are torn by *Weltschmerz*. Show me a nineteen-year-old boy who is perfectly happy and you show me an idiot. I rarely get a cheerful theme except from freshmen. Nine tenths of them are expressions of deep concern and distress. A boy's college years are the years when he finds out that life is n't what he thought it, and the finding out is a painful experience. He discovers that he and his fellows are made of very brittle clay: usually he loathes himself; often he loathes his fellows.

"College is n't the Elysium that it is painted in stories and novels, but I feel sorry for any intelligent man who did n't have the opportunity to go to college. There is something beautiful about one's college days, something that one treasures all his life. As we grow older, we forget the hours of storm and stress, the class-room humiliations, the terror of examinations, the awful periods of doubt of God and man—we forget everything but athletic victories, long discussions with friends, campus sings, fraternity life, moonlight on the campus, and everything that is romantic. The sting dies, and the beauty remains.

"Why do men give large sums of money to their colleges when asked? Because they want to help society? Not at all. The average man does n't even take that into consideration. He gives the money because he loves his alma mater, because he has beautiful and tender memories of her. No, colleges are far from perfect, tragically far from it, but any institution that commands loyalty and love as colleges do cannot be wholly imperfect. There is a virtue in a college that uninspired administrative officers, stupid professors, and alumni with false ideals cannot kill. At times I tremble for Sanford College; there are times when I swear at it, but I never cease to love it."

"If you feel that way about college, why did you say those things to us two years ago?" Hugh asked.

"Because they were true, all true. I was talking about the undergraduates then, and I could have said much more cutting things and still been on the safe side of the truth. There is, however, another side, and that is what I am trying to give you now —rather incoherently, I know."

Hugh thought of Cynthia. "I suppose all that you say is true," he admitted dubiously, "but I can't feel that college does what it should for us. We are told that we are taught to think, but the minute we bump up against a problem in living we are stumped just as badly as we were when we are freshmen."

"Oh, no, not at all. You solve problems every day that would have stumped you hopelessly as a freshman. You think better than you did four years ago, but no college, however perfect, can teach you all the solutions of life. There are no nostrums or cure-alls that the colleges can give for all the ills and sicknesses of life. You, I am afraid, will have to doctor those yourself."

"I see." Hugh did n't altogether see. Both college and life seemed more complicated than he had thought them. "I am curious to know," he added, "just whom you consider the cream of the earth. That expression has stuck in my mind. I don't know why—but it has."

Henley smiled. "Probably because it is such a very badly mixed metaphor. Well, I consider the college man the cream of the earth."

"What?" four of the men exclaimed, and all of them sat suddenly upright.

"Yes—but let me explain. If I remember rightly, I said that if you were the cream of the earth, I hoped that God would pity the skimmed milk. Well, everything taken into consideration, I do think that you are the cream of the earth; and I have no hope for the skimmed milk. Perhaps it is n't wise for me to give public expression to my pessimism, but you ought to be old enough to stand it.

"The average college graduate is a pretty poor specimen, but all in all he is just about the best we have. Please remember that I am talking in averages. I know perfectly well that a great many brilliant men do not come to college and that a great many stupid men do come, but the colleges get a very fair percentage of the intelligent ones and a comparatively small percentage of the stupid ones. In other words, to play with my mixed metaphor a bit, the cream is very thin in places and the skimmed milk has some very thick clots of cream, but in the end the cream remains the cream and the milk the milk. Everything taken into consideration, we get in the colleges the young men with the highest ideals, the loftiest purpose.

"You want to tell me that those ideals are low and the purpose materialistic and selfish. I know it, but the average college graduate, I repeat, has loftier ideals and is less materialistic than the average man who has not gone to college. I wish that I could believe that the college gives him those ideals. I can't, however. The colleges draw the best that society has to offer; therefore, they graduate the best."

"Oh, I don't know," a student interrupted. "How about Edison and Ford and—"

"And Shakspere and Sophocles," Henley concluded for him. "Edison is an inventive genius, and Ford is a business genius. Genius has n't anything to do with schools. The colleges, however, could have made both Ford and Edison bigger men, though they could n't have made them lesser geniuses.

"No, we must not take the exceptional man as a standard; we 've got to talk about the average. The hand of the Potter shook badly when he made man. It was at best a careless job. But He made some better than others, some a little less weak, a little more intelligent. All in all, those are the men that come to college. The colleges ought to do a thousand times more for those men than they do do; but, after all, they do something for them, and I am optimistic enough to believe that the time will come when they will do more.

"Some day, perhaps," he concluded very seriously, "our administrative officers will be true educators; some day perhaps our faculties will be wise men really fitted to teach; some day perhaps our students will be really students, eager to learn, honest searchers after beauty and truth. That day will be the millennium. I look for the undergraduates to lead us to it."

CHAPTER XXVI

THE college year swept rapidly to its close, so rapidly to the seniors that the days seemed to melt in their grasp. The twentieth of June would bring them their diplomas and the end of their college life. They felt a bit chesty at the thought of that B.S. or A.B., but a little sentimental at the thought of leaving "old Sanford." Suddenly everything about the college became infinitely precious—every tradition; every building, no matter how ugly; even the professors, not just the deserving few—all of them.

Hugh took to wandering about the campus, sometimes alone, thinking of Cynthia, sometimes with a favored crony such as George Winsor or Pudge Jamieson. He did n't see very much of Norry the last month or two of college. He was just as fond of him as ever, but Norry was only a junior; he would not understand how a fellow felt about Sanford when he was on the verge of leaving her. But George and Pudge did understand. The boys did n't say much as they wandered around the buildings, merely strolled along, occasionally pausing to laugh over some experience that had happened to one of them in the building they were passing.

Hugh could never pass Surrey Hall without feeling something deeper than sentimentality. He always thought of Carl Peters, from whom he had not heard for more than a year. He understood Carl better now, his desire to be a gentleman and his despair at ever succeeding. Surrey Hall held drama for Hugh, not all of it pleasant, but he had a deeper affection for the ivy-covered dormitory then he would ever have for the Nu Delta house. He wondered what had become of Morse, the homesick freshman. Poor Morse. . . . And the bull sessions he had sat in in old Surrey. He had learned a lot from them, a whole lot. . . .

The chapel where he had slept and surreptitiously eaten doughnuts and read "The Sanford News" suddenly became a holy building, the building that housed the soul of Sanford. . . . He knew that he was sentimental, that he was investing buildings with a greater significance than they had in their own right, but he continued to dream over the last four years and to find a melancholy beauty in his own sentimentality. If it hadn't been for Cynthia, he would have been perfectly happy.

Soon the examinations were over, and the underclassmen began to depart. Good-by to all his friends who were not seniors. Good-by to Norry Parker. "Thanks for the congratulations, old

man. Sorry I can't visit you this summer. Can't
you spend a month with me on the farm . . . ?"
Good-by to his fraternity brothers except the few
left in his own delegation. "Good-by, old man,
good-by . . . Sure, I 'll see you next year at the reunion." Good-by. . . . Good-by. . . .

Sad, this business of saying good-by, damn sad.
Gee, how a fellow would miss all the good old eggs
he had walked with and drunk with and bulled
with these past years. Good eggs, all of them—
damn good eggs. . . . God! a fellow could n't appreciate college until he was about to leave it. Oh,
for a chance to live those four years over again.
"Would I live them differently? I 'll say I would."

Good-by, boyhood. . . . Commencement was
coming. Hugh had n't thought before of what
that word meant. Commencement! The beginning. What was he going to do with this commencement of his into life? Old Pudge was going
to law school and so was Jack Lawrence. George
Winsor was going to medical school. But what
was he going to do? He felt so pathetically un-
prepared. And then there was Cynthia. . . .
What was he going to do about her? She rarely
left his mind. How could he tackle life when he
could n't solve the problem she presented? It was
like trying to run a hundred against fast men when
a fellow had only begun to train.

Henley had advised him to take a year or so at

Harvard if his father proved willing, and his father was more than willing, even eager. He guessed that he 'd take at least a year in Cambridge. Perhaps he could find himself in that year. Maybe he could learn to write. He hoped to God he could. . . .

Just before commencement his relations with Cynthia came to a climax. They had been constantly becoming more complicated. She was demanding nothing of him, but her letters were tinged with despair. He felt at last that he must see her. Then he would know whether he loved her or not. A year before she had said that he did n't. How did she know? She had said that all he felt for her was sex attraction. How did she know that? Why, she had said that was all that she felt for him. And he had heard plenty of fellows argue that love was nothing but sexual attraction anyway, and that all the stuff the poets wrote was pure bunk. Freud said something like that, he thought, and Freud knew a damn sight more about it than the poets.

Yet, the doubt remained. Whether love was merely sexual attraction or not, he wanted something more than that; his every instinct demanded something more. He had noticed another thing: the fellows that were n't engaged said that love was only sexual attraction; those who were engaged

vehemently denied it, and Hugh knew that some of
the engaged men had led gay lives in college. He
could not reach any decision; at times he was sure
that what he felt for Cynthia was love; at other
times he was sure that it was n't.

At last in desperation he telegraphed to her that
he was coming to New York and that she should
meet him at Grand Central at three o'clock the
next day. He knew that he ought n't to go. He
would be able to stay in New York only a little
more than two hours because his father and mother
would arrive in Haydensville the day following, and
he felt that he had to be there to greet them. He
damned himself for his impetuousness all during
the long trip, and a dozen times he wished he were
back safe in the Nu Delta house. What in hell
would he say to Cynthia, anyway? What would
he do when he saw her? Kiss her? "I won't
have a damned bit of sense left if I do."

She was waiting for him as he came through the
gate. Quite without thinking, he put down his bag
and kissed her. Her touch had its old power; his
blood leaped. With a tremendous effort of will
he controlled himself. That afternoon was all-
important; he must keep his head.

"It 's sweet of you to come," Cynthia whispered,
clinging to him, "so damned sweet."

"It 's damned good to see you," he replied
gruffly. "Come on while I check this bag. I 've

only got a little over two hours, Cynthia; I 've got to get the five-ten back. My folks will be in Haydensville to-morrow morning, and I 've got to get back to meet them."

Her face clouded for an instant, but she tucked her arm gaily in his and marched with him across the rotunda to the checking counter. When Hugh had disposed of his bag, he suggested that they go to a little tea room on Fifty-seventh Street. She agreed without argument. Once they were in a taxi, she wanted to snuggle down into his arm, but she restrained herself; she felt that she had to play fair.

Hugh said nothing. He was trying to think, and his thoughts whirled around in a mad, drunken dance. He believed that he would be married before he took the train back, at least engaged, and what would all that mean? Did he want to get married? God! he did n't know.

When at last they were settled in a corner of the empty tea-room and had given their order, they talked in an embarrassed fashion about their recent letters, both of them carefully quiet and restrained. Finally Hugh, shoved his plate and cup aside and looked straight at her for the first time. She *was* thin, much thinner than she had been a year ago, but there was something sweeter about her, too; she seemed so quiet, so gentle.

"We are n't going to get anywhere this way, Cyn-

thia," he said desperately. "We 're both evading.
I have n't any sense left, but what I say from now
on I am going to say straight out. I swore on the
train that I would n't kiss you. I knew that I
would n't be able to think if I did—and I can't; all
I know is that I want to kiss you again." He
looked at her sitting across the little table from
him, so slender and still—a different Cynthia but
damnably desirable. "Cynthia," he added hoarsely,
"if you took my hand, you could lead me to
hell."

She in turn looked at him. He was much older
than he had been a year before. Then he had been
a boy; now he seemed a man. He had not changed
particularly; he was as blond and young and clean
as ever, but there was something about his mouth
and eyes, something more serious and more stern,
that made him seem years older.

"I don't want to lead you to hell, honey," she
replied softly. "I left Prom last year so that I
would n't do that. I told you then that I was n't
good for you—but I 'm different now."

"I can see that. I don't know what it is, but
you 're different, awfully different." He leaned
forward suddenly. "Cynthia, shall we go over to
Jersey and get married? I understand that one
can there right away. We 're both of age—"

"Wait, Hugh; wait." Cynthia's hands were
tightly clasped in her lap. "Are you sure that you

want to? I 've been thinking a lot since I got your telegram. Are you sure you love me?"

He slumped back into his chair. "I don't know what love is," he confessed miserably. "I can't find out." Cynthia's hands tightened in her lap. "I 've tried to think this business out, and I can't. I have n't any right to ask you to marry me. I have n't any money, not a bit, and I 'm not prepared to do anything, either. As I wrote you, my folks want me to go to Harvard next year." The mention of his poverty and of his inability to support a wife brought him back to something approaching normal again. "I suppose I 'm just a kid, Cynthia," he added more quietly, "but sometimes I feel a thousand years old. I do right now."

"What were your plans for next year and after that until you saw me?" Her eyes searched his.

"Oh, I thought I 'd go to Harvard a year or two and then try to write or perhaps teach. Writing is slow business, I understand, and teaching does n't pay anything. I don't want to ask my father to support us, and I won't let your folks. I lost my head when I suggested that we get married. It would be foolish. I have n't the right."

"No," she agreed slowly; "no, neither of us has the right. I thought before you came if you asked me to marry you—I was sure somehow that you would—I would run right off and do it, but now I

know that I won't." She continued to gaze at
him, her eyes troubled and confused. What made
him seem so much older, so different?

"Do you think we can ever forget Prom?" She
waited for his reply. So much depended on it.

"Of course," he answered impatiently. "I 've
forgotten that already. We were crazy kids,
that 's all—youngsters trying to act smart and
wild."

"Oh!" The ejaculation was soft, but it vibrated
with pain. "You mean that—that you would n't
—well, you would n't get drunk like that again?"

"Of course not, especially at a dance. I 'm not a
child any longer, Cynthia. I have sense enough
now not to forfeit my self-respect again. I hope
so, anyway. I have n't been drunk in the last year.
A drunkard is a beastly sight, rotten. If I have
learned anything in college, it is that a man has to
respect himself, and I can't respect any one any
longer who deliberately reduces himself to a beast.
I was a beast with you a year ago. I treated you
like a woman of the streets, and I abused Norry
Parker's hospitality shamefully. If I can help it,
I 'll never act like a rotter again. I hate a prig,
Cynthia, like the devil, but I hate a rotter even
more. I hope I can learn to be neither."

As he spoke, Cynthia clenched her hands so
tightly that the finger-nails were bruising her tender
palms, but her eyes remained dry and her lips did

not tremble. If he could have seen *her* on some parties this last year. . . .

"You have changed a lot." Her words were barely audible. "You have changed an awful lot."

He smiled. "I hope so. There are times now when I hate myself, but I never hate myself so much as when I think of Prom. I 've learned a lot in the last year, and I hope I 've learned enough to treat a decent girl decently. I have never apologized to you the way I think I ought to."

"Don't!" she cried, her voice vibrant with pain. "Don't! I was more to blame than you were. Let 's not talk about that."

"All right. I 'm more than willing to forget it." He paused and then continued very seriously, "I can't ask you to marry me now, Cynthia—but—but are you willing to wait for me? It may take time, but I promise I 'll work hard."

Cynthia's hands clenched convulsively. "No, Hugh honey," she whispered; "I 'll never marry you. I—I don't love you."

"What?" he demanded, his senses swimming in hopeless confusion. "What?"

She did not say that she knew that he did not love her; she did not tell him how much his quixotic chivalry moved her. Nor did she tell him that she knew only too well that she could lead him to hell, as he said, but that that was the only place that she could lead him. These things she felt positive

of, but to mention them meant an argument—and
an argument would have been unendurable.

"No," she repeated, "I don't love you. You see,
you're so different from what I remembered.
You've grown up and you've changed. Why,
Hugh, we're strangers. I've realized that while
you've been talking. We don't know each other,
not a bit. We only saw each other for a week
summer before last and for two days last spring.
Now we're two altogether different people; and we
don't know each other at all."

She prayed that he would deny her statements,
that he would say they knew each other by instinct
—anything, so long as he did not agree.

"I certainly don't know you the way you're talking now," he said almost roughly, his pride hurt
and his mind in a turmoil. "I know that we
don't know each other, but I never thought that
you thought that mattered."

Her hands clenched more tightly for an instant
—and then lay open and limp in her lap.

Her lips were trembling; so she smiled. "I
didn't think it mattered until you asked me to
marry you. Then I knew it did. It was game of
you to offer to take a chance, but I'm not that
game. I couldn't marry a strange man. I like
that man a lot, but I don't love him—and you don't
want me to marry you if I don't love you, do you,
Hugh?"

"Of course not." He looked down in earnest thought and then said softly, his eyes on the table, "I 'm glad that you feel that way, Cynthia." She bit her lip and trembled slightly. "I 'll confess now that I don't think that I love you, either. You sweep me clean off my feet when I 'm with you, but when I 'm away from you I don't feel that way. I think love must be something more than we feel for each other." He looked up and smiled boyishly. "We 'll go on being friends anyhow, won't we?"

Somehow she managed to smile back at him. "Of course," she whispered, and then after a brief pause added: "We had better go now. Your train will be leaving pretty soon."

Hugh pulled out his watch. "By jingo, so it will."

He called the waiter, paid his bill, and a few minutes later they turned into Fifth Avenue. They had gone about a block down the avenue when Hugh saw some one a few feet ahead of him who looked familiar. Could it be Carl Peters? By the Lord Harry, it was!

"Excuse me a minute, Cynthia, please. There 's a fellow I know."

He rushed forward and caught Carl by the arm. Carl cried, "Hugh, by God!" and shook hands with him violently. "Hell, Hugh, I 'm glad to see you."

Hugh turned to Cynthia, who was a pace behind them. He introduced Carl and Cynthia to each other and then asked Carl why in the devil he had n't written.

Carl switched his leg with his cane and grinned. "You know darn well, Hugh, that I don't write letters, but I did mean to write to you; I meant to often. I 've been traveling. My mother and I have just got back from a trip around the world. Where are you going now?"

"Oh, golly," Hugh exclaimed, "I 've got to hurry if I 'm going to make that train. Come on, Carl, with us to Grand Central. I 've got to get the five-ten back to Haydensville. My folks are coming up to-morrow for commencement." Instantly he hated himself. Why did he have to mention commencement? He might have remembered that it should have been Carl's commencement, too.

Carl, however, did not seem in the least disturbed, and he cheerfully accompanied Hugh and Cynthia to the station. He looked at Cynthia and had an idea.

"Have you checked your bag?"

"Yes," Hugh replied.

"Well, give me the check and I 'll get it for you. I 'll meet you at the gate."

Hugh surrendered the check and then proceeded to the gate with Cynthia. He turned to her and asked gently, "May I kiss you, Cynthia?"

For an instant she looked down and said nothing; then she turned her face up to his. He kissed her tenderly, wondering why he felt no passion, afraid that he would.

"Good-by, Cynthia dear," he whispered.

Her hands fluttered helplessly about his coat lapels and then fell to her side. She managed a brave little smile. "Good-by—honey."

Carl rushed up with the bag. "Gosh, Hugh, you 've got to hurry; they 're closing the gate." He gripped his hand for a second. "Visit me at Bar Harbor this summer if you can."

"Sure. Good-by, old man. Good-by Cynthia."

"Good-by—good-by."

Hugh slipped through the gate and turned to wave at Carl and Cynthia. They waved back, and then he ran for the train.

On the long trip to Haydensville Hugh relaxed. Now that the strain was over, he felt suddenly weak, but it was sweet weakness. He could graduate in peace now. The visit to New York had been worth while. And what do you know, bumping into old Carl like that! Cynthia and he were friends, too, the best friends in the world, but she no longer wanted to marry him. That was fine. . . . He remembered the picture she and Carl had made standing on the other side of the gate from him. "What a peach of a pair. Golly, would n't it be funny if they hit it off . . ."

He thought over every word that he and Cynthia had said. She certainly had been square all

right.   Not many like her, but "by heaven, I knew
down in my heart all the time that I did n't want
to get married or even engaged.   It would have
played hell with everything."

CHAPTER XXVII

THE next morning Hugh's mother and father arrived in the automobile. He was to drive them back to Merrytown the day after commencement. At last he stood in the doorway of the Nu Delta house and welcomed his father, but he had forgotten all about that youthful dream. He was merely aware that he was enormously glad to see the "folks" and that his father seemed to be withering into an old man.

As the under-classmen departed, the alumni began to arrive. The "five year" classes dressed in extraordinary outfits—Indians, Turks, and men in prison garb roamed the campus. There were youngsters just a year out of college, still looking like undergraduates, still full of college talk. The alumni ranged all the way from these one-year men to the fifty-year men, twelve old men who had come back to Sanford fifty years after their graduation, and two of them had come all the way across the continent. There had been only fifty men originally in that class; and twelve of them were back.

What brought them back? Hugh wondered. He thought he knew, but he could n't have given a reason. He watched those old men wandering slowly around the campus, one of them with his grandson who was graduating this year, and he was awed by their age and their devotion to their alma mater. Yes, Henley had been right. Sanford was far from perfect, far from it—a child could see that—but there was something in the college that gripped one's heart. What faults that old college had; but how one loved her!

Thousands of Japanese lanterns had been strung around the campus; an electric fountain sparkled and splashed its many-colored waters; a band seemed to be playing every hour of the day and night from the band-stand in front of the Union. It was a gay scene, and everybody seemed superbly happy except, possibly, the seniors. They pretended to be happy, but all of them were a little sad, a little frightened. College had been very beautiful—and the "world outside," what was it? What did it have in store for them?

There were mothers and fathers there to see their sons receive their degrees, there were the wives and children of the alumni, there were sisters and fiancées of the seniors. Nearly two thousand people; and at least half of the alumni drunk most of the time. Very drunk, many of them, and very foolish, but nobody minded. Somehow every one seemed to realize that in a few brief days they were trying to recapture a youthful thrill that had gone forever. Some of the drunken ones seemed very silly, some of them seemed almost offensive; all of them were pathetic.

They had come back to Sanford where they had once been so young and exuberant, so tireless in pleasure, so in love with living; and they were trying to pour all that youthful zest into themselves again out of a bottle bought from a bootlegger. Were they having a good time? Who knows? Probably not. A bald-headed man does not particularly enjoy looking at a picture taken in his hirsute youth; and yet there is a certain whimsical pleasure in the memories the picture brings.

For three days there was much gaiety, much singing of class songs, constant parading, dances, speech-making, class circuses, and endless shaking of hands and exchanging of reminiscences. The seniors moved through all the excitement quietly, keeping close to their relatives and friends. Graduation was n't so thrilling as they had expected it to be; it was more sad. The alumni seemed to be having a good time; they were ridiculously boyish: only the seniors were grave, strangely and unnaturally dignified.

Most of the alumni left the night before the graduation exercises. The parents and fiancées remained. They stood in the middle of the campus and watched the seniors, clad in caps and gowns,

line up before the Union at the orders of the class
marshal.

Finally, the procession, the grand marshal, a professor, in the lead with a wand in his hand, then
President Culver and the governor of the State,
then the men who were to receive honorary degrees—a writer, a college president, a philanthro-
pist, a professor, and three politicians—then the
faculty in academic robes, their many-colored hoods
brilliant against their black gowns.   And last the
seniors, a long line of them marching in twos headed
by their marshal.

The visitors streamed after them into the chapel.
The seniors sat in their customary seats, the faculty
and the men who were to receive honorary degrees
on a platform that had been built at the altar.
After they were seated, everything became a blur
to Hugh.   He hardly knew what was happening.
He saw his father and mother sitting in the transept.   He thought his mother was crying.   He
hoped not. . . . Some one prayed stupidly.   There
was a hymn. . . . What was it Cynthia had said?
Oh, yes: "I can't marry a stranger."   Well, they
were n't exactly strangers. . . . He was darn glad
he had gone to New York. . . . The president
seemed to be saying over and over again, "By the
power invested in me . . ." and every time that he
said it, Professor Blake would slip the loop of a

colored hood over the head of a writer or a politician—and then it was happening all over again.

Suddenly the class marshal motioned to the seniors to rise. They put on their mortar-boards. The president said once more, "By the power invested in me . . ." The seniors filed by the president, and the grand marshal handed each of them a roll of parchment tied with blue and orange ribbons. Hugh felt a strange thrill as he took his. He was graduated; he was a bachelor of science. . . . Back again to their seats. Some one was pronouncing benediction. . . . Music from the organ —marching out of the chapel, the surge of friends— his father shaking his hand, his mother's arms around his neck; she *was* crying. . . .

Graduation was over, and, with it Hugh's college days. Many of the seniors left at once. Hugh would have liked to go, too, but his father wanted to stay one more day in Haydensville. Besides, there was a final senior dance that night, and he thought that Hugh ought to attend it.

Hugh did go to the dance, but somehow it brought him no pleasure. Although it was immensely decorous, it reminded him of Cynthia. He thought of her tenderly. The best little girl he'd ever met. . . . He danced on, religiously steering around the sisters and fiancées of his friends, but he could not enjoy the dance. Shortly after eleven he slipped out of the gymnasium and made one last tour of the campus.

It was a moonlight night, and the campus was mysterious with shadows. The elms shook their leaves whisperingly; the tower of the chapel looked like magic tracery in the moonlight. He paused before Surrey Hall, now dark and empty. Good old Carl. . . . Carl and Cynthia? He wondered. . . . Pudge had roomed there, too. He passed on. Keller Hall. Cynthia and Norry. . . . "God, what a beast I was that night. How white Norry was—and Cynthia, too." Cynthia again. She 'd always be a part of Sanford to him. On down to the lake to watch the silver path of the moonlight and the heavy reflections near the shore. Swimming, canoeing, skating—he and Cynthia in the woods beyond. . . . On back to the campus, around the buildings, every one of them filled with memories. Four years—four beautiful, wonderful years. . . . Good old Sanford. . . .

Midnight struck. Some one turned a switch somewhere. The Japanese lanterns suddenly lost their colors and faded to gray balloons in the moonlight. Some men were singing on the Union steps. It was a few seniors, Hugh knew; they had been singing for an hour.

He stood in the center of the campus and listened, his eyes full of tears. Earnestly, religiously, the men sang, their voices rich with emotion:

"Sanford, Sanford, mother of men,
Love us, guard us, hold us true.
Let thy arms enfold us;
Let thy truth uphold us.
Queen of colleges, mother of men—
Alma mater—Sanford—hail!
Alma mater—Hail!—Hail!"

Hugh walked slowly across the campus toward the Nu Delta house. He was both happy and sad —happy because the great adventure was before him with all its mystery, sad because he was leaving something beautiful behind. . . .

Afterword

By R. V. Cassill

Soon after its publication early in 1924 *The Plastic Age* became a best seller and the center of buzzing controversy. Evidently it struck a public nerve already inflamed by journalistic exploitation of the catchwords and boiler-plate situations said to typify the Jazz Age. The author was an instructor at Brown University when notoriety surprised him. He is reported to have received hundred of letters from individual correspondents applauding him for tearing the veil of hypocrisy from around the depravities of college life, berating him for spoiling the game by publicizing it, or seeking further specification about what really happened to clean-cut boys sent to Ivy League colleges to be perfected as gentlemen. Reporters besieged him. He became an informal counselor to concerned alumni, and administrative echelons moved to fish in the waters he had inadvertently helped to muddy. He was let go from his teaching job at Brown—not, according to the enduring consensus of those who survived his departure, because he *had* written a risqué and sensational book that tarnished Brown's reputation along with others, but because he was the sort of person who *would* do such a thing. (Such delicate distinctions are requisite in institutions cherishing a reputation for academic freedom.) Like Professor Henley of the novel, Marks was a mild but persistent adversary of "uninspired administrative officers, stupid professors, and alumni with false ideals" (p. 307), as much of his later writing indicates. In the spring of his departure from Brown a Providence paper quoted him as saying: "The average college teacher hasn't enough mental energy to spit intellectually; he dribbles."[1] Such parting shots are the privilege of a man who has a best seller on his hands.

A "photoplay" starring Clara Bow, the "It Girl" of Hollywood in the 1920s, was made from *The Plastic Age* and released in 1926. And for the rest of his productive life Marks was victim and beneficiary of the curious eruption of misprision and misunderstanding which attended his first major venture into print. On its appearance a hyper-stimulated minister from Ann Arbor wrote him: "It is honest, daring, direct with brutal directness, frank almost to the point of sensationalism. But it is life, life. . . ."[2] Marks knew better than that. When an admirer of one of his later books wrote him asking where he could get a copy of *The Plastic Age* (by then out of print), the author advised

[1] *Providence Journal*, 9 March 1924.
[2] *Boston Globe*, 18 May 1924.

him urgently not to read it, explaining that it was "dated."[3]

Certainly it is neither daring, brutal, nor frank by any of the measures suitable to serious criticism, literary or cultural. And if it is honest (as it seems to me to be), the honesty is muted by an authorial diffidence quite appropriate to limited talents for observation and to the ingenuousness of a mind that had not yet questioned whether "idealism" was the right epithet for a facile, popular lip service to sexual asceticism. It may—it does—depict "life, life," but life as it is seen through the clouded lens of academic provincialism and parochial conventions. Surely it was intended to be primarily an anatomy of collegiate manners with only enough character portrayal to give an emotional tint to conflicts with which the author was preoccupied in his teaching career. When, in the thirties, he called it a dated book, he observed: "The period of which it is written is dead."[4] With the onset of the Depression and the imminence of a new war, campus manners had certainly taken on a new look.

For the reader of our times the novel may seem high as game hung for half a century before the feast. So take it as camp if you will, or as a nostalgia trip if the American past seems a Disneyland where one can hide out from the intractable present. But still consider that

[3] *New Haven Register*, 24 January 1937.
[4] Ibid.

it might be read as a Rosetta stone or as a fossil organism turned up from a not very deeply buried stratum of the persisting national agon. Decoding archaisms of vocabulary and narrative tactic is part of the pleasure of reading it, as it is a requirement for perceiving how these bones must have lived in the flesh of flappers and hot collegians.

I take it to be a clue of some significance that the narrative form is about as ingenuous as the moral frame applied to drinking and "going all the way" in sex. A contemporary reviewer noted: "Its narrative thread consists of school terms as they pass."[5] It is essentially a chronicle—that most obvious and primitive of choices for a writer aiming at honesty—almost as innocent of proportioning, foreshadowing, highlighting, dramatic arrangement, peripety, or thematic refinement as an untreated diary might be. If Hugh's story comes to a climax in the quandaries of his involvement with Cynthia—and without this there would be no resolution except the acquisition of a diploma at commencement—the skimpy rendition of her character, amounting to a lack of curiosity about the female in her nonsocial dimensions, leaves that affair grossly one-sided. "'Cynthia runs with a fast crowd, and she smokes and drinks . . .'" (p. 249), Norry Parker specifies. To tell the truth, we learn little about her beyond that. Yes, we find out that her pur-

[5] *New York Times Book Review*, 3 February 1924.

suit of fun, her past and the "'awful pace'" (p. 288) at which she parties are, for her, irreconcilable with the prospect of an enduring match with Hugh. In a very rare transition to her point of view we are told "she knew only too well that she could lead him to hell, as he said, but that was the only place she could lead him" (p. 320). There is a pale suggestion that had she led him "to hell" he might have discovered her not to be virgin—"If he could have seen *her* on some parties this last year . . ." (p. 320).

But what does she make of this chap who is so patently glad to be freed of her threat to his purity? Does she not feel a comparable relief in returning to her gambols? The inelastic method of narration will not permit us an informed guess about such pertinent questions, so we are left with Professor Henley's hobbled assessment that "she is a very brave girl" (p. 281) for renouncing Hugh, and that is not enough.

Surely we chafe at the implication of a self-evident wrong in her desire for his body—"strong and blond and clean"—as we chafe at the glib assurance with which love is neatly opposed to "sex attraction" (p. 265) or at the skewed euphemism of leading Hugh "to hell" if he yielded to her appetite. If Cynthia were half the girl I conceive she might have been, she would have chafed as well and been glad to be rid of the ninny, however clean and blond. Yet, just as such speculations rip the seams of the moral straitjacket Marks strapped on his chief character, they get no support at

all from the straitlaced, monocular narrative strategy.
The puritan austerity of the technique conspires with
the puritan idealism it represents in making broader
alternatives unthinkable. We can follow only Hugh's
evolving and calcifying attitudes.

One is reluctant to say that the attitudes he shapes
in college amount to the education of an individual. Is
it not closer to the mark to see them as the preparation
of a citizen, or as a model of decency in a nation that
has no higher gods? The pieties confirmed in Hugh are
the liberal academic clichés of our century, seen while
they still retained an aura of freshness, spiced with the
popular optimism flowering after the First World War.
Hugh is wrong in telling Professor Henley that college
has not prepared him for problems in living (p. 308). It
is exactly such problems he has been prepared for
rather than those which obsess the scholar, the hero,
the sage, or the saint. He has been prepared to tempo-
rize with all the ultimate challenges of existence as
he temporized with Cynthia and her inconvenient
impulses.

We follow the structuring of his attitudes about
sports, fraternities, bull sessions, parents, roommates,
liquor, disillusion, "moral laxity" (p. 165), the role of
poetry, and the ends of education itself—to find him
enlightened on all these subjects, but not to a degree
which should imperil him or jolt the carriage wheels of
American Destiny. As for sports, he finds they have a
valuable place in college life if they are not overem-

phasized. Fraternities recruit by standards of money, family, athletic skill, and prep school background, but can express a collective conscience. Bull sessions thrive on smutty talk but open the door to candor and personal reform. Liquor is a temptation that can be overcome. Disillusion turns a young man to the consolations of poetry. The purpose of poetry is to be beautiful and to advertise the beauty of the world to "'people who appreciate all of it'" (p. 163). The purpose of education is to meliorate the inevitable coarsening of young men as they inevitably learn the nature of life.

To remark that such attitudes are popular or vulgar adulterations of high thinking is to slide past the point. Indeed they are. Matthew Arnold foresaw a higher destiny for poetry than that it should stimulate an appreciation of beauty. Socrates did not assume that an examination of life would reveal that "'the college man [is] the cream of the earth'" (p. 308). Whitman did not write to kindle in young American gentlemen a repugnance for drunken girls who "'wanna pet'" (p. 214). When Norry says, "'I don't want beauty debased. I want to fight when orchestras jazz famous arias. Well, petting is jazzing love; and I hate it'" (p. 271), Hugh not only sees what he means but helplessly concurs—as he might not have if Sanford College had given him a better education.

The real point, for us latter-day readers committed to spelling backward the charms that enthralled us in our institutions and adulterated pride, may well be that our Sanford Colleges did the job for which they were intended by the conditions of the democracy, tailoring attitudes as the age demanded. Here again I would emphasize the *decency* in all things to which Hugh is schooled and which has served as a pillar of fire for so many educators in these last decades—for in giving full value to such decency we might finally estimate its value and its price.

It is a decency that erodes all social impediments to human liberty without clarifying a vision of what individual liberty might grasp for, lead to. Hugh will never knowingly contribute to the oppression of the racially disadvantaged, the poor, the young, the old, the female, or students. He will unwaveringly deplore oppressors and when need be fight them, on the campus, in government, in the market place, or on the beaches. He will always side against materialism and selfishness, as he will always appreciate beauty and truth and love. He will trust the future to remedy the shortcomings of past and present. He will never suspect the mortgages he has laid on that future.

His decency finds apt expression in the wish that the dislodged Cynthia might strike up a situation with Carl Peters. There is charity in such a wish, good will toward people who are not of Hugh's "kind." But as we recall that Carl disappeared from Hugh's ken suffering from a venereal infection, we may more than faintly suspect an unconscious will to punish the un-

clean vessel in the fancy that Carl might embrace her.
How many other snakes may lurk under the stone of
Hugh's idealism?

In his junior year Hugh becomes an enthusiast for
poetry. He is thrilled by his teacher Blake who "taught
poetry almost entirely by reading it, only occasionally
interpolating an explanatory remark, and he read
beautifully" (p. 229). Appreciative as Hugh may be of
this mode of teaching, it does not stir him to suspect
that Cynthia may be the most palpable incarnation he
will ever see of La Belle Dame Sans Merci. Poetry will
never sting him with intimations of what he misses. At
the end of the novel there is, indeed, a note of bitter-
sweet melancholy for what has vanished in the fog of
his college years. "Midnight struck. Someone turned a
switch somewhere. The Japanese lanterns suddenly
lost their colors and faded to gray balloons in the
moonlight" (p. 331). But Hugh is no knight palely
loitering beside a lake where no birds sing. The "great
adventure" (p. 302) is still to come—or so he has been
schooled to believe.

If there is a single aspect in *The Plastic Age* that dates
it more than any other, it must be the infusing faith in
the future as a panacea, rectifying mistakes, compen-
sating for losses, overcoming pettiness, cowardice, and
ignorance. The great American adventure is not over,
it is still to come. But even if it were, would Hugh
recognize it when it came? And if it is already past?

How wrestle with the angel if the angel comes without identifying wings and has already been ignored?

It will not do to make too much of the Cynthia who peeps in and out of this less-than-monumental fiction, and I am not quite prepared to insist she is a terrible angel who passed while Citizen Hugh was too calfish to grapple with her, or even that she is the fatally Beautiful Lady for whom the Romantics kicked away the base decencies of the common world. This period piece should not be fluffed up as a prophetic novel. But we read all the signs of past times for prophecy, curious if not desperate to know how we came to our present condition. Now in America we are shaken in our confidence that we are a decent people, though we have yielded so much for the sake of decency. The colleges that prepared our decent attitudes appear now to run by social and economic inertias, lacking that naïve aspiration toward a millennium voiced by Marks's Professor Henley. And in the denial of Cynthia is there not a seismographic trace of the cataclysmic error, the original sin of those who deified decency? Whether or not an author has intended allegory, we allegorize as we read. Cynthia allegorizes as glamour and passion, mistakenly rejected as damnation. After such ignorance, what forgiveness?

I have never seen Clara Bow in the photoplay made from this book. I am sure there would be less temptation for me to think of Clara Bow as a figure in an allegory of sacred and profane love than there is to think of Cynthia that way. In any case it would grieve me to see Clara Bow again in a crackly old film. It would only remind me that if she had *It*, she took it with her when she quit us, as surely as Cynthia did when she slipped away from Hugh.

Textual Note

The text of *The Plastic Age* published here is an exact photo-offset reprinting of the first edition (New York and London: The Century Co., 1924). No emendations have been made in the text.

Lost American Fiction Series

published titles as of September 1980
please write for current list of titles

Weeds. By Edith Summers Kelley. Afterword by Matthew J. Bruccoli.

The Professors Like Vodka. By Harold Loeb. Afterword by the author.

Dry Martini: A Gentleman Turns to Love. By John Thomas. Afterword by Morrill Cody.

The Devil's Hand. By Edith Summers Kelley. Afterword by Matthew J. Bruccoli.

Predestined. A Novel of New York Life. By Stephen French Whitman. Afterword by Alden Whitman.

The Cubical City. By Janet Flanner. Afterword by the author.

They Don't Dance Much. By James Ross. Afterword by George V. Higgins.

Yesterday's Burdens. By Robert M. Coates. Afterword by Malcolm Cowley.

Mr and Mrs Haddock Aboard. By Donald Ogden Stewart. Afterword by the author.

Flesh Is Heir. By Lincoln Kirstein. Afterword by the author.

The Wedding. By Grace Lumpkin. Afterword by Lillian Barnard Gilkes. Postscript by the author.

The Red Napoleon. By Floyd Gibbons. Afterword by John Gardner.

Single Lady. By John Monk Saunders. Afterword by Stephen Longstreet.

Queer People. By Carroll and Garrett Graham. Afterword by Budd Schulberg.

A Hasty Bunch. By Robert McAlmon. Afterword by Kay Boyle.